THE HAUNTING OF MEADE MANSION

SKYLAR FINN

*I*t was January in Colorado, and a fierce wind carried snow down the mountains, blanketing Boulder. A single streetlamp lit the long and rambling private lane which led up a steep hill to the old Meade House. It had sat uninhabited at the top of the hill for as long as anyone could remember until its current owner, Matilda Meade, moved in and opened her home to local children in need. The homeless population led to runaways and abandoned children, who often found themselves at Meade House when they would have otherwise been left out in the cold.

On this particular night, as the blizzard raged outside, Matilda fixed hot cocoa for the children while Cynthia, her assistant, dutifully set out grilled cheese cut into crust-less triangles on the dining room table. The two youngest, Bobby and Tricia, were brother and sister just a year apart in age. They sat at the high wooden kitchen table, legs swinging. Tricia watched the window with worry as the snow blew past, giving a little jump each time the wind howled. Bobby was oblivious, absorbed in the work of eating his grilled cheese.

Andrea, the oldest, had come to Meade House only days before. She was reluctant to leave her parents, who often slept in the park or the woods behind the library, changing locations often enough not to be detected. One unlucky night, a passing bicycle cop shined a light into their tent. Andrea was placed in custody with Child Protective Services. Within a day, she found herself in the backseat of an old Buick, bumping up the long lane to Meade House. The caseworker told her how lucky she was: it often took months to place a child even temporarily, but Matilda just happened to have a spot open up.

Andrea fidgeted with her hair, not eating. Matilda placed a mug of hot chocolate in front of her and smiled warmly.

"You're not eating," she said. "Whatever is the matter, dear?"

"I—" Andrea started to say but was cut short by a loud bang. The power went out and the whole house went dark. Tricia and Bobby screamed. Tricia began crying loudly. She was afraid of the dark.

"There's nothing to worry about, it's just an outage," came Matilda's voice in the dark. "Cynthia, take this flashlight. I'll go to the fuse box and see if I can get it back on or if it went out with the storm. If it's the storm, I'll have to get to the backup generator. Take the children upstairs to the attic. It has the fewest windows."

The bright beam of the flashlight popped on. Cynthia picked up Tricia and reached for Bobby's hand. "Come on, everyone. We'll just go upstairs and wait for the storm to pass. It will be over before you know it." She led them out of the kitchen as Andrea trailed behind.

In the attic, Cynthia pulled the door shut securely behind them. Tricia and Bobby huddled together on top of the toy chest. Andrea sat cross-legged on the old rug decorated with trains. Across the room, the beady red eye of the carousel horse glinted. Andrea hated that horse.

"When will the storm be over?" asked Tricia, her voice quavering.

"It's hard to say, dear," said Cynthia. "But it's almost morning now, and when the sun comes up, the snow will melt and the power will come back on. In the meantime, we're all here together. Everything will be fine."

Downstairs, an earsplitting scream reverberated off the walls. There was a crash, and it sounded like something large and heavy had tipped over. Andrea flinched. It didn't sound like everything was fine.

"What happened?" Bobby cried.

Cynthia glanced towards the attic door. "I'm sure it's nothing. Maybe Matilda fell. I'll go check on her. Andrea, watch out for the young ones. I'm going to lock you in."

Cynthia left before Andrea could ask her the many questions that raced through her mind, like *who screams like that because they fell?* and *if it's nothing, why are you locking us in?*

The attic door closed behind Cynthia and Andrea heard the lock click into place. The children wept softly. Andrea tried to think of something reassuring to say.

"Hey guys, you want to play a game?" she asked.

"In the dark?" asked Bobby.

"We'll play hide-and-seek. We're going to hide and Cynthia's going to find us when she gets back, okay?" She ushered the children into the toy chest. "You guys stay here and be as quiet as possible, like little mice. Okay?" She put her locket on the edge of the lid before closing it so it couldn't shut all the way and trap them.

Downstairs, a second scream cut through the air. More crashes sounded. Footsteps creaked up the stairs. Andrea closed her eyes briefly, trying not to cry. The footsteps paused on the second-floor landing, then resumed.

"Andrea?" came Tricia's terrified voice from inside of the toy chest.

"It's okay," she said. "We're just playing a game, remember? Stay there and keep quiet."

Andrea shined the flashlight around, looking for a place to hide. The beam of light landed on the old armoire across the room. She approached the armoire, the flashlight shaking in her hand. She hated Miss Cynthia for leaving them. She had never felt more frightened in her life.

Andrea climbed into the armoire, pulling the doors shut behind her. For a moment, the space was illuminated, then she clicked the flashlight off and was plummeted into darkness. Outside the attic door, the footsteps grew louder as they slowly ascended the steps: *thud, thud, THUD THUD.* Andrea trembled inside the armoire. The attic door creaked open. The footsteps approached the center of the room and paused. Andrea waited. The footsteps came toward the armoire. The doors opened. Andrea screamed.

Inside the toy chest, Tricia and Bobby held each other, shaking and crying. Tricia screamed when she heard Andrea as Bobby frantically tried to shush her. The heavy footsteps approached the toy chest.

The lid was thrown open. The children screamed and screamed. They would never have stopped, had their screams not been cut violently short.

2

$\mathscr{E}$mily sat at her laptop, staring at the blinking cursor. It had been this way for weeks now. She either hated everything she wrote and dragged it straight into the trash or couldn't write anything at all.

The door to the studio apartment opened and Emily sighed with relief. She and Jesse had been married for seven years, but the knowledge he was home never ceased to reassure her. Jesse's upbeat nature countered her constant pessimism, and he always encouraged her no matter how poorly her work was going.

Jesse came in and placed the mail on the desk. He was covered in plaster dust. On the weekends, he and his band played gigs around town, but during the week he was up to his neck in whatever construction work he could get to make ends meet. Kissing Emily on the head, he went over to the small galley kitchen and placed two grocery bags on the counter.

"Hungry?" he asked.

"I'm starving," said Emily. "Jess? What is this?"

Sandwiched between her latest unpaid student loan bill

and yet another credit card bill with FINAL NOTICE stamped across the outside was a letter from the landlord.

"Huh?" asked Jesse. "I dunno, just the usual bloodsuckers, I guess."

"Jesse, this one's actually important," she said, slitting the envelope open. "I mean like, in a more immediate sense." Emily scanned the letter and sighed. "So, we need to re-sign the lease or give our thirty-day notice."

Jesse ran a hand through his tousled dark hair. "What's the trouble? We re-sign, right? No way we're coming up with the deposit for a new place."

"He wants to raise the rent by a hundred dollars," said Emily. She felt the added tension on top of the frustration she already felt about her work. Their sable Sheltie, Widget, seemed to sense her distress. She trotted across the room, her little black nails clicking on the tile, and jumped into Emily's lap. She buried her hands in Widget's fur and tried to calm down.

"A hundred dollars!" Jesse spat grape soda across the counter. "How? Why? This place is just as crappy as it was last year. What changed?"

Emily shrugged, unable to form a response. They were barely getting by as it was. They had at least always been able to pay rent until now, but this would send them over the edge.

Emily's phone vibrated, rattling on the desk. Emily picked it up: an unknown number with a Colorado area code.

"Hello?" she said uncertainly.

"Is this Emily Meade-Martinez?" said an unfamiliar voice on the other end of the line.

"This is she," Emily said cautiously. She generally didn't answer unknown numbers out of the assumption that a collections agent lurked on the other end of the line, but this voice was polished, refined, and clipped: more like a posh butler than a bill collector.

"This is J.R. Watkins of Watkins, Taft, and Simms, Attorneys at Law," said Watkins.

"Oh no," said Emily. "Are we being sued?" In the kitchen, Jesse's eyes grew wide.

"Sued?" Watkins sounded puzzled. "Heavens, no. If anything, I would say this is quite the opposite of litigation. I'm an estate lawyer, and I worked for your aunt, Matilda Meade?"

"Yes, that's her," said Emily, puzzled. "I thought she disappeared?"

"A while back, yes. Very unfortunate. The police have yet to recover her body, but I've been informed there is zero reason to think her alive: no activity on any of her accounts, no known communication with anyone that she knew, and her house has sat abandoned for some time now."

"Oh," said Emily, wondering what this had to do with her. "I'm sorry to hear that." Emily had never known her aunt, who for reasons unknown was estranged from everyone in her mother's family. Emily had only met her once as a child.

Jesse mouthed *what's going on?* at her. Emily gave a little half shrug, mouthing *no idea.*

"To clarify, I should probably state that her death has been declared in absentia," continued Watkins. "Which means that, for all intents and purposes, she is now deceased. I'm sorry to be the bearer of bad news, but on a less sad note, I'm also calling to tell you that you're in Ms. Meade's will."

"I am?" Emily was totally confused. She hadn't seen her aunt in twenty years, not since she was a kid. What was she doing in her will?

"Yes. It seems that she wanted you to have her house."

"Her *house*?" Jesse jumped on the couch with Emily and Widget and tried to put his ear next to the phone. Emily gave him a look and put the phone on speaker.

"Oh yeah," said Jesse. "Or you could just do that."

"I'm sorry?" came the polite tone of J.R. Watkins, attorney at law.

"Nothing. That was just my husband, Jesse. So, wait, you mean to tell me Aunt Matilda left me her entire house?"

"The house and the accompanying property," said Watkins. "It's quite a good bit of land for this area, especially with the housing market here. Lovely place."

"I'm sure it is," said Emily. "I'm just not quite understanding how this all happened. I haven't spoken to my aunt in years."

"Yes, Ms. Meade did mention she had some familial difficulty, but she spoke quite fondly of you nonetheless. And she was very generous, something of a local philanthropist. It was in her nature to be giving beyond what any of us normally expect."

"That's incredible," said Emily. "I mean, wow. This is just so unexpected. We'll need to discuss this and get back to you, if that's all right."

"Of course," said Watkins. "The property is yours to do with as you see fit...regardless of what you might choose. Good day."

"Good day," Emily echoed without thinking before pressing the button to hang up. Jesse immediately burst out laughing.

"'Good day'?" he repeated. "Who is this guy, Mr. Belvedere?"

"Some rich lawyer giving me my rich aunt's house," said Emily. "Do you know what this means?"

"Um, we get Mr. Belvedere to sell the joint and buy ourselves a sick place here?"

"Jesse, as of next month, we have no place to live. We can't sell the place remotely and wait for the money to come through while we sleep on a park bench here. We should just go out there, look at the place, see if there's anything worth keeping, then sell out and figure things out from there."

"Move? To your aunt's place?" Jesse looked appalled. "Are you crazy? Do you know how cold it is in Colorado?"

Emily pulled up the average temperatures in Boulder on her computer. "It actually doesn't look that bad."

"There's like a forty-degree range there, daily! That's like living in a desert on top of a mountain. Have you ever even lived above sea level? Let alone..." He leaned over and looked at her screen. "Five thousand feet? Why don't we just move to the Himalayas?"

"We don't have a free house in the Himalayas," said Emily. "Look. We don't have the money to stay here. A month from now, we're going to have to decide whether we move into my parents' basement or yours. And if you want to be in your thirties, married, and living in your parents' basement, I think we've acquired different priorities. So, unless you suddenly get signed to a major label or I write an entire novel in about a week, there's no quick fix for the mess we're currently in. Except for this."

Jesse, frustrated but unable to form a counterpoint, fell silent. Emily, sensing her window of opportunity, continued.

"Look, it's not forever. We go there for the winter, renovate it, sell it, then buy whatever house we want, wherever we want. We won't have to pay rent. I'll have time to work on my novel, and you can work on your music whenever we're not doing stuff for the house."

Jesse sighed, tugging at his hair till it stuck straight up. "Let me get this straight. You want to move to Colorado for the winter to fix up some creepy old building a dead lady gave you while you try to write the Great American Novel? Does any of this sound familiar to you?"

"This isn't *The Shining*! We'll be in the middle of a town, in a totally normal house. I'm sure everything will be perfectly fine—"

"—said everyone in every horror movie ever," said Jesse.

"Do you have any better ideas?" said Emily. She knew she had him there.

"No," admitted Jesse. "I don't."

"It's this or the basement," said Emily.

Jesse shuddered. Her parents—austere, formal, and convinced their daughter could have done better than a musician-by-night/foreman-by-day—made Jesse deeply uncomfortable. His parents, while loving and accepting people, unceasingly harangued the pair about grandchildren. Emily didn't mind the propaganda, but Jesse wanted them to be in a better place financially before they even considered it. And his mother was relentless.

"Okay, okay, fine," he said. "Six months and we're out. No matter what happens."

"Six months," Emily repeated. "No matter what."

Widget barked as if in agreement with them, and Emily hugged her as a feeling of relief washed over her: no more rent hanging over their heads, and a chance to catch up and maybe even get ahead. She felt like their luck was finally starting to change.

IT ONLY TOOK a week for them to pack their scant belongings. They rented a small truck, loaded their few boxes, and climbed into the front seat with Widget between them.

"Good-bye, crappy studio in a questionable part of town," said Jesse as he turned the key in the ignition. "We won't miss you at all."

Emily felt a pang, although it wasn't for the apartment. It was the realization they'd be leaving behind everything they'd always known in exchange for the unknown. Anything could happen. It was both thrilling and terrifying.

It was a thirty-hour drive to Colorado, and they alternated driving and sleeping in shifts. When it was Emily's turn, she watched the landscape pass through the window, feeling the distance between their old lives and new increase more and more with each passing mile. As she drove, she wondered if this could be the thing to change their fortune: would Emily be able to write again? Would Jesse find a band he could play with? Would they ever get out of debt?

When they were both awake, they speculated on what their new lives might bring.

"You know, this reminds me of the Gold Rush, or the Oregon Trail," said Jesse. "People who head out West to find their fortune?" He seemed to be warming up to the idea. "It's funny how that hasn't changed since the old days."

"We just have a moving van and smart phones instead of a covered wagon and cholera," said Emily.

"Remember the game? In elementary school? My family always died of cholera."

"You have to play as the banker," said Emily. "It's the secret to winning. That way you have enough money for buffalo meat and bullets and when half your family drowns in the river or you lose one of your wagon wheels, you can afford to replace it."

Jesse snorted. "We're never gonna be the banker."

"I don't know," said Emily, gazing out the window at the mountains in the distance, her first glimpse of the Rockies. "Maybe our luck is finally about to change."

AFTER SEVERAL WRONG turns and a pit stop at a coffee shop advertising high altitude roasts, Emily pointed excitedly out the window at the street sign denoting the private lane that led to the Meade House.

"There!" she yelled, startling Jesse, who spilled hot coffee on his leg. "There it is!"

"Ow," he complained. "Give a guy a little warning."

"Sorry," said Emily. "I got excited."

Jesse flicked the turn signal on and drove the moving truck up the long, rocky incline leading to the house. It was steeper than Emily expected, and she held onto Widget so the dog wouldn't slide out of her lap.

"It's not that steep," said Jesse.

"I'm not used to this," said Emily. "I'm used to beaches and swamps."

She watched the house approach through the windshield. It was sturdy brick, stone, and wood, with a chimney extending from the side and a wide front porch. The grass looked dry and dead, and there were no lush trees or tropical plants to shield the house from the glaring sun overhead.

Jesse pulled to a stop in the driveway and grinned rakishly at her. "Moment of truth," he said.

Emily forced a smile. She suddenly realized how far from home they were, and it made her feel strangely isolated in a way she'd never known.

They jumped out the truck. Widget immediately leapt down and tore off, running around in circles and barking. Emily wished she could run in circles to release some of the nervous energy she felt. Her fingertips were tingling and in spite of the long drive and the fatigue she expected to feel, instead she felt keyed up, nervous, and wired. She stared up at the house. It was much larger and more imposing than the pictures had made it out to be.

Jesse, usually the one to lead the charge into the fray, paused beside her and looked up at the house the same way.

"It's a little…spooky," he finally said.

Emily shrugged. She didn't want to agree and acknowledge that from the outside, the house was less than inviting. Not on top of all the uncertainty she already felt. To speak it out loud would make it real.

"It's just old," she said dismissively, setting off across the lawn towards the front door as Jesse followed. "A coat of paint, some walkway lights, more plants, maybe an archway over the front walk and it will feel like home in no time." Jesse looked at her pointedly. "Temporarily, of course," she amended.

They paused on the massive stone porch, in front of the imposing wooden door. An iron door knocker shaped like a lion roaring decorated the center. Emily studied it curiously.

Jesse looked at her. "Are you going to knock? Cause I don't think there's anybody to hear you."

"I'm just looking at it. Hold your horses."

She reached into her purse, rummaging for her keys, and pulled out the one for the house: FedExed to them last week, courtesy of one J.R. Watkins, Esq. "Are you ready for the moment of truth?"

"I kinda need to use the bathroom, so in other words, yeah," said Jesse.

Emily put the key in the lock and turned it. The door swung silently inward, revealing only the inky black darkness within. Emily took a deep breath and stepped inside.

he first thing Emily noticed was the smell: there was something about the smell of an old house that was hard to define, specific to very old buildings. It was the smell of dust, brick, and stone, combined with the larger sense of the many lives who had passed through the walls.

Directly across from the front door, a large mirror hung on the wall, reflecting their tired faces. To the right was a coat rack. To the left was another door. Emily pushed it open and saw a living room with wood floors and massive windows. An old stone fireplace was situated at the center of the room. Matilda's furniture, maroon tufted armchairs and a long navy couch, made the room seem even darker than it already was. Heavy drapes hung from the windows, blocking out the harsh light that shone through the thin mountain atmosphere. The center of the room was dark, too dark to see what was in it. Emily groped around on the wall and flipped the switch. A heavy chandelier blazed with light.

Over the fireplace, a portrait of Matilda hung, posed proudly with a group of solemn-looking children gathered around her. Jesse stepped closer to it, studying the portrait briefly, before turning to Emily.

"Well, this isn't weird at all," he said fake-brightly.

Emily, absorbed in the way a thin shaft of light extended from the window and hung in the center of the room, barely heard him. Widget ran ahead of her, skidding across the dusty wooden floor and nearly careening into a closed door that led off the living room. Next to this door was a set of French doors, closed to what looked like a dining room with a second (albeit smaller) chandelier hanging from the ceiling.

"Geez," said Jesse. "What's with all the doors?"

"Do you want door number one, or doors number two and three?" asked Emily.

Jesse glanced back and forth between the closed wooden door in the corner of the living room and the French doors.

"I'll take doors number two and three," he said, heading toward the French doors. "It's kinda like the difference between swimming in a pool and swimming in a lake, you know what I mean?"

Emily watched him walk into the dining room. She headed to the opposite end of the room and opened the mystery door. It led to a hallway with more doors leading off of it. She stepped into the hallway. To her immediate left was a door leading back into the dining room; she could hear Jesse inside, exclaiming about the size of the windows. Down the hall lay the unknown. Emily chose the unknown.

The house had not been decorated for many years, that much was obvious. The garish linoleum in the hallway was a lurid advertisement for the seventies, and the kitchen wasn't much of an improvement. The countertops were burnt orange and the walls were an unsubtle shade of avocado. A hideous fringed lampshade decorated the hanging light swinging gently over the old mahogany table. Through the window over the sink, the Flat Irons posed, stately and majestic. Emily paused in the doorframe to regard them as Jesse popped through a swinging door at the opposite end of the room.

"It's like the whole place goes in a circle," he declared. "Get a load of this interior design, though. This is gonna have to go. Was your aunt Mrs. Brady or what?"

"I kind of like it," said Emily, going back to the hallway to continue her exploration.

"Are you for real? It's like we came here in a time machine! Plus, we gotta sell it, not live in it forever." He poked her in the back.

"I know, I know. No one's going to make you live in Colorado forever. I promise."

At the end of the hallway was a bathroom: antique claw foot tub, heavy old windows, and a little round mirror over the tall, stately sink. The floor was an alternating pattern of black-and-white squares, like a chessboard. The light was a large heavy bulb that hung from a chain. Emily turned to the door next to the bathroom. It was another old wooden door, this one with two doorknobs: one at regular height, the other set high in the door just above Emily's head.

"Weird," she muttered.

"Did your aunt have four arms?" asked Jesse.

"Jesse, she's dead," said Emily. "Please try to have a little respect."

"Sorry," he said, abashed.

"That is, presumed dead," added Emily, turning the lower knob. "I mean, she could still be living in the walls, watching us as we speak..." Jesse was easily spooked by her off-the-cuff hypothetical scenarios, and she had learned over time that they were far more effective than nagging or criticizing him.

"Emily!" protested Jesse. "Knock it off!"

Emily stopped when she opened the door. The room was a library, the shelves lined with books, with a fireplace in the center of the room and a desk in the corner. There was a green-shaded banker's lamp on the desk and a red leather armchair in the corner. Emily gazed at the room like she was in love.

"I think I just found my office," she said.

"Yeah, that or a really sweet practice space," said Jesse, going in and flopping down on the brown leather couch in front of the fireplace.

"You can practice in the basement," said Emily absently as she approached the bookshelf on the far side of the room.

"Wow, thanks Em. That's quite the consolation prize."

Emily studied the dusty leather volumes on the shelf. They were all titles she didn't recognize and had never heard of. She was just about to pull one down when a loud banging noise sounded from the front of the house. Emily jumped and dropped the book in her hand, which fell to the floor with a thud. She looked over at Jesse, who stared back at her.

"What did you say about your aunt living in the walls?" he said.

"I'm sure it's just…the postman," she said, going toward the front of the house.

"Or maybe it's just the wind," suggested Jesse, following her.

"Or that," agreed Emily.

"I was actually implying that it's probably a crazed murderer, which is usually what happens when people say it's just the wind, but whatever."

"Can you at least pretend to be positive about the situation?" asked Emily. "You know, the one where we live in this giant house for free?"

"I'm sorry, Em," said Jesse, catching her from behind and wrapping his arms around her. He buried his face in her hair. "From now on, I'll pretend this place doesn't utterly creep me out. Deal?"

"Deal," said Emily.

The banging sounded again and Emily jumped, startling

Jesse with her reaction even as she realized it was the ornate lion's head door knocker.

"Who would be knocking at the door?" she asked. "We don't know anyone here."

Jesse shrugged, apparently committed to his vow not to rag on the house or its possible weirdness. Emily stopped in front of the mirror in the foyer and peered through the peephole. A man in a forest green polo and glasses stood squinting at the door. She opened it.

"Who are you?" he said. He looked mystified by the sight of her.

"Who are *you*?" said Emily, offended. "*We* live here."

"I'm the property's handyman, Richard," he said. "Been coming out to this place for the last twenty years. I've never seen you before. Nobody's lived here since—" he stopped, as if recalling a painful memory. "Well, since Ms. Meade disappeared. I didn't think anyone would."

"I'm Matilda's great niece, Emily," she said. "This is my husband, Jesse." She glanced down as Widget squeezed between their legs and sniffed Richard's shoe. "And this is our dog, Widget."

"Well, hello there," said Richard, giving Widget a much warmer reception than he had Emily. "Aren't you cute."

Emily stepped outside and Jesse came out after her. Widget took off in the yard. Richard watched her chase a squirrel.

"Careful about letting your dog outside without a leash," he said. "There are a lot of wild animals out here you folks aren't used to, depending on where you're from."

"Animals?" said Emily, alarmed. "What kind of animals?" Jesse whistled for Widget and she ran back to the porch.

"Bears. Coyotes. Deer, mostly, but a few predators here and there. Sometimes pets go missing. Just keep an eye on her and don't let her wander too far." Jesse took a treat from his pocket and tossed it inside the house for Widget.

"Didn't know Ms. Meade had a niece, even a great one," said Richard, regarding Emily curiously. "She never did talk much about her family. I assumed she didn't have one."

Emily felt uncomfortable, as if she was the one responsible for Aunt Matilda's estrangement from her mother and grandmother. "I only met her once. I just found out she left the house to us a couple of weeks ago."

Comprehension dawned on Richard's face. "Oh. So, you don't know then."

"Know what?" said Jesse immediately. *I told you so*, she could practically hear him thinking.

"About what happened," said Richard. "The night they disappeared."

"They?" asked Emily.

"Well, her and the children. And another young woman about your age who helped her out with the kids."

"Kids? What kids?" said Emily. "I thought she didn't have any children."

"She didn't. The town's children were her children. The ones nobody wanted, or had and couldn't afford to keep. She took them in, gave them a room and space to play. Made sure they went to school and ate well. She gave them a home." Richard shook his head. "Makes it even more terrible, what happened here."

"But what happened?" asked Jesse, exasperated. "Is this place built on a sacred burial ground, or what?"

Richard sniffed, displeased. "Not sure what you mean by that, but to be honest with you, nobody's entirely sure what happened. One morning, I had some extra firewood I brought up to the property for Matilda and the three kids, and that assistant of hers—never could remember her name —and the house was just as dark and cold as could be. That's when I called the sheriff." Richard gazed at the Flat Irons in the distance, looking pensive. "When he got here, there was no sign of Matilda or the kids. That assistant of hers was also missing. Searched the house from top to bottom, but there was no sign of them anywhere."

"They just vanished? Two women and three kids?"

"Up in smoke. Into thin air, like they were here one minute and gone the next. Folks couldn't believe somebody would hurt that sweet old lady and the kids she took care of, especially after all she'd done for the town. We formed search parties, put up posters. Local news aired broadcasts, asking for information. A few of the wealthier ones put up a reward. We went up into the mountains and looked for them there. But they were nowhere. It was almost as if they'd never existed."

At these words, Emily felt a deep chill that had nothing to do with the setting sun or the rapidly plummeting temperature. Beside her, Jesse was motionless. For the first time, Emily considered what *death in absentia* might mean.

"They never found any sign of them?" she said. "And they have no idea who might have been responsible?"

"None whatsoever," said Richard. "Then people started asking questions: just what was she doing up here with those kids in the first place? Who else could have hurt them? I think people got suspicious. After that, the standard myth was that if anyone was behind it, it was probably her. Not that I believe that. But you can see why I was so surprised to find anybody here. I didn't think anyone would want to live here after all that."

Seeing the shock and fear on their faces, he hastily added, "That was then, of course. I'm sure whoever might have been responsible is long gone from here. I expect you two will be safe as houses."

Richard's tone was less than convincing, and judging from the expression on Jesse's face, he was clearly unconvinced. And if she was truly honest with herself, neither was Emily. She knew Matilda had vanished, but she just assumed that maybe the old lady fell down hiking and her body hadn't been recovered. Things like that happened all the time out here, didn't they? But to disappear with three children and another adult—that seemed like something else altogether.

"Sun's going down," said Richard abruptly, changing the subject. "You folks probably aren't used to it yet, but it gets real cold at night, even in the fall. You might want to build a fire at night to keep warm till it's time to turn the heat on for the winter."

"Thank you, Richard," said Emily. "We'll do that."

"Stay safe," he said, before retreating from the porch to the sanctuary of his pick-up truck in the yard. Emily thought he pulled out a little more quickly than normal.

"'Stay safe'?" echoed Jesse. "After he tells us everybody who lived here got sucked into another dimension or eaten by cannibals? I'm less than reassured."

Emily wrapped her arms around her more tightly, shivering. "Let's go in and build a fire, like he said. I'm not used to the cold."

They went inside and approached the fireplace and stared at it.

"Um...have you ever actually built a fire?" ventured Emily.

"No. Why, have you?"

"Definitely not," said Emily.

Jesse shrugged. "Have no fear, dear. That's what YouTube is for."

Twenty minutes later, after looking up How to Build a Fire, Emily and Jesse had created a modest but pleasant blaze. The only food they had was from the cooler they brought across country, so they had a makeshift meal of salami, crackers, cold Coke, and iced tea. It was actually kind of cozy, in spite of the unspoken words hanging between them.

"So..." Jesse finally said, clearly cautious after their earlier exchange but unable to keep it in any longer. "Are we gonna talk about what Crazy Richard said? Or pretend that it's not, like, unusual at all that everybody who lived here before us disappeared, never to be seen again?"

"What makes you think he's crazy?" asked Emily.

"That's what you took from my question?"

"I'm just saying, he seemed kind of normal to me. Unless you think that he's a suspect." Emily could feel the cogs in her creative wheelhouse spinning. As bad as she felt about whatever happened to Matilda, maybe this was the chance to finally overcome her writer's block.

"A suspect? In what?" Jesse glanced around like he expected a murderer to come flying out of the old cuckoo clock on the mantel.

"The disappearance," said Emily. She was careful to label it *the disappearance* and not *the horrible murder whose perpetrator is still at large*. It had been hard enough getting Jesse out here in the first place.

Jesse shrugged. "I dunno, spooky guy, weird house, bunch of missing or possibly dead people? Seems like basic arithmetic to me."

"Yeah, but if he did something, why would he hang around after? Wouldn't he leave town?"

"Maybe he's got a split personality, like Norman Bates. Maybe he thinks he's your aunt and lives in the basement."

No sooner had Jesse uttered these words than a resounding crash sounded somewhere below their feet.

4

Emily and Jesse huddled together at the top of the basement steps as if on a life raft, the inky darkness beneath them like an ocean. To make matters worse, Widget took one look at the basement and immediately ran in the opposite direction.

"This seems ill-advised," said Jesse. "After what we just heard? Maybe we should just leave."

"It could have been anything," said Emily. "Raccoons, something falling from a shelf. You know what it probably wasn't? Richard dressed up like Matilda. Now come on."

Emily descended the steps ahead of Jesse, flashlight in hand. The string hanging at the top of the stairs had illuminated nothing, and Emily hoped there would be a second light somewhere at the bottom. She hated basements, and this one was no exception.

"What do you see?" whispered Jesse. "Anything?"

"Nothing yet," said Emily in a normal tone of voice, determined to keep things as un-weird as possible.

She swept the beam back and forth across the cement floor. Like any basement, it seemed to be filled with old junk: tennis rackets, speakers, a boxy computer monitor, and a tube TV. Relics from a previous time. Emily fixed an old gramophone in the beam of her flashlight.

"Look at that, Jess! We should take it up and use it, right?"

"Right," said Jesse. "Totally."

Finally, in the center of the room, Emily's flashlight landed on a second skinny piece of string, connected to a bare lightbulb overhead. She pulled it, relieved when it illuminated the basement in its harsh white light.

"Hey!" said Jesse behind her. "Look at this!"

Emily turned to see a wooden table covered in carpentry equipment, old paintbrushes, and cans of paint. Jesse was examining a circular saw. "I can really use this stuff, then sell it once the house is done. This is definitely going to come in handy."

Emily wandered the length of the basement, pausing occasionally to look closer at various objects she saw: a ship in a bottle, an oversized hourglass, a wrought iron lantern. At the end of the row of junk, she saw the source of the noise: a window set high in the wall had blown open and banged against the frame in a sudden gust of wind.

"Hey Jesse, do you see a ladder anywhere?" she called. "We need to shut this window."

After a few minutes of searching, Jesse located a stepladder behind a torn fishing net and dragged it over to the window. He climbed up it and pulled the window shut, securing it with a rusty old latch.

"Gonna have to fix this latch," he called down to Emily, pulling out his phone and starting a list in Notes. Emily was relieved. Distracted by the physical demands of the house, maybe he would forget about the more sinister implications revealed by Richard's story.

Upstairs, they put out the fire and got ready for bed. The upstairs was still a relatively unknown area, so they entered the first room they found with a functioning light and dropped their backpacks on the floor. Jesse took his boots off and was asleep the moment his head hit the pillow. Emily took longer, examining various tchotchkes that lined the dresser: ceramic lambs and faceless shepherds.

In the bathroom, she examined her tired face and concluded she needed to drink more water and get some sleep. Once she climbed into bed, she fell asleep nearly as quickly as Jesse had.

THE ROOM WAS DARK. Emily sat up when she heard music playing downstairs. Her first thought was that Jesse, unable to sleep, had gone downstairs to practice. She glanced over and saw that Jesse was still fast asleep next to her.

"Jesse?" He stirred slightly, then resumed snoring. Emily sighed. Jesse slept the sleep of the dead.

She slipped her feet into fleece-lined slippers. Widget watched her, alert, from the center of the bed. She jumped down and clicked after Emily as she left the room and went downstairs.

The music grew louder. Emily realized it was coming from the parlor. This was one of the rooms she had yet to explore.

Emily went down a dark hallway towards the green glow of a light she didn't recall leaving on. The gramophone stood in a corner, piping out a slightly sinister-sounding tune. Emily rubbed her eyes. They hadn't brought the gramophone upstairs. Had they? Maybe Jesse went back and got it after they left the basement.

Emily approached the gramophone. Behind it hung the picture that must have been the basis for the portrait over the fireplace. Emily squinted, leaning towards it. There was something different about the photo.

In it were Matilda and the kids, just as they were in the portrait over the fireplace. But there was a fifth figure with them: a pale, slight, unsmiling girl. Matilda's assistant?

Something moved in the corner of Emily's eye. She turned her head and bit back a scream. Reflected in the black glass of the window across the room, the young woman stood solemnly behind Emily's left shoulder. She whirled around. Widget barked loudly.

There was no one there.

AFTER EMILY HAD TURNED out the light and turned off the gramophone, she went back upstairs and crawled into bed. Had she seen someone outside, through the glass? Had it been her own reflection, refracted and doubled by some trick of the light? Emily felt sure there was some reasonable and logical explanation. There had to be.

This was what she told herself as she drifted off into a fitful sleep.

THE NEXT MORNING, Jesse left for the hardware store to pick up a replacement latch for the window in the basement. Emily made coffee and shut herself in the office. As always, she stared at the blinking cursor on the blank white screen. As always, the words wouldn't come.

Emily closed the screen and got up, restless. It was difficult not to feel spooked by what she thought she saw the previous night. She told herself it was a byproduct of a restless imagination and Richard's scary stories. People went missing all the time. It wasn't that uncommon an occurrence.

Emily decided she would procrastinate dealing with her writer's block by going through Aunt Matilda's things and determining what could be sold. Since she and Jesse had only explored the first floor and she didn't relish the idea of returning to the basement alone, she decided she would start at the top and work her way down.

As much as she'd rationalized the previous evening's

events, she decided to take Widget with her in case she got scared. The dog hesitated at the foot of the attic steps. Emily, having anticipated this based on Widget's reaction to the basement, had a pocket full of treats and lured Widget the rest of the way by leaving one on each step until they were upstairs. Lulled by the treats, Widget forgot her earlier reservations and enthusiastically explored the attic. She sniffed the various pieces of antique furniture and the dusty clothes hanging on a rack.

Emily, following Widget's lead, flipped through the clothes on the rack. They were all at least thirty years out of date and would have been at home in any vintage store. Next to the rack of clothes, a white wicker end table held an ornate silver jewelry box. Emily flipped it open and a tiny ballerina, dressed in a pink tutu and pink satin shoes, spun in a circle while the jewelry box played Greensleeves. Something about the song seemed vaguely sinister in the attic, and Emily quickly flipped the lid shut, cutting off the sound.

Beneath the single round window opposite the attic door was an old roll top desk, and on the desk was a black manual typewriter. Emily felt the same delight she had regarding the library for the first time: it was as if it had been placed here, just for her.

Emily walked over to the desk and examined the typewriter. Old as it was, it appeared to be in perfect working order.

Widget barked. Emily turned to see her sitting in front of the armoire in the corner, staring at it. Emily felt an unpleasantly chilly sensation and decided it was time to go downstairs. She hefted the typewriter into its case and headed for the door, whistling for Widget, who didn't need to be told twice.

IN THE OFFICE, Emily meticulously arranged the typewriter

and a fresh ream of white paper in the center of the desk. She pulled the chain on the banker's lamp and rolled a fresh piece of paper into the typewriter. Her hands hovered over the keys as she waited for her customary blank feeling to descend on her brain, barring all creative thoughts but the one of her imminent failure.

Instead, her fingers settled gracefully on the keys and she wrote with a fluidity that she had not for months, so much so that she felt scarcely aware of what she was writing. Prior to her writer's block, Emily often felt that writing came so naturally that she wasn't fully in control of the ideas she had or what she wrote—but this was something else altogether. It was as if she wasn't even there; as if she was hovering over some distant shore, watching herself in the water below from far above.

Emily closed her eyes briefly and opened them at the sound of a truck door slamming. It was Jesse, back from the hardware store. She blinked and rubbed her eyes. She felt as if she was coming out of a trance.

Emily stretched and yawned, hearing the cuckoo pop out and chime the hour in the living room: six times. How had that happened? That meant she had been in the office for over four hours. She unrolled the current page from the typewriter and scanned it, eyes racing over the words.

I'M SCARED. *I thought that being here would make me feel safe, but it doesn't. I feel like something weird is going on, like there's something somebody isn't telling me. Everyone told me I was so lucky to be here, but I don't feel that way. I feel like something is wrong.*

Matilda and Cynthia seem nice enough, but when I look at them for too long, they look away. I can tell that they're hiding something, I just don't know what. If I look at them for too long, I can tell their eyes are lying.

I walked around the house yesterday because I was bored and there was nothing to do. I thought, at least there's this huge old house to explore. Cynthia caught me looking in a closet and almost lost her mind.

"What are you doing?" she said, like I had just murdered somebody.

"Nothing." I was scared and felt guilty. Maybe they would kick me out. "I was just looking for something I could draw with."

She ended up being okay, just took me to the kitchen and gave me butcher paper and some colored pencils, but it was so weird the way she freaked out like that. All because I opened a closet with a bunch of tea towels in it.

At night, I can sometimes hear them whispering in the front parlor. It has an old heating grate, the kind that carries sound, and it's connected to the one in my room. I can't make out every word because it's getting cold and they turned the heat on, so it's hard to hear over the air gushing up through the vent. Most of what they talk about seems to be about money. I don't get it. If she has this big giant house on a hill, isn't she rich?

I miss my parents. I know that I'm supposed to live in a house and go to school, but at least I know they loved me. I didn't like not being like other kids, but I liked having a family. I want to go to the park and visit them. Matilda says, "not yet," but not when. Which is another thing I feel like I'm being lied to about.

I wish I could run away, but I know they'd just find me and make me come back here.

EMILY FROWNED. She had no recollection of writing this. The first paragraph could have been her feelings about the move, but the rest of it seemed to be about the house—about Matilda and Cynthia, whoever that was. Maybe the second caretaker Richard had mentioned? If it was, did that mean that she was the woman in the photograph?

It had occurred to Emily to write about the house, because what better inspiration than a spooky old mansion on a hill? But she hadn't meant to write this. She would have changed the names around. She would have changed the situation, out of respect for the dead.

This narrator sounded young: a kid, and as a general rule, Emily didn't write child protagonists. They always sounded like an older person pretending to speak in the voice of a kid, and it sounded false. But this sounded like it could be taken from a diary—the diary of any young girl. Well, maybe not just any young girl. Maybe one who was stuck in a new situation she didn't ask for, one that made her uncomfortable. A girl who was forced to deal with the decisions that the adults around her made, ostensibly for her benefit. But how much to her benefit had it really been?

Emily often asked herself these questions about a character as she wrote, but this was different somehow. This didn't feel like a character she had created. Sometimes, characters seemed to have a life of their own, as if they had their own agendas and desires and Emily was merely a conduit for their will. But ordinarily, she was at least aware of what she was writing as she wrote it.

The typewritten pages disturbed her, and rather than reading anything else she'd written, she turned the sheaf of papers on the desk next to the typewriter facedown and got up to go to the kitchen and talk to Jesse. She closed the office door firmly shut behind her.

JESSE WAS IN THE KITCHEN, making stir fry on the stove. As usual, Emily felt relieved at the very sight of him. She hugged him from behind and then dropped into a seat at the table like a sack of bricks.

"Long day at the salt mines?" Jesse kidded her as he added peanut oil to the pan.

"Something like that," said Emily.

"Me too," he said. His back was to her, so he couldn't see

the odd expression on her face. "You wouldn't believe how hard it is just to find a latch for these old timey houses. I looked for hours! It doesn't help that there's only like two hardware stores in the entire town. The entire town! Some old-fashioned, family-run joint and a Home Depot over at the 29th Street Mall."

"Huh," said Emily, staring out the window.

"I ran into our friend Richard at the mom and pop shop. Asked me how the house was, then stared at me like I was going to run into the street screaming. I'm telling you, the dude's weird. There's something off about that guy."

"Maybe he just..." Emily closed her eyes and suddenly lost the will to finish her sentence. She was feeling very tired all of a sudden.

"Just what?" Jesse turned, really looking at her for the first time. "Babe? You all right?"

"I'm just so tired. That old gramophone from the basement woke me up last night. I guess it turned itself on or something? I don't know how those things work. I didn't even realize you brought it up to the parlor." Emily opened her eyes to find Jesse looking at her strangely.

"That thing from the basement? I didn't bring that upstairs."

Emily stared at him in total confusion. "But it's there. I saw it. Do you think maybe Richard—" Her reply was cut short by a pounding on the back door, rattling the glass panes. She and Jesse turned to see two tall black silhouettes at the door. Emily screamed.

5

*J*esse immediately picked up the long-handled wooden spoon he used to cook, wielding it like a weapon. Emily grabbed the fire extinguisher off the floor and threw aside the curtain over the glass panes of the door.

Two tall, attractive, well-coiffed people peered at them through the glass: a man and a woman. They were dressed head to toe in black. Backlit by the yellow overhead porch light, they looked like shadows.

"Hello!" The woman rapped lightly on the glass. "Do you have a moment to speak with us?"

Emily unlocked the door and opened it. They looked like replicants: black suits, black eyes, and shining black hair. The only thing to distinguish them from one another was the fact that the woman was Chinese and the man had pale skin like a vampire. Maybe he was Transylvanian. Emily chuckled inwardly at her little joke, and the pair regarded her inquisitively.

"Darla Chinn," said the woman confidently, extending her hand. Her nail polish was a deep vermillion, her nails manicured stiletto points.

"And I'm Roger Oglethorpe," said the man, extending her hand. "How do you do?"

They shook Emily's hand, then Jesse's.

"We're from Three Star Properties," said Darla. "Perhaps you've heard of it?"

"No," said Emily. "I can't say that I have."

"We're a local property management company, specializing in dealing with unique or...*unusual* properties," said Roger demurely. "We've been very interested in this house for some time now."

"Very interested," echoed Darla.

"May we come in for a moment?" asked Roger. "We don't wish to intrude, but we have a proposition for you that we think might be *very* much worth your while."

Emily looked at Jesse. He shrugged.

"Sure," said Emily. She stepped aside to let them in.

Roger and Darla slithered through the opening and sat themselves at the kitchen table. Emily and Jesse leaned against the counter, watching them warily.

"So," said Darla over steepled fingers. "How are you liking this place?"

"We were shocked to see anybody living here, frankly," said Roger, not giving them the chance to respond. "I mean, after everything that happened..."

Darla slid her eyes to the left, watching him. As he trailed off, she chimed in, as if on cue, "The murders, yes. So unfortunate."

"Murders?" said Jesse. "We heard they disappeared."

"Well, technically, they *did* vanish," Darla amended her earlier statement. "But I think it's fairly obvious that when three little children mysteriously disappear out of nowhere who the obvious culprit is."

"You're saying Matilda did something to them?" Emily asked.

"Well," said Roger delicately, "most of the town feels that

33

it's a foregone conclusion."

"Sometimes people aren't who we think they are," said Darla. "Of course, I would never want to speak ill of your family. But it would be dishonest of me to pretend that we don't all assume that something terrible happened here."

"What do people think happened?"

"Well, whether she took those kids, or took them and did something to them and then vanished herself—that's largely a matter of speculation," said Roger.

"But if I were you, I'd want to get rid of this place as quickly as possible," said Darla, shaking her head. "I don't even know how you can stand to be here."

"Just coming up here gives me the heebie jeebies," said Roger, adding "As a matter of professional opinion, of course."

"I TOLD you there was something weird about this place!" Jesse had barely closed the door behind them when he whirled on Emily, waving the spoon for emphasis. "And not just the place—the entire situation. This is totally a murder house!"

"Well, of course they're going to say that," said Emily. "They want to buy us out as cheaply as possible. Did it ever occur to you that they might be lying in order to freak us out?"

"Yes, they might be lying. But that's something we can find out so easily! All we have to do is Google it. Why would they lie about something that easy to prove?" Jesse smacked himself in the forehead, hit with the realization for the first time. "We didn't look up anything before we came here! Why didn't we Google any of this?"

"Why would we?" said Emily, taking out her laptop. "We were moving into a house we already technically owned. What was there to research?"

Emily opened her MacBook and Googled MEADE HOUSE COLORADO. The first hit was the local paper, an article titled *Murder in the Mountains?* with the subheading of *Five Disappear, Foul Play Suspected.*

MATILDA MEADE, *a local philanthropist who used her wealth to take care of local children in need, went missing last night between 10 p.m. and 7 a.m. She was reported missing by a maintenance man who works on the property. Police said there was no sign of a struggle. Nor was there any sign of Ms. Meade, her assistant Cynthia Harkness, or the three children who resided there. Police are reluctant to either confirm or deny suspicions of foul play, but eyewitness accounts confirm that no bodies have been recovered from the scene.*

"SO BASICALLY, everybody in the house went missing, and everyone who lives here thinks Matilda did it," said Jesse, reading over Emily's shoulder.

"It's a pretty reasonable assumption, I guess," said Emily, closing the laptop. "All things considered." She felt strange. It was one thing to think that her aunt, who for whatever reason had taken a liking to her, had left her this place for Emily to do whatever she wished with it. It was another to think that Matilda, who had died or disappeared under mysterious circumstances, might be responsible for harming three children and another adult—then left her the house in which she committed these crimes. Had she known the full set of circumstances prior to moving, would she still have taken the house? Emily thought guiltily of how desperate she felt before they moved. Some small part of her felt it was better not to know whether or not she would have taken the house regardless of its obscene history.

As if reading her mind, Jesse said, "Can we really afford to change our minds, though?"

Emily pinched the bridge of her nose, as if fending off an oncoming migraine. "As horrible as it sounds, I don't know that we can. We spent what little we had left moving out here. We put even more into the idea of fixing this place up. I don't know, maybe we should just try to hurry up and sell the place so we can leave."

THAT NIGHT, Emily found herself unable to sleep. She stared at the ceiling while Jesse snored beside her. She was restless at the thought of the day's events and worried she would have another nightmare. She decided to get up and make a cup of tea.

In the kitchen, Emily heated up water in the electric kettle. She selected a blue mug from the cabinet and poured hot water over the teabag, adding a generous dollop of honey. Against her better judgment, she carried the tea into the library. That day's pages lay face down on the desk where she had left them. She flipped them over.

THE HOUSE IS MAYBE *the prettiest I've ever seen. It's a million times bigger than our house before everything went wrong. I don't remember it well, but I remember it was small and had a lot of bugs in it.*

Matilda's house is on a hill and sometimes there are animals in the yard. There's a ton of rooms to explore, but the basement scares me so I stay away from that.

There's a playroom upstairs in the attic where I go with the kids sometimes. There's a toy chest for them and a big old closet-looking thing filled with old clothes that I like to dress up in. It's always warm in the attic no matter how cold the rest of the house is. Matilda says this is because heat rises.

I hope that after I start school, maybe I can go and see my parents again. I asked Matilda and she said, "we'll see." I hope that I get to HELP ME HELP ME HELP ME HELP ME

STARTLED, Emily dropped the pages. Reaching forward as if they might bite her, she flipped them over, one by one: HELP ME HELP ME HELP ME HELP ME. It went on like that for six pages. Eventually, the story resumed in the place Emily read when she came out of her trance.

Emily imagined herself at the typewriter yesterday, typing these words over and over with no awareness of what she was doing. She felt sick.

Shoving the papers in the desk's single drawer, she locked it with a tiny gold key in the keyhole and dropped the key into the pocket of her robe. This was exactly what Jesse had joked about, only now it was real. He would never want to stay if he knew how crazy she was acting. She wasn't sure that she did, either. Only that having these people after the house made her realize how valuable it truly was. What would Aunt Matilda say if she sold it after a week? She obviously had her reasons for not wanting to sell to them. Maybe they were the ones behind whatever had happened to her and the children.

Emily paused at the doorway and looked at the typewriter. *Whatever happened to her and the children...*Were the strange things she had written indicative of something more than stress? Was one of the children trying to communicate with her? From...wherever they were now?

She pushed the thought aside. It sounded like something she would write. *Fiction isn't life,* she chided herself. Then again, she thought, sometimes truth was stranger than fiction. Either way, the thought of purposely using the typewriter again and having something similar happen made her skin crawl.

She closed the office door and went back upstairs, determined to forget about what she read. She would get on with fixing the house with Jesse, sell anything of value, and they would get out and never come back.

With that reassuring thought in mind, she was able to fall deeply asleep.

No dreams or nightmares had woken Emily in the night, and she awoke, refreshed and ready to start a new day.

"You look happy," said Jesse. He was at the stove, cooking eggs.

"I am happy," said Emily, giving him a peck on the cheek. She poured a hot mug of steaming coffee from the fresh pot on the counter. Even the hideous color of the kitchen barely bothered her today.

"Going to do some writing?" asked Jesse.

Emily shuddered inwardly. "No, I think I'm going to tackle some more cleaning today," she said in a would-be casual tone. "Maybe go through the stuff in the attic. I think a lot of the old furniture is antique. We could get a nice chunk of change for it on eBay."

"I like where you're going with this," said Jesse. "I'm going back to that Small Town Hardware R Us place I found yesterday to get the latch. Old Man Wigglesworth ordered it for me express."

"I'm sorry, what did you say his name was?" asked Emily. "Old Man Wigglesworth?"

"That's not really his name, that's just what I call him. It's like, everybody around here acts so quaint and it's driving me mad."

"It bothers you that people are nice here?" asked Emily, amused.

"It doesn't *bother* me, it's just kinda Stepford, you know? Either you have weirdos lurking in the bushes telling you murder stories and trying to steal your house, or you have the guy who runs the hardware store, offering you lemonade and talking to you about his geraniums. These people need to pick a way to be and stick with it. In cities, everybody's a jerk. At least it's consistent."

"Your logic never ceases to amaze me," said Emily. "I'll see you at lunch."

"See you in a few," said Jesse. "Hours, that is. Holler if you need me."

"Will do." Emily watched as he went down the back stairs and over to his truck. She immediately felt her apprehension rise as soon as he backed out and headed towards town.

The sooner you do this, the sooner you can get out of here, she reminded herself. *Ideally forever*.

IN THE ATTIC, the unexpected warmth soothed Emily of her initial fears and she decided to start next on the far side of the attic, away from the corner that held the typewriter.

Emily went to the window, armed with glass cleaner and a roll of paper towels. She attacked the thick coating of dust on the glass, vigorously spraying and wiping. It was on her third pass that she saw the girl.

She was small and frail, no more than ten, though she could have been as young as eight. Her hair hung down her face in long and unkempt tangles. She wore a long pale nightgown. She stood in the yard below the house, and even from this distance, Emily could see her sad, dark eyes. Who was she? A neighborhood child?

Emily remained frozen to the spot, unable to move, certain if she so much as blinked, the girl would vanish before her very eyes. The girl remained fixed in her spot, staring at Emily.

She tried to open the window, but it was painted shut. Frustrated beyond belief, she ran to the attic door.

It was locked.

6

*E*mily frantically banged on the door. She rattled the knob to no avail. She was stuck.

She was not a particularly claustrophobic person, and anyway, the attic was large. But something about the idea of being stuck inside it with no visible means of escape after everything else she'd experienced terrified her beyond all reason. She started to yell for help, but would anyone hear her?

Emily ran to the window, reaching into her pocket for her phone. Her pocket was empty, and Emily pictured the kitchen table downstairs, where she'd left her phone that morning. She cursed and tried opening the window again. It seemed like it had never been opened, as if it was permanently glued shut. The feeling of being trapped increased. She banged on the window.

The girl was gone.

"Help!" she yelled. There was no one to hear her.

Emily ran back towards the door, promptly tripping on a child's rug decorated with trains and stubbing her toe on an old toy chest. A hollow clunk emitted from the wooden floor and Emily glanced down, seeing a tarnished gold locket on a thin, delicate chain.

Emily reached down and picked up the locket. She opened it and saw two photographs of a man and a woman around her and Jesse's age. She closed the locket, wondering if it had belonged to one of the children.

She looked around the attic. There was an old carousel horse leaning in the corner. For some terrible reason, its designer had thought it advisable to give it glittering red rubies for eyes. They glinted menacingly in the weak late autumn sunlight of the attic. Emily wondered if she could use it as a battering ram.

Hefting the horse up (it was heavier than it looked), she tucked it under one arm. She backed up to the far side of the attic across from the door so she could get a running start. She took a deep breath and squared her shoulders: *I will get out of this attic*, she thought. She took off running, her socked feet sliding a little on the wooden floor. She was two feet from the door when it flew open.

Emily skidded to a stop and almost fell over. The horse stopped, inches from impaling Richard, who stared at her with wide round owl eyes behind his spectacles.

"Doing a bit of jousting?" he asked.

EMILY TURNED on the electric kettle. She had offered Richard a cup of tea out of remorse for nearly running him through with a fake plastic horse.

"I really thought it was stuck," she said.

Richard nodded kindly. "Old house like this, it's temperamental. Weather can do that—humidity, or cold. Sometimes you can't even open your door for the wind up here. It's not surprising. Nothing to feel bad about."

"Yeah, lucky I didn't dismember you with that creepy carousel horse," she said. "I'd definitely feel bad about that."

Richard laughed. "Oh, I don't expect you would have done too much damage. Aside from all that, how are you folks doing? How are things with the house?"

Emily shrugged. "They're okay, I guess." She certainly didn't want to get into her strange dreams, mysterious type-writer activity, or random children appearing in the yard. Richard would think she was crazy. Or maybe he wouldn't. Emily wasn't sure which one would be worse.

"Just okay?" he said gently. He seemed to know she wasn't telling him everything.

"Richard," she said. "What can you tell me about Matilda? And about the children who lived here? Before they, you know—disappeared."

Richard scratched his chin. "Well, I worked on this property a long time. I maintained it when there was nobody living here, and I maintained it after your aunt moved in. Nice lady. Kind and warm. You couldn't ask for a sweeter person to work for. And generous, too. It wasn't enough for her to have this great big old space all to herself. No, she opened her home to those kids and treated them like they were her own. Gave them a chance they might never have had otherwise. And the kids, they were just as sweet as can be—little boy and girl, brother and sister I think they were, and another girl who hadn't been here as long."

"Another girl?" Emily felt the hair on the back of her neck rise. "How old was she?"

"Nine, ten? Not too sure. Saddest eyes I ever saw. I don't know what she went through before she came here, but she had already had a hard life. Just makes it that much worse what happened to her."

"But what happened to them? I don't understand. You just came up here one day and they were gone?"

"Last I saw of them was the night of the big storm. Blizzard knocked the power out for a couple days. That was why it took us so long to understand they were missing, you see. Folks were wrapped up in dealing with that."

"And you said he found no trace of them? They were just...gone?"

"No sign of a struggle, nothing broken or smashed—it was like they just up and disappeared."

"But who would want to hurt them?"

Richard shrugged. He leaned over the table, closer to Emily.

"You ask me, it was those damn property managers."

"Darla and Roger?" asked Emily, startled. Taking advantage of people, yes. She definitely believed they were capable of that. But murder?

"You think they're capable of kidnapping? Or murder? Or both?"

"Take that with a grain of salt, now. And you didn't hear it from me. But I think those scoundrels are capable of just about anything if it means a profit for them."

"But why?"

"They don't care about anything but money. They don't care about this town or the people in it. We're just in the way, as far as they're concerned. It's like Monopoly to them: buy up all the property, build hotels on it, and charge people as much as possible so they send them into bankruptcy. They're snakes. Matilda wouldn't sell to them. I hope you won't, either."

"I wasn't planning to," said Emily.

"Good. Don't let them get away with it. Be careful, though. You folks seem like a real nice couple, and I don't want to see anything happen to you two."

As well-meaning as he was, the statement made Emily deeply uncomfortable. The prospect that whoever had harmed Aunt Matilda and the children was still at large—even worse, still nearby and after whatever they'd try to take from Matilda before—filled Emily with a fear like none she'd ever felt.

The sound of wheels on gravel alerted her that Jesse was home. She sighed with relief. A slight dread accompanied it. It was time to tell Jesse what was going on.

"Well, thank you so much, Richard," she said. "I really appreciate all your insight and your help getting out of the attic." Remembering the night before, she added, somewhat tentatively, "And for bringing that old gramophone up from the basement."

"The what?" said Richard, politely confused. He reached into his pocket as he got up from the table and handed her his card. "You folks need anything, if you ever get into trouble or anything else, you call me now, you hear? Day or night."

"Day or night," echoed Emily and watched as he opened the back door and went down the steps, tipping his cap to Jesse as he walked by. If Richard hadn't brought up the gramophone, and neither had Jesse—who had?

Jesse came in with several bags from the hardware store and deposited them on the counter.

"What did he want?" he asked curiously.

"I got stuck in the attic," Emily admitted. "He heard me yelling and came to let me out."

"Stuck in the attic?" said Jesse. "But how?"

"I don't know. One minute, I was cleaning the window, and the next I just…couldn't get the door open."

"Was it stuck?"

"I guess so. I tried to bash it open with a carousel horse and almost took out Richard."

"Eventful day," said Jesse with a little laugh, removing a carton of orange juice from the fridge. "Anything else you want to talk about?"

"How did you know?"

"You've been acting pretty strange," said Jesse. "At first, I thought it was just the altitude. But it's more than that. I know you're not sleeping. And you just—don't seem like yourself, is all. I mean, I know you pretty well."

"I know," said Emily. She felt ashamed for keeping everything from Jesse as long as she had. "I just didn't want to affirm everything you said about coming here. And it sounds completely crazy." She told him about seeing the woman in the window and the girl standing in the front yard. She told him about the things she had written on the typewriter and her general feeling of overall wrongness.

He listened patiently without asking any questions or interrupting, then said, "I'm sorry you've been dealing with that, Em. I wish you would have told me. Do you think maybe the stress of moving is getting to you? I mean, you're totally isolated in this old house with just me and Widget for company, and she won't even go into half the rooms in the place. There's no one for you to talk to besides me or that weirdo handyman. The stress of the move, trying to write your novel—I don't want to say it might be a projection of your imagination, but what else could it be?"

In spite of the fact that she'd been telling herself very similar things for the past several days, Emily was insulted at the implication that it might be all in her head. "Jesse, I know what I saw! I'm not making this up. How can you say that?"

"I know, and I believe you," he said hastily. "It's just that you're so good at telling a story—you can scare me without even trying—and you haven't been able to write for a while, so, you know. Maybe it's coming out in other ways."

Emily considered this. She knew that people who were unable to sleep for long periods of time sometimes had waking dreams. Maybe her writer's block had resulted in something similar. But that wasn't enough to explain what she'd seen. Emily shook her head.

"No, I've considered that, and there's definitely something

weird going on," she said. "I think you might have been right about this place."

"That's funny, cause I'm starting to think that *you* were," he said. "This is a great opportunity. I know it's not ideal, but what is? I think maybe we need to see this thing through."

"That's it?" Emily was shocked. "You're like the number one conspiracy theorist of all the things wrong with this house. You don't think there's anything weird about what I just told you?"

"It's definitely weird, all right. I just don't think it's weird enough to warrant giving up our lottery ticket, you know? I mean, if you're truly uncomfortable, then obviously we need to have a larger discussion. But I really don't think it's going to take me long to get the work done. Let's just see how it goes for the next couple of days and then we'll reconvene. And also—I got hoagies."

"Okay, I guess," said Emily. She wasn't remotely satisfied or reassured. It all seemed very logical and reasonable, but why didn't she feel any better?

THE NEXT DAY, Jesse stuck around the house to fix the window in the basement and Emily was relieved. Just knowing he was there and she wasn't alone in the house was enough to calm her down.

It wasn't enough to return to the typewriter, of which she'd had just about enough, but she decided it *was* time to take her office back. Hastily stowing the typewriter back in its ominous cracked black case, she shoved it behind the couch and sat down at her desk. She opened her laptop and hit the power button, rubbing her arms while she sat waiting for the computer to boot up. It was freezing in here.

Emily thought of her seasonally inappropriate clothing in the bedroom upstairs. Florida was not exactly known for its winter gear, and Emily knew she was unprepared to deal with the temperature change. She just figured she'd pick up stuff from a local store when they got there, but with all the chaos of the last few days, she'd never gotten around to it. Maybe Matilda had something she could wear.

Emily went upstairs to the door at the end of the hallway. She felt weird about going into Matilda's room, even though she'd left it to her: it, and everything in it. Even if Matilda had died of natural causes, it still would have felt strange going through her things. Knowing that she didn't made it somehow even worse.

Emily pushed the door open with a creak. It was a pleasant, welcoming room with its own small fireplace. A sleigh bed took up one wall and a bookcase filled with mysteries took up another. There was a long dresser with a vanity mirror and two matching bedside tables ornamented with Tiffany lamps.

Emily wondered if maybe she had been letting her imagination get the better of her. Standing in Matilda's bedroom in broad daylight with nothing strange or mysterious happening, it seemed like everything was perfectly normal.

Emily went to the armoire. It was the identical twin to the one in the attic. She opened the heavy wood doors and peered inside.

Matilda's clothes were neatly organized by color, spanning from neutral autumn tones to bright pastel spring hues. Her shoes were lined up along the bottom beneath the clothes. Emily reached in and pulled out a thick, cozy cardigan, slipping it on over her thin chambray shirt.

"That's better," she murmured with a sigh of relief.

No sooner had she uttered these words than the window blew open with a loud report like a rifle, the sash banging furiously against the wall. An impossibly strong gust of wind rushed into the room, knocking over the lamps on the bedside table and pulling the books from the shelves. It blew so hard Emily could barely walk across the room to close the window, and she fought to take each step. The wind blew her backward and she fell onto the floor. There was a loud, shaking sound, and Emily looked up in horror to see the armoire listing from side to side like it was drunk. With an endless loud creak, it tipped forward.

Emily screamed and rolled to the side just as the armoire crashed onto the floor in the very space she'd been only seconds before. The wind suddenly ceased. Emily fought to catch her breath as adrenaline pumped through her veins.

Struggling to her feet, she caught a glimpse of her face in the mirror over the dresser: her own tangled hair and wild eyes followed her across the room as she ran for the door and thundered down the stairs.

Emily went straight to the basement door, where the sounds of the circular saw whining carried up the steps and into the hallway. She shivered as she descended the steps towards the workbench where Jesse, goggles on, oblivious, operated the saw. She plunged her hands into the pockets of Matilda's cardigan to warm them, startled when her hand wrapped around a small, hard object. Emily stopped at the bottom of the stairs and pulled it out.

Clutched in her hand was a black spiral bound book: Matilda's diary.

$\mathcal{F}$orgetting her plan to tell Jesse what happened, Emily sank to the bottom step of the basement and immediately began to read. She felt as though she was inside of one of her novels. She needed to know what was going to happen next.

THE VULTURES WERE HERE AGAIN today, clawing at my door looking for scraps. Will they never cease? I would think they would know by now that I will never, ever sell to them—no matter what they offer.

It pains me to admit how tempted I've been in the past. Maintaining this place hasn't been easy for a woman alone, let alone with the children to take care of. I would never let on to anyone how hard it gets at times, not even Cynthia—but she's been getting curious. She seemed to buy my story about the electric company accidentally taking four thousand dollars out of my account instead of the four hundred I owed them as the reason for her check bouncing last week, but I think Cynthia might be shrewder than she pretends to be.

Between the bank, Cynthia, the property managers, and that meddlesome Richard always poking his nose into my business, I've got a full plate on my hands, and that's not even counting the responsibility of the children. This is all really for them. I would have no purpose without them. I'm so grateful to them, really. I don't know what I would do if I failed them. I don't think I could live with myself.

"EM?"

Emily jumped, flying at least a foot in the air. The diary thudded to the ground beside her. She'd been so absorbed in the story, she hadn't even heard Jesse approach her.

He lifted the goggles off his head. "Whatcha doin'?"

"I found Matilda's diary," she said.

Jesse stared at the small black notebook on the ground. "Where'd ya get that?"

"Her room," she said. She felt a flash of annoyance at his questioning look. "I needed a sweater, okay? I was cold."

Jesse held up his hands with an air of surrender. "I didn't say anything."

"But you didn't believe me," she said. "When I told you what I saw." She hadn't realized how much it had been bothering her until she said it out loud. She felt tears form in the corners of her eyes.

"Hey, hey," said Jesse, taking her into her arms. "Don't cry. I'm sorry. I didn't mean to make you feel like I didn't believe you."

"But you don't," said Emily, drying her eyes.

"It's not that," said Jesse. "It's just like, it was one thing to joke about, you know? It was bad enough knowing something happened here. But thinking that there's still something weird going on—it's like, too much, you know? I guess I just don't want to believe it."

Emily stared at the little book in her lap. "Maybe there's something in here that will tell us what happened. I wish we could just ignore it, but it's not going away. I tried to pretend it wasn't happening, too, and it didn't do me any good. If anything, I think that it just made everything even worse."

"Okay," said Jesse. "How about this: you build a fire with our newly acquired YouTube skills, and I'll pick up food. We'll meet up in front of the fireplace and maybe we can go through the diary and find out what happened to Matilda. Deal?"

"Deal," said Emily.

She regretted it almost immediately when she realized it would leave her stranded in the house alone, but she felt too proud to tell Jesse that. Instead, she waited till he left, then called Widget into the living room. She barricaded them in the room by closing the many doors that led in and out of it.

She went to the fireplace to build another fire, preferably a massive, roaring one, but there was scarcely enough wood left for even a small fire. She decided to look outside to see if there were any firewood bundles stored somewhere on the property. It occurred to her that there might be some in the basement, but she didn't relish the prospect of going downstairs without Jesse home.

Behind the house, there was an old toolshed at the far edge of the lawn. Emily imagined something popping out at her as soon as she opened the door. She shuddered, deciding to leave that as a last resort. The stairs from the kitchen door to the yard had a small alcove beneath, which seemed an obvious and logical place to store firewood. It was darker than she would have liked, but it seemed like a preferable alternative to exploring the toolshed.

Emily activated the light on her flashlight app as she crouched and slipped under the stairs. She shone the light around all the corners under the porch before shuffling forward, hunched over. She approached what she thought was a small bundle of wood, only to find it was nothing more than a black garbage bag covering a pile of bricks. Emily shone her light on the pile, squinting. Behind it, there was a wooden rectangle in the wall. Upon closer inspection, she realized it was a door.

Emily reached for the narrow wooden strip set into the door's surface and turned it clockwise. The door swung inward. Emily hurriedly set the bricks to the side and pulled the door open the rest of the way. She peered into the opening. Set into the side of the house was a long, dark passageway. It was impossible to tell where it led to without going in.

Emily paused at the entrance. Clearly, this was a terrible idea: she had no idea what was in the walls of this house. Maybe it was filled with rats, or bodies, or more ghosts. Yet she felt a strange pull she couldn't account for, one that led her forward. In spite of what the townspeople said, after reading Matilda's diary, Emily couldn't accept that she had bad intentions towards the children. Maybe some evidence lay within the house's walls that would exonerate her.

The passage was narrow and low, just wide and tall enough for a child to walk upright and an adult to walk bent over. Emily swept the beam of her light back and forth, revealing a series of narrow twists and turns. At one point, the passage appeared to tilt swiftly upward, as if on an incline. Emily moved forward, running one hand along the wall as she went. At the first bend, she was surprised to feel another roughly hewn latch under her hand. Turning it, she poked her head through and was surprised to see that it opened up to a corner of the cellar. She closed the door again and continued along the passageway, which now sloped upward and then turned left. At the turn, she found another door: this one inside the pantry in the kitchen. Emily closed the door and continued.

The secret passage led all over the house, with each door opening to a different room: the parlor, the living room, Aunt Matilda's bedroom, and a second bedroom, decorated for a young girl. The doors were all concealed within closets or behind furniture: a couch and a chair, in the living room and parlor respectively; the closets in Matilda's room and the second bedroom.

At the door into the second bedroom, the passageway abruptly bisected: ahead, the passageway sloped gently down an incline, presumably back into the living room. Behind Emily, across from the small door, there was a ladder: *the attic?* she wondered.

Just then, she heard the front door open and shut. "Hello?" Jesse called from somewhere below her.

Emily assumed he couldn't hear her from within the walls, so she exited the passageway in Andrea's room and ran down the stairs. Jesse stared at her as she entered the kitchen. Glancing at her reflection in the kitchen window, she saw that her hair was sticking up crazily and she was covered in dust bunnies.

"Jesse, you'll never believe what I found!" she said breathlessly.

"Was it Richard's soul?" Jesse rested two bags of something savory-smelling on the kitchen table.

"There's a secret passageway in the walls and it leads all over the house! There are doors into practically every room."

"Why do I find this information less than reassuring?"

"This means that maybe Matilda wasn't responsible," said Emily. "I mean, anyone who knew about the passage could have come into the house at any point and taken all of them! They might have been asleep in their beds. That's why no one heard anything, and that's why there were no signs of a struggle."

"And this is a good thing?"

"It clears her name and proves she didn't do it," said Emily triumphantly before adding thoughtfully, "we just have to figure out who did."

"Maybe it's time we revisit the question of the property management company," said Jesse. "I mean, it would be a quick fix and an easy out."

"Jesse, we can't! Matilda flat-out refused to sell this house to them, no matter what. Richard thinks they might have something to do with what happened to her and the kids. We can't just give them the house, it would be like letting them win. And whatever money they give us would be nowhere near what this place is worth."

"I don't know, babe," said Jesse, tugging at his hair. "I mean, what else can we do? Start running a haunted Airbnb and hope all the freaks show up to get their paranormal jollies? Cause I'm not really seeing a whole lot of alternatives here."

"There has to be another way," said Emily. "I don't think Matilda or this girl are trying to hurt us. I think they want us to help them. I think they want us to find the people who hurt them and bring them to justice."

"Emily, you can't be serious. That's like combining the efforts of the Ghostbusters with everybody on *CSI*! Normal people, people like us? We're not meant to go around solving crimes and bringing people to justice. Can't we just go to the cops?"

"And say what? 'My dead aunt wants us to bring her killer to justice?' They're not going to buy it, Jesse. They're going to think we're crazy or wasting their time or both."

"Well, what are we supposed to do?"

Emily contemplated the diary. "There must be something we're not seeing."

"I don't know if I want to see it. Can we just leave and come back later?"

"We don't have anything to go back to," Emily reminded

him. The two sat in momentary silence, reflecting on this unhappy fact. Jesse was the first one to speak.

"All right," he said. "What can we do? Is there somebody else we can talk to? Somebody else that knew them, besides Richard or the cops? Somebody else who might have known what was going on?"

Emily thought of the locket.

"Yes," she said, surprising herself with the certainty she felt. "I know exactly who."

BOULDER CREEK WAS low that time of year, and in spite of the cold, the banks were littered with people in the grass: people with backpacks, people with tents. They were mere feet away from the happy people who traversed the park, exclaiming over the Christmas lights that had gone up in early November. They were miles away from having a warm bed to sleep in that night.

Emily and Jesse made their way across the lawn, peering closely at the occasional couple as Emily checked their likenesses against the photographs inside the locket. She stopped, distressed, pausing beneath a tree growing out of an overhang near the water's edge. Jesse came to a sudden halt beside her.

"Jess, what if they're not here? Maybe they're in a different spot, or maybe they picked up and left town—" As she spoke, the locket suddenly grew so hot in her hand that she dropped it off the overhang and it promptly disappeared below.

"The locket!" Now Emily was even more distressed. She had just lost the most valuable possession of a dead girl who tragically lost her life under unknown circumstances. She was trying to help her, and she couldn't even get that right. Emily stumbled down the muddy bank after the locket and Jesse followed.

"Maybe we should go back—" he started as Emily came to a halt.

Beneath the tree, in the small shelter the overhang provided, were a couple. They looked up at Emily and Jesse with mild alarm. Emily and Jesse clearly weren't cops, but they weren't anyone the couple recognized, either. Emily saw the locket glinting on the ground in the moonlight. She picked it up.

"Excuse me," she called, cautiously approaching the pair. "Um, my name is Emily, and I was just wondering if I could ask you about your daughter."

"Andrea?" The woman sat up. There was a mingled note of hope and despair in her voice. "Do you know what happened to Andrea?"

"Are you Andrea's mother?" asked Emily, opening the locket. "Is this you?"

She held the locket out to the woman. Tears sprang to her eyes as she looked at the necklace. She held it out to the man seated next to her. He looked equally overwhelmed with grief.

"They took her away," he said suddenly. "They said we couldn't care for her, and maybe that's true. But we did love her, very much. And they didn't tell us where she'd gone. And they didn't tell us if we'd ever see her again, or if they'd ever bring her back—" His voice broke and he stopped, too overcome to go on. His wife placed a reassuring hand on his back.

"We asked," she said. "We asked and asked, but they wouldn't tell us anything. And then when they did, they questioned us. They said Andrea had disappeared, and they thought she had run away or that we had taken her. They asked us if we'd gone up to that house and done something to the people that lived there." Her voice shook with right-eous indignation. "They took our daughter away and then accused us of hurting the people they gave her away to. I

56

wouldn't have done that. I wanted my child to have a better life. Who doesn't?"

"I believe you," said Emily. "I want to find out what happened to Andrea. Is there anything you could tell us that might help?"

The couple exchanged a glance. They seemed to hesitate.

"We're on your side," said Jesse encouragingly.

"She came to see us once," Andrea's mother said wistfully, fondly. "Told us how much she missed us and how she wished she could come back. She said she had to go back to those people, so she wouldn't get us into trouble. But that she just wanted to say how much she loved us. She wanted to make sure that we were safe."

"Such an amazing, wonderful, loving child," said her father, his voice stricken with grief. "She wanted to make sure *we* were safe. When she was the one in danger…"

"We asked her if she was all right up there," said Andrea's mother. "In that big old house on the hill. You want to know something strange about that place? Everyone said how wonderful it was, it and the woman who owned it. But all the times we walked past, I never saw anybody come out of it. Anybody that went in, they never came out. Nobody but that old maintenance man."

"She said they were treating her fine," said Andrea's dad. "Said there were two sweet children she took care of some-times. But who was taking care of Andrea?"

"We asked about the older ones, the adults, and she wouldn't tell us anything," said Andrea's mom. "She clammed right up and said she had to go. There was something wrong, I could tell. I just don't know what."

"You will tell us if you find her, won't you?" asked Andrea's father. "Will you bring her back to us? If you find Andrea?"

"Yes," said Emily. "I'll do whatever I can."

Even as she said the words, her heart was breaking. She knew she was making them a promise she couldn't keep.

They were silent on the ride back to the house until they pulled into the driveway, awash in the red and blue flashing lights of the sheriff's cruiser.

___

8

*E*mily jumped from the cab of the truck and ran toward the front door. Richard was standing on the porch, twisting his hat in his hands.

"I called them as soon as I saw," he said.

"Saw what?" asked Emily. She looked over and saw the front window's shattered glass. Emily ran inside, calling Widget's name. The little dog came running at the sound of her voice, and Emily stooped to hug her.

Stepping carefully among the broken glass, Emily bent to pick up the large rock that had sailed through the large bay window, turning it to see the black lettering painted on the side:

CURIOSITY KILLED THE CAT.

EMILY STARED at the rock in shock. Who could have done this? She already suspected Matilda's disappearance had been the result of foul play and that the person responsible might still be around—with a similar agenda for Jesse and Emily. But now they had incontrovertible proof that the villain was dangerously close.

She looked through the window. The sheriff had rounded the side of the house with a flashlight, stopping in the front yard to talk to Jesse and Richard. Emily went outside, bringing Widget with her so she wouldn't cut her paws on the glass.

"Richard here saw the glass and called us up," the sheriff was saying. Emily read the name on the pocket of his shirt: OGLETHORPE.

"Are you related to Roger Oglethorpe?" she said suddenly.

The sheriff turned, surprised. "Unfortunately," he said, before resuming his assessment of the damages to the house. "It looks like it's just petty vandalism, but given the house's history, I wanted to perform a more thorough investigation myself."

"Why would anyone want to vandalize this place?" asked Jesse.

"Well, from where I stand, it could be a couple of different things. I got these damn kids running around in gorilla masks, spray-painting anarchy symbols on all the construction sites in town—some kind of rebellion against all the new property development happening. Or it could be one of the townspeople. One of the ones still angry about what happened here."

"Why would they be angry at the house and the people living in it now?" asked Emily. "I mean, shouldn't they be angry at the people who took them?" *Or killed them*, she added silently.

Sheriff Oglethorpe paused before answering, as if deciding how much to tell them. "Some folks didn't think it was somebody from the outside," he said finally. "There were some who thought the problem lay within the walls, so to speak."

Emily thought his caginess might have something to do with not wanting to speak ill of her aunt in front of her. "Sheriff Oglethorpe, I know there were people in town who didn't like Matilda. Can you be a little more specific? At this point, I'm just concerned for my own safety."

"Oh, I don't think it's anything that serious," said Sheriff Oglethorpe. "If anything, I think they're just trying to scare you folks."

"Who?" asked Jesse.

"When the news van came up here to report the story, some folks showed up with their little hand-drawn signs," said Sheriff Oglethorpe. "Mind you, in this town, people will protest somebody opening a restaurant that uses straws or a store that sells soda pop. So that's hardly surprising. For the most part, your aunt had a reputation as a kind and generous woman who cared about children, which is what I believe. And if we'd recovered any bodies, I don't think anyone would be speculating on what might have happened. But, because we didn't, there were some that thought maybe she took those kids."

"Took them where?" said Emily. "She was already caring for them here. Why take them someplace else?"

The sheriff shrugged. "Some say she was having money problems and that maybe faking her death was a way out of it. They might think you're part of their little conspiracy theory—fixing up the house to sell it and give it to Matilda, wherever she's at, in exchange for your cut of the profits."

"That's ridiculous," said Emily.

The sheriff chuckled. "Well, of course it is. I'm not saying that it's reasonable. Not everyone gave credence to those rumors." He scratched his chin, looking pensive. "I find it very unlikely that Matilda—or anyone who was in the house that night—is still alive, unless they're criminal masterminds, or spies. No one gets declared dead in absentia without a thorough investigation."

"So, what do we do here?" said Jesse. "We're trying to fix the place and sell it, not put more money into it because of vandals."

"I'll have somebody come through and check on the place a couple times a day, especially when the sun goes down," said the sheriff. "I think if whoever did this knows you're under our surveillance, it will discourage them from causing you folks any further trouble."

"But how serious is this?" asked Emily. "Are we in any danger?"

"No, no, nothing like that. Folks get on their high horse and want to prove their little point. It's nothing for you to worry about." The sheriff smiled at her. He turned to the cruiser, obviously done with the situation.

"Is that it?" Jesse called after him.

"That's it," said the sheriff. He closed the door of the cruiser, started the ignition, and pulled away.

"Don't expect him to be of much assistance," said Richard bitterly from the shadows of the house.

Emily jumped. She had forgotten he was there. "Why not?" she asked.

"Never did find out what happened to Matilda, Cynthia, and those kids," he said. "You ask me, he's just passing time till he can retire and collect his pension. Most of the conversations I've had with him have been about his place in Vail." Richard abruptly turned and headed down the driveway for his truck.

Emily turned to Jesse. "What do you think?"

He shook his head. "I think we should fix this place up ten times faster than we planned and get the hell out of Dodge."

AFTER THEY SWEPT the glass from the floor and threw it away, Emily and Jesse got ready for bed that night in pensive silence. It seemed that they were truly between a rock and a hard place. This situation was becoming far worse than even the money problems they had back in Florida, where at least they were safe from vandals and possible murderers. But it didn't change the fact that this was the only place they had to live.

"Jesse," Emily began as they got into bed. She knew her suggestion wouldn't be well-received. "Maybe we should ask my parents for help."

Jesse looked at her, openly horrified. "Em! No *way*. We can't! They already think that I'm a total failure and you never should have married me. This will be more fuel for the fire."

Emily sighed. "I know, I know. I don't like it, either. Do you think they consider my job a real job? They wanted me to be an accountant and crunch numbers for the family firm. But look at the alternative. Should we really allow pride to dictate our decisions? After all this?"

Jesse was silent for a moment, considering. Pride was a huge point of contention for Jesse. He wanted to be entirely self-sufficient and reliable. To admit to being anything less would kill him.

"Here's the thing," he said. "Let's just say that theoretically —*very* theoretically—maybe this place is haunted. Which means there are invisible entities bothering us, or, like you said, trying to contact us. They're not physically here and they can't really do anything to us." Emily thought of the armoire falling over and shuddered. "I mean, like—it's our house. Not theirs. Not anymore. I'd be really mad to give up a chance at our future because of something invisible, like angry spirits or whatever."

Emily allowed herself to imagine it: the house fully restored, the check in their bank account, a brand-new place. If they could just stand up to the people trying to intimidate them, they could have it all.

As for the ghosts, if they found out what happened to

them, it might give their spirits a chance to rest. Solving the mystery would also protect Emily and Jesse from the people who hurt Matilda and the children. But who were they? Where were they? And what were they up to now?

"It's not the ghosts I'm worried about," said Emily. "I'm worried about the people throwing rocks through our window. I'm worried about the sharks trying to buy this place, who coincidentally happen to be related to the sheriff."

"I am, too," said Jesse. "But if they wanted to do something bad to us—if they wanted to make us disappear—wouldn't they have done something way worse than throw a rock through the window?"

"That's true," said Emily. "I guess it was more like a warning. But it's almost like they knew we talked to Andrea's parents. How would they know that?"

"They would have to be watching us very closely," said Jesse.

"So maybe we should just pretend everything is normal and we're not trying to find out what happened here," Emily said. "We'll just go back to working on the house."

"And the sooner we finish," started Jesse.

"The sooner we can leave," finished Emily.

With this reassuring conclusion in place and Widget curled up between them, Emily leaned over to turn out the light.

"PLEASE DON'T HURT THE CHILDREN," Matilda's voice, pleading and desperate, drifted up the stairs. "Take whatever you want—you can have anything in the house! If it's not enough, I'll pay you. Just please don't hurt the kids!"

Everything was dark. Emily could hear, but she couldn't see. She heard loud crashes downstairs and the voice of Matilda. Momentarily, it was joined by Cynthia.

"Matilda? What's going on? Is everything—" Cynthia's voice was cut off by her prolonged scream.

Inside the darkness, Emily's breath was rapid and shallow. She heard footsteps on the stairs. Her heart pounded in her chest. From somewhere nearby, she could hear the sound of children crying. The sound was muffled, as if hidden somewhere close.

The footsteps grew closer. Emily had never felt this kind of fear: it was all-consuming, a certain dread that the sound might be the last thing she would ever hear.

The attic door creaked open. Emily closed her eyes, though it made no difference in the dark. She wished with every fiber of her being that she could see her parents again.

Something creaked in front of her: a door opening in front of Emily's face, letting in a narrow shaft of light. Emily screamed.

Emily sat bolt upright in bed, drenched in sweat. It was several minutes before her breathing returned to normal. She patted Widget until she calmed down. Jesse, as usual, was sleeping the sleep of the dead.

Was it just a nightmare, borne from the unconscious suggestion of what happened in the house? Or was it a memory?

Emily swung her legs over the side of the bed and slid her feet into fleece-lined slippers. Grabbing her thick fuzzy robe from the bathroom door's hook, she wrapped it tightly around her. She cautiously crept down the stairs toward the library. She was relieved when Widget willingly followed her without food-based incentives.

Emily built a fire in the library's fireplace, reassured by the cheery light it provided. She reached behind the couch and pulled out the cracked black case that held the typewriter. She set it on the desk and carefully lifted the typewriter out, rolling a fresh sheet of blank white paper into the roller.

If her theory was correct, Andrea used the typewriter to contact Emily in order to tell her what happened. As unsettling as she found the idea, the prospect of continuing her life in the house with a fistful of suspicions and no certain idea of what transpired within these walls was intolerable. If Andrea used the typewriter to contact Emily the first time, maybe she would do it again.

Except this time, Emily would be ready for it.

She sat in front of the typewriter. Before placing her fingers on the keys, she reached into the pocket of her robe and pulled out a flat flask of whiskey. She took a small swig for courage. The whiskey was strong and burned reassuringly all the way down. Emily took a deep breath, steeling herself.

She placed her fingers on the keys.

9

*A*t first, nothing happened. The fire crackled merrily in the background. Widget yawned and settled herself on the sofa, leather creaking as she turned in circles before curling up into a ball. The only other sound was the wind outside as it blew fiercely down the mountain.

Emily felt foolish. Maybe she *had* written the other pages on the typewriter. Maybe there were similar explanations for all the strange and frightening things that had happened in the house since she and Jesse moved in, and she'd just overreacted. The reflection in the parlor had been her own. The girl in the yard had been a Girl Scout out of uniform, saddened by how few boxes of cookies she'd sold. The dream had been nothing but a dream, the product of the mythology regarding the house and what happened here. The incident in Matilda's room had really just been the wind, the door to the attic had just become stuck, and she needed to stop inventing wild stories when there was a perfectly reasonable explanation for all of this—

Emily's fingers fell upon the keys as if they belonged to someone else. She no longer had the trance-like feeling she'd felt before, and it was strange and somewhat horrifying to watch her hands fly along the keys like they belonged to someone else. It was as if Emily was merely a marionette having her strings pulled by an unknown entity.

MY NAME IS Andrea and I lived here before you. Matilda and Cynthia took care of me. Sometimes I took care of Bobby and Tricia. They were the other kids who lived here. But I couldn't protect them. I tried so hard, but I couldn't keep them safe. Matilda and Cynthia had been acting funny for a while. I spied on them by listening in on their conversations when I could, but I couldn't find out that much stuff except what they said about money, which they complained about. Two people were always coming by the house trying to get Matilda to sell it to them, but she wouldn't. One day I came downstairs and heard her yelling at them. Cynthia made me go out to the yard to play. That night, something bad happened. I don't know who did it, I couldn't see their faces. I hid the kids and I tried to hide, but they found me. I don't remember anything after that till I woke up in the house, but nobody could see me or hear me and I just want to leave but I can't please help me help me help me

EMILY WRENCHED herself away from the desk, unhinged by the surge of emotions overwhelming her. They seemed to run all the way to her fingertips. Breathing hard, she stared at the page in front of her. *Something bad happened...I couldn't see their faces...I just want to leave...help me.*

Emily felt colder than she ever had in her life. She huddled on the hearth by the fire and stoked it with the poker, tossing in rolled-up newspapers and pieces of card-board from the nearby recycling can until the fire blazed high, warming her against the chill of the library. She almost wished she had never come downstairs to use the typewriter. It was too much. But now that she had, she felt like there was no way she could ignore the pleas of the little girl. Emily felt certain she was the girl from her dreams; the one she'd seen in the front yard. The one whose parents wept for, wanting nothing more than to have her back.

She didn't think the ghost knocked over the armoire. This ghost was a child who just wanted help, and Emily couldn't accept that she might have tried to hurt her. But if it hadn't been Andrea, who had it been? Matilda? Cynthia? Or something else?

Emily suddenly felt more tired than she'd ever felt in her life. Widget jumped up and followed, her tags jingling, as Emily shuffled slowly from the study. It was all she could do to drag herself upstairs and collapse into bed, where she promptly fell into a dark and dreamless sleep.

THE NEXT MORNING, blindingly bright sunlight poured through the open blinds and fell across Emily's sleeping face. Flinging a hand up to block the harsh rays, she rolled over and hid her head beneath the pillow. She would never get used to how brightly the sun shone here, as if living in the mountains were on par with building a home on the sun itself.

Emily heard Jesse's truck start up in the front yard. She removed the pillow from her head and squinted at the clock: noon. She never slept this late at home.

Emily shuffled downstairs and into the kitchen like a sleepwalker. She was thrilled to see that Jesse had left a fresh pot of coffee brewing. She poured a cup and opened the pantry to see if there was any food or if she'd have to go to the store.

On the table, Emily's phone buzzed. She kept it on vibrate so the inundation of calls from various collections agencies wouldn't startle her throughout the day. She glanced over briefly, then went back to the pantry, unwilling to deal with them this early in the morning. The phone stopped. It immediately buzzed again.

Emily let the door fall shut with a sigh. She'd just have to put the phone on silent, that was all. When she picked it up, she saw the name across the top of the screen: three simple letters capable of inciting either utmost comfort or undeniable dread.

"Mom?"

"Emily, where have you been? It's been two weeks since you moved out to that godforsaken house. I've called you countless times to make sure you're alive, and what do I get in response? *Text messages!* If I've told you once, I've told you a thousand times, texting is not an acceptable alternative to communication. I've been worried sick, and so has your father, of course—"

"How is Dad?" asked Emily, desperate to get a word in edgewise.

"Worried sick! Just as I am. And still building those infernal *birdhouses*, if you can imagine anything more lurid. What eyesores, my God. I'd love to sneak into the yard in the night and light them all on fire. But of course, he'd know it was me. Tell me, Emily: what on earth are you doing camped all the way out there in that hideous box of tinder?" She lowered her voice confidentially. "Is it Jesse? Are you having problems? Are you considering a...separation?"

Wouldn't you love that, Emily thought. "No, Mom. We're not having any problems." Marital ones, anyway, she added silently. "When I found out Aunt Matilda left the house to me, we just wanted to come check it out and see if it was worth anything." Emily felt guilty. Maybe her mother was upset Matilda had left Emily the house instead of her.

This, however, was not the case. "Oh my goodness, Emily, I can't believe you went out there. I understand, of course, the property might be of some value, but honestly, your father would have gladly handled the sale remotely. That way, you could have avoided having anything to do with that crazy old bat."

"Mom!" Emily was shocked. "She's missing. I'm pretty sure she might be...dead."

"Well, that doesn't surprise me in the slightest. I always knew Matilda would come to a bad end. She never wanted to settle down and have a family, at least not in the traditional sense; thought she was above getting married or even working a day in her life—it made my mother crazy. Especially when their grandmother left Matilda the house instead of her. And then she turned it into some sort of *orphanage* for wayward children? I can't imagine how they must have damaged it. I mean, is it even worth anything?"

Emily was overwhelmed. She knew her mother had little idea of what had happened in the house to Matilda and the kids; even so, she seemed like the height of insensitivity at that moment. But maybe she could at least tell her why no one in the family spoke to Matilda anymore. That was one thing Emily had never understood, and maybe answering that would be the key to understanding Matilda and figuring out what happened to her. What was the terrible thing Matilda wouldn't consider doing, the one that had seemed like the only way out?

"Is that why nobody talked to Aunt Matilda anymore?" Emily asked. "Because Matilda got the house instead of Grandma?"

Her mother snorted. "That was hardly the calamity you'd think it was. That house was in the family a long time; no one actually wanted to *live* there. We all assumed it was old and probably filled with mold besides. It was a well-known fact that Matilda would never marry, and so it was likely done to ensure she had some kind of property to her name. I don't think my mother was overly broken up about it. She had simply grown tired of dealing with Matilda's hardheaded obstinance. She always said you couldn't have a conversation with her about anything. I assume that was why they drifted apart."

"That's it?" Emily asked. "They stopped talking because Matilda was stubborn?"

"Well, yes. Families are something you're born into; when you get older and have a choice, you don't always want to know them anymore. They were very different people, and they simply grew apart."

"That's so sad," said Emily, imagining Matilda alone with her problems for no better reason than the fact that her sister found her annoying.

"Speaking of family," said Emily's mother, suddenly severe. "If you plan to have one, and Jesse's not supporting you, you still have time to change your mind. Marriage is hardly the binding arbitration it once was, and I assure you, my girl, there are any number of men who would be overjoyed—"

"Mom, I have to go," Emily said hurriedly, before the Divorce Jesse and Worthier Possible Suitors Shall Arise discussion could commence. "Jesse's here, and he's, um, starting a business. So, we need to discuss our, uh—start-up capital." She didn't know what it was about her mother that caused her to compulsively lie, but the need was irresistible all the same.

"Jesse? A business?" She could practically hear the raised eyebrow in her mother's voice. "My, my. How…unexpected. What kind of business?"

"I have to go," said Emily wildly. "He's here with the home inspector, we're selling the house and putting the money into our start-up. I'll explain later."

"Well, okay, dear," said her mother, sounding taken aback. "Do keep me updated. And call if anything goes wrong in that miserable viper pit. I'm sure it's riddled with rat holes and dry rot."

"OkayMomthanksgottagoloveyoubye," Emily said all in

one breath. After she hung up, she sat at the kitchen table, sweating. Amazing how talking to her mother had the same effect on her as talking to a ghost.

"OUR START-UP?" said Jesse. It was late afternoon when he and Emily reconvened over lunch to recap that morning's events. "What start-up?"

"I don't know! She just kept talking about money and what were we doing and I just wanted to invent something that might placate her—"

"You could sacrifice me to an active volcano and it wouldn't placate the angry god that is your mother," said Jesse. "Did anything else happen? Besides this imaginary start-up of ours?"

"Well." Emily bit her lip and gazed down at the table. She was reluctant to disclose that she'd spent the previous night purposely communing with the ghost. It was one thing when she didn't have a choice, but to purposely invite the very contact they'd been trying to pretend didn't exist seemed like something that might not go over well.

"What's up?" said Jesse, watching her closely.

"I used the typewriter again. To see if I could contact Andrea," Emily said in a rush.

"What?! Why? I mean, why would you want to hear her on purpose? I get that we have some kind of poltergeist and some of this stuff is just unavoidable, but I don't think you should invite it in for tea, you know what I mean?"

"I know. It's just that I had another nightmare, and it was almost like I had to know what happened. I just want to help her, Jesse. I feel so bad for those kids. What if no one ever finds out what happened to them? How can Andrea's parents live with that?"

Jesse ran a hand through his hair till it was sticking up. "I get what you're saying. I definitely feel for them. I really do. I guess I'm more concerned about helping *us*. Who's gonna help us if things get any worse? Probably not a ghost. And what are we going to do for this person, anyway? She's not even a person anymore."

"I know it sounds crazy. I do. I just have this feeling like if we *can* help her, and Matilda and the others, maybe all of this will stop."

"I hope you're right," said Jesse.

Richard knocked on the back door. Emily and Jesse jumped, startled by his sudden and unexpected presence. Emily got up and opened the door.

Richard cleared his throat and chuckled uncomfortably. "Sorry, I didn't mean to show up uninvited. Just wanted to see how you folks were doing."

"Everything's been pretty normal," said Emily. "Just another day in the woods."

"Mountains, in this case," said Jesse.

Richard looked relieved. "Oh, good. You're such nice people, I'd hate to hear that those crazies downtown were bothering you. You ask me, it was those lunkheads in gorilla masks, running around terrorizing folks and calling themselves anarchists. If it were up to me, I'd have them all thrown in jail."

"What's all that about?" asked Emily.

"Oh, you know. 'Keep Boulder weird,' that whole shtick. I'd settle for 'normal but still affordable,' but evidently, it's not a choice." Richard sighed, then immediately brightened. "I got something for you all out in the truck."

Emily and Jesse exchanged a glance, then followed Richard down the back stairs and into the side yard where his truck was parked.

10

*H*e threw the canvas cover off the flatbed, revealing rows and rows of neatly bundled firewood.

"Oh, Richard!" Emily was moved. "That's so sweet of you to think of us." Firewood was expensive, and Emily didn't relish the prospect of excavating what remained of their savings account to buy more.

"First snow of the season's on its way," said Richard. "I can smell it in the air."

"I can see it on my phone," said Jesse, studying his screen. He glanced back up at Richard, looking vaguely troubled. "How much does it snow here, anyway?"

"Oh, it's not near as bad as you would think. It'll drop below freezing some nights, but those are the nights it doesn't snow. And when it does, it may seem like a lot, but a Chinook wind will come through and melt it all away the next day. If *that* doesn't do it, the sun will come out the next day and take care of the rest."

"Well, that's good to know," said Jesse.

"It does get awful cold at night, though. And it must be a nightmare trying to keep this whole place heated. I figured it might just be easier for you to build a few fires till the snow passes."

"We really appreciate it," said Emily. "That's so kind of you."

"Sure thing," said Richard as he hefted the bundles off the truck and set them in the driveway. "You need help carrying these in the house?"

"I got it," said Jesse abruptly. Emily glanced over to see the obstinate expression on his face and sighed. *Here we go.*

"All right. Hope it keeps you warm. You have my number, if you need anything." Richard waved as he climbed into his truck.

Jesse practically had smoke coming from his ears. "Does he think I can't get enough firewood for the two of us? I know how to collect wood. I can cut down an entire tree!"

Emily bit her lip. She was actually holding back a smile, but there was no way she wanted Jesse to see that. "I think he was just trying to help."

"I don't need his help! I'm going out to the yard. Have you seen how many dry sticks and branches there are out there? There's enough kindling to last us the winter!"

"Okay, Jesse," said Emily. "Whatever you say."

Jesse stormed off, disappearing around the side of the house. Widget ran after him, barking merrily at what she thought was a rousing game. Emily surveyed the bundles of wood lying in the driveway.

"Well, I guess I'll just take these in, then," she said to no one.

JESSE RETURNED TRIUMPHANTLY with an armful of branches he found in the yard. It was nowhere near as substantial as the supply Richard left them, but he seemed so pleased with himself Emily never would have said anything to that effect. Instead, she helped Jesse build a fire in the living room with his newly gathered tinder, discreetly noting the nearby proximity of store-bought firewood. Then she went to the kitchen to boil a kettle of water for tea.

"This isn't so bad," said Jesse an hour later. After his foray to the hardware store, he'd stopped by the supermarket, purchasing graham crackers, chocolate, and marshmallows. He had speared one with one of his sticks from the yard and roasted it with the studied carefulness of a master. "You want a s'more?"

"Obviously I want a s'more," said Emily. "Do you even have to ask?"

Jesse made her an especially gooey one. They split the remainder of her flask and pulled out the sofa bed. It was so warm and cozy Emily could almost forget all the strange and terrible things that had happened.

"I wish it could always be like this," she said as they gazed into the fire.

"I know what you mean," said Jesse.

They drifted to sleep as the cuckoo clock chirped midnight.

EMILY AWOKE NEAR DAWN. It was still pitch black outside. Her eyes were half closed, and through them she saw that the door connecting the living room to the hallway had drifted open in the night. Emily sat up, rubbing her eyes. The fire had dwindled and a cruel draft wafted in through the open door.

She sat up and steeled herself to dash across the room, shut the door, stoke the fire, then dive back into bed. Next to her, Widget sat like a sentry: still as a stone, staring at the door. Emily followed her gaze and froze.

Framed in the doorway hovered a tall shadow. Emily felt as though it had been there, watching them, for some time.

It was her first impulse to scream and wake up Jesse. Her

second impulse was to promptly bury herself under the covers and hope it would go away. *Widget will protect us*, she thought wildly. But something else told Emily that neither action would do her much good.

"What do you want?" whispered Emily. Her breath was visible in the icy cold room.

The shadow was silent. Emily had a terrible feeling she knew just what it wanted.

Wrapping herself in the topmost quilt, Emily shuffled toward the door. The shadow glided down the hallway. It paused at the foot of the stairs. Emily swallowed her fear and followed it.

It slithered up the stairs and glided to the door at the end of the hall. It paused outside Matilda's room before sliding in.

Emily, terrified but determined, followed. She saw the shadow lingering in front of the old steamer trunk at the end of Matilda's bed. She didn't want to go any closer. She squeezed her eyes shut, her hands in fists at her side. When she opened her eyes, the shadow was gone and the trunk's lid stood open.

Frowning, Emily approached the trunk and peered inside. On top of a neat row of blankets, nestled on a chenille throw, was a small black laptop.

Emily was surprised. She assumed when she found the typewriter that Matilda had shunned all technology.

She tucked the computer under one arm and hurried down the stairs. She closed the door tightly when she got back to the living room, then stoked the fire. Jesse rolled over and sighed in his sleep. Emily curled up under the blankets as the sky lightened from navy blue to gray. The snow continued to fall.

She opened the laptop.

. . .

THE COMPUTER PROMPTED her for a password, and Emily stared blankly at the screen. She realized she didn't even know Matilda's birthday. She tried her mother's, then her grandmother's. She even tried her own. None were the correct password. Beyond that, Emily was stumped. She realized how little she actually knew about the woman whose house she lived in.

Emily closed the laptop and pulled the covers over her head. Even with the fire rebuilt, the room was freezing. She didn't think that she would ever fall asleep with the cycle of thoughts swirling in her brain: what she had just witnessed combined with the endless series of other strange things that had occurred.

When she woke up, it was without recollection of ever having drifted off. Bright white light filled the room. The drapes were open and Emily, squinting, saw several feet of snow blanketing the ground. And still more snow came down, seemingly endless, buffeted by currents of wind that sent it spiraling into large, heavy drifts against the side of the house.

The heat was on—the thermostat set to seventy-five—but the temperature of the house matched the frigid chilliness outdoors. Emily wrapped a blanket around her shoulders and went to stoke the fire again, closing all the doors to the living room. They had all drifted open in the night.

"Hey, what's going on?" asked Jesse, sitting up and looking out the window at the endless expanse of snow. "When did that happen?"

"While we were sleeping," said Emily.

"Yeah, but this means—"

"This means we can't leave," said Emily. "Not until the snow stops. And by the looks of it out there, it's not going stop anytime soon."

They brought the rest of the firewood in and piled it up next to the hearth. Jesse examined the thermostat then went to the basement to check the heater. Emily thought darkly that there was nothing wrong with the heater. She knew there was something else behind the coldness of the house.

Emily opened Matilda's laptop again and stared at the screen in total frustration. Chewing her lip, she tried *Andrea* then *Emily* then *Richard*—

Emily heard a distant scream from downstairs. She jumped up, the laptop falling to the ground with the crash. She ran to the hallway just as Jesse appeared at the top of the basement stairs, wild-eyed and pale as—well, as a ghost.

He slammed the basement door shut and pulled a chair in front of it.

"I just saw something in the basement," said Jesse.

"What did you see?" asked Emily.

"I don't know! It was like a shadow, but huge and terrible and it wasn't my shadow, it was moving on its own—"

Jesse looked over Emily's shoulder and screamed. Emily whirled around and saw it: the shadow, the one she had seen the previous evening, glided past her along the wall and disappeared down the hallway after turning the corner to the parlor.

There was a popping noise, and all the lights went out.

"Now do you believe me?" she said.

THEY GATHERED ALL the candles they could find and lit them in the kitchen before bringing them to the living room where the fire still blazed.

"Do you think it's afraid of fire?" said Jesse fretfully. "Like maybe if we stay in this room, we'll be okay?"

"I think it's Matilda," said Emily. "I think she needs our help."

"Who cares!" Jesse was practically shouting. "I get that we had our problems back home, but I can't deal with giant shadow people chasing me around a house that isn't even mine! We've got to get out of here, *tonight*." He pulled up his phone and frantically looked up flight times, then flung his phone across the room in total frustration. "There are no flights out! Everything's canceled."

Inwardly, Emily rolled her eyes. Anyone could have concluded that with a single glance outside. However, she didn't want to agitate Jesse any further. Aloud, she said only, "Maybe the snow will let up by morning."

"But what if it doesn't? What if it just keeps snowing and snowing and the ghost kills us and Richard finds our frozen bodies—"

"Ghosts can't kill people," said Emily reasonably. She was trying to reassure Jesse, but also herself. "They're not, you know...*solid* enough to do that."

"How do you know?" asked Jesse, running from window to window. He reminded her of Widget when she heard them come home but didn't know which door they were coming through. "They're not even supposed to exist! Who knows what they can do? Wait, what's Richard doing?" Jesse stopped abruptly by the side window overlooking the yard.

"Richard? Is he out there?" Emily went to the window and stood next to Jesse, peering out into the snowy darkness.

"He has snow shoes! Maybe he'll let us borrow them!"

"And do what? Walk back to Florida?"

"How can you joke at a time like this? We need a Plan B. Listen, I'm getting those snow shoes. Can you look through the closets and see if Matilda owned skis? Just in case. We'll ski to a bed and breakfast if we have to. I don't even care."

Emily sighed. "Whatever you say, Jesse."

He wrenched the front door open, grimacing at the wind and snow that blew into his eyes, before throwing himself out the door.

Emily decided to search for the skis, if for no other reason than to honestly tell Jesse she couldn't find any when he returned. She couldn't fathom that Matilda and the children had spent a lot of time skiing in the mountains.

Emily went to the hall closet with the tea towels, the one Andrea described the first time she wrote on the typewriter. She didn't recall seeing a pair of skis behind the mops and brooms, but maybe it was just because she hadn't been looking for skis.

The door was stuck. Emily rattled the handle, then with a loud wrenching sound, she pulled the door open.

There were no skis, but there, at the bottom of the closet, she saw a small door leading to the hidden passage. Maybe there was something she had missed in her first pass, when Jesse came home and interrupted her before she could reach the attic: an important clue that would reveal what had happened the night Matilda disappeared. After calculating the time it would take Jesse to wade through the snow, argue with Richard about his snow shoes, and wade back, Emily made a decision.

She dropped to her knees, opened the door, and disappeared inside.

JESSE WADED through the knee-high snow, gasping as he struggled to inhale the thin, freezing air. Running through snow was even harder than running through sand, and the toolshed looked like it was impossibly far away.

He squinted against the fat flurries that blew in his face. He could see Richard just ahead of him, gliding across the snow's surface on his snow shoes like a water bug on a lake. At least, he *thought* it was Richard. The man was so bundled up it was impossible to tell.

Richard approached the toolshed on the edge of the property. Removing a set of keys from his pocket, he opened the padlock on the door and disappeared inside. Jesse hastened his approach. It was cold and wet, and the snow had already soaked through both his boots to his socks.

When Jesse reached the doorway, he was startled to find that Richard was nowhere in sight. Instead, he found the empty shed lit with a portable lantern. The lantern was sitting on the floor of the shed, next to a square hole in the ground.

"What the—" Jesse got closer and looked into the hole. A series of rungs embedded in the side led down into a void.

Jesse didn't know what Richard (or whoever it was) was doing in that hole, but he didn't want to find out. He looked around for the snow shoes. He'd just take them and go back to the house, that was all. But something else was bothering him. What had Emily said? About the house, and what she had found...*There's a secret passageway in the walls and it leads all over the house...there are doors into practically every room... anyone who knew about the passage could have come into the house at any point and taken all of them...*

What if this was part of the network of tunnels and it led to the walls inside of the house? What if Richard—or maybe not Richard at all—was making his way to the house right now, with Emily unaware and by herself?

He reached for his phone. His pocket was empty.

"Shit," Jesse mumbled, remembering how he'd thrown it across the living room when he discovered that there were no available flights. "I really don't want to do this," he muttered, even as he was already in motion. He took off his enormous parka so he could fit inside the narrow opening and placed it on the ground. He picked up the lantern and lowered himself into the hole.

HER SECOND TIME in the walls of the house, Emily felt over-whelming fear and dread combined with what was unmis-takably a tug of excitement. If this was one of her novels, this would be the penultimate chapter, when the stakes were at their highest: would the heroine escape? Would she solve the mystery and win the day?

Emily paused as she heard a strange thudding noise, one that seemed to come from the vicinity of the basement. It was hard to tell from inside the walls. Whatever it was, she didn't want to encounter it.

Emily crawled faster through the passageway, bypassing the doors that led to the kitchen and parlor. She ascended the incline that led up the stairs past Matilda's bedroom until she reached the small door that opened to the inside of Andrea's closet. Instead of opening it, she tested the rungs of the small ladder opposite the door. It seemed steady enough.

She scaled the ladder to find out where it would lead.

Jesse climbed down the metal rungs of the ladder with the lantern's handle between his teeth, trying to not think about all the things he couldn't see. He didn't think there were bugs; it was too cold and dry, and he hadn't seen a single insect since they moved to Colorado. But there were worse things than bugs. Jesse remembered the shadow from the basement and almost stopped and climbed back out of the hole. Then he remembered Emily, alone in the house, and pushed forward.

He dismounted the ladder at the bottom, jumping down lightly onto a hard, packed surface that felt like dirt. He raised the lantern to examine his surroundings. Even with the bright light clenched in his fist, he could scarcely see more than a foot ahead of him. It appeared he was in a long and narrow tunnel of the same tightly packed earth he was standing on. He couldn't see or hear anyone ahead of him.

Shining the light ahead, he went forward into the darkness.

. . .

Emily climbed the ladder, coming to a stop when she reached a trapdoor above her head. There was a wooden latch on the inside of it similar to the one on the other passage doors. She turned it clockwise and pushed. Her effort was met with resistance, and Emily momentarily panicked. What if she had to go back and risk running into whatever she heard? Whatever she told Jesse about ghosts not being able to hurt people, Emily didn't want to confront the shadow inside a dark and narrow tunnel within the house. What if it was on its way here now?

The door gave way, and Emily saw that it was hidden beneath the rug decorated with toy trains. She pushed the rug aside and swung the door upward so it rested on the floor of the attic.

Emily crawled out of the trapdoor and closed it behind her, covering it back up with the rug. She figured if anything was following her, it could probably pass through solid objects (she'd thought this earlier, watching Jesse frantically wedge the chair under the basement door), but it gave her some peace of mind, anyway.

Emily heard something coming from the corner of the attic. It sounded like music. Spooked, she went closer to see what it was.

It was the jewelry box. It stood open for its slowly spinning ballerina. Or at least, she had been a ballerina.

Until someone had cleanly decapitated her head.

Jesse ran through the passageway, sweating in spite of the cold. He was afraid he wouldn't make it to the house in time. What if Richard did something to Emily? He always knew there was something weird about that guy. What if it wasn't Richard at all?

Jesse stopped when the light from his lantern fell on a small door set in the wall. He opened it, revealing a dusty corner of the basement. Jesse wondered if Richard had exited here and crept up the stairs; then he remembered the chair he had wedged under the door earlier. He felt a small thrill at his own precognitive brilliance, then froze. A shuffling sound echoed in the passage somewhere above his head. Whoever it was, they were still in here.

And Emily still didn't know.

EMILY STARED at the ballerina as she performed her slow pirouette of death, the sinister music of the music box tinkling on a loop. Who had done it? Was it one of the living, or one of the dead? And what was that sound behind her?

Emily could hear a steady scrape: the sound of boots on a wooden ladder. She looked at the rug, where she'd rolled it neatly back over the trapdoor. Who else knew about the passageway besides her and Jesse? But she hadn't told Jesse how to get in from the outside, and she didn't see why he would come in that way. It had to be someone else.

Emily frantically dialed Jesse. She could hear the phone ringing downstairs, echoing in the huge old drafty house. What if Jesse was still outside? She had to get downstairs.

Behind her, the trapdoor thudded and the rug began to rise. Emily felt nostalgia for the huge and horrible black shadow skating along the wall. This somehow felt worse, and imminently more threatening.

She flung the attic door open. Above her, the trapdoor hit the floor of the attic with a loud thud, the same noise it had made when she swung it open and emerged from the hidden passage.

Emily ran for the stairs.

11

*J*esse clambered up the passage when it sloped gently upward. He paused briefly while he struggled to catch his breath on the landing. The light of his lantern fell on a rectangle in the wall. Jesse pushed it open. The room was pitch black and impossibly small. He held his lantern higher and realized he was inside the pantry in the kitchen.

Jesse burst out of the pantry into the kitchen and ran into the hallway, calling Emily's name.

"Jesse?" He heard her voice on the stairs and had never been more relieved in his life. She thundered down the stairs and ran into his arms. "There's someone here! They're in the house!"

"I know, I was coming back to warn you. I thought it was Richard, but now I'm not so sure."

They heard the sound of heavy footsteps above their heads.

"We have to get out of here," Jesse said.

"But the snow—"

"I put chains on the tires when we got here," Jesse said. "If we can just make it to the truck, maybe we can get out of here. I'd rather take my chances out there than in here."

They ran for the kitchen door, pushing it open against the snowdrift that formed against the other side. Slipping and sliding down the coated wood stairs, they ran across the side yard for Jesse's truck. The truck was buried under mounds of fluffy white snow.

Jesse tossed her the keys. "Get in the driver's side and start the engine while I clear the windshield and shovel out the wheels."

Emily ran to the truck and clambered into the driver's side. Jesse grabbed a shovel from the flatbed of the truck and dug at the snow around the wheels. Emily put the key in the ignition and turned it. The engine briefly sputtered to life and then died.

"No!" Emily pounded the wheel and tried to start the truck again. Nothing.

"Jesse!" she called. He didn't hear her over the howling wind. She jumped to the ground, landing in a huge pile of snow, and waded her way over to him. "The truck won't start!"

Jesse looked at her in disbelief. Ice crystals formed in his eyebrows and beard, and she thought randomly of the Claymation Jack Frost in the Christmas special she watched every December as a child.

"He must have done something to it," Jesse shouted over the wind. "Sabotaged it somehow." He opened the passenger door and got in the truck. Emily got in the other side. They closed their doors against the wind. It was still cold, but now they were no longer being snowed on and could hear each another without interference from the elements.

Emily was scared, in a different way than she'd been seeing the ghosts of Matilda and Andrea. It was different from the fear she felt hearing the man in the attic. Now, she was frightened of the elements. She had never felt a cold like this. They weren't dressed for the weather. Where they came from, it didn't even snow. She doubted they would make it halfway to town before they developed hypothermia. Emily looked up at the dark house where Matilda had met her dark fate. Was she destined for the same end?

SHE TOOK her phone out and dialed 911.

"911, what is your emergency?" A pleasant, reassuring female voice answered.

"I'm at my house and I'm trapped by the storm, but someone broke in and they're still in the house," Emily said in a rush.

"Are you in a safe place?"

"Kind of? I mean, not really. For now, I guess?"

"Try to find a safe hiding place and remain as quiet as possible. Do you own a firearm?"

"No," said Emily. For the first time in her life, she wished that she did.

"Okay. Find a secure place to wait, as safe as you can, then call me back if you're able to. We'll get someone out there to you as soon as possible."

She looked at Jesse. "She says we should hide."

Jesse looked around the yard. "We're too exposed in the truck, unless we hide in the flatbed and cover ourselves with the tarp. But if he looks for us there, we'd be sitting ducks. He can easily get into the toolshed. He's already in the house. There's no way we can go back inside."

"We have to," said Emily.

Jesse looked at her incredulously. "Why would we do that?"

"Widget," she said.

EMILY AND JESSE had always been compatible for the reason

that they agreed about most things. Often their agreements were unspoken and automatically assumed. For this reason, there had been no discussion over whether they would return to the house to get Widget before they hid: Widget was part of their family, and neither of them was willing to leave her behind.

Now, the couple crouched beneath the porch under the back stairs. "It comes out at the basement first," said Emily.

"I know he's not in the basement," said Jesse. "He might have tried that first, but the door to the upstairs was jammed."

"We should hurry," said Emily. "Before he realizes we're not in the house."

As they ran along the inside of the wall, Emily was unable to stop herself from picturing the man in the house inside the walls with them. She didn't hear anything, but that didn't mean he wasn't there.

They came to the door that led to the basement and opened it, stepping onto the cold cement. Jesse held the lantern up. It cast a small circle of yellow light on their immediate surroundings.

A sharp creak of the floorboards resounded directly overhead.

"He's still here," said Jesse.

Emily looked around frantically. Where was there a hiding place big enough for two people?

The light in the basement flickered on and off with a buzz.

"The power's coming back on!" said Jesse.

Emily stared at the light. "I don't think it is, Jess."

The light flickered on once, twice, three times. The third time, Emily saw it: a warped old chest in the far corner of the basement, next to Jesse's carpentry tools.

"Look!" Emily pointed to the chest just as the light flickered out again. They made their way across the basement, trying not to walk into anything or kick anything over and alert the intruder to their presence. Emily felt her way blindly in the darkness, groping along the carpentry table and hoping she wouldn't inadvertently grab the circular saw. Finally, her toes hit something hard and hollow, and she grasped for the handles, pulling the chest open.

Jesse helped Emily into the chest, then moved to close the lid over her.

"Jesse, what are you doing?" she protested, holding her hand against the lid.

"There isn't room for both of us," he said. "You're going to hide in here and I'm going to get my sledgehammer and hide in the secret passage. If the guy comes downstairs before the cops come..." He didn't finish his sentence, but then, he didn't need to.

He smiled at Emily reassuringly as he closed the lid over her head. Emily heard his footsteps retreat to the other side of the basement and the creak of the passage door opening. She heard it close with a click.

Emily listened for any sounds above them that would indicate the intruder's location. She curled into a ball in the darkness and tried not to hyperventilate. Was this how Matilda had died? And Cynthia? And the children? Hidden in a small, confined space, trapped like rats, while the murderer lurked somewhere in the house?

* * *

SHERIFF OGLETHORPE SAT at his desk as the snow swirled past the windows. He sipped his coffee and cracked the spine of his favorite novel, Stephen King's *The Shining*. There was no place he'd rather be on a snowy evening like tonight. Inevitably, something would come up: a fender-bender or an accident from some fool trying to drive in this weather, and he'd have to slog his way through the cold night and the snow. But for now, he could sit back and enjoy the storm.

"We've got a call," said Stacy, the dispatch operator.

Oglethorpe was unsurprised. He'd just reached an especially gripping passage, his favorite—the part where Danny discovers room 237—so naturally, it was now that something had to interrupt his reading.

Oglethorpe sighed. "What seems to be the trouble?" he said.

"Something happening at that old Meade place on the hill. Says there's a break-in and the intruder's still in the house? I didn't know anybody was up there."

Sheriff Oglethorpe swung his feet off his desk onto the floor. "Young couple just moved there with their dog. God only knows what's happening there now. Let's hope we can avoid a scandal this time, shall we? I'm up for re-election."

The sheriff pulled his fleece-lined hat on, settling the flaps securely over his ears and finishing his coffee.

"Don't forget your scarf," said Stacy brightly.

"Thank you, Stacy," said Oglethorpe, wrapping it around his neck several times and knotting it firmly around his throat. He pulled on his fleece-lined gloves and trudged towards the door of the station.

"Gosh, I sure hope those people are okay," said Stacy. "That house just seems like it's nothing but trouble, doesn't it?"

The sheriff shrugged. "They're out-of-towners. Probably just got frightened by the storm. I'm sure it's nothing to worry about."

* * *

EMILY HAD NEVER FELT SO helpless in her life. What was taking the police so long?

It was so dark inside the chest within the dark basement

that Emily could scarcely tell the difference between when her eyes were closed or open. She tried not to picture Matilda's last moments of life, or Andrea's. Still, the images crept in, unbidden. Like memories, but something more than memories, all at once.

She was concealed in a dark place where no light penetrated. She waited in stark terror while a set of footsteps approached the stairs.

Emily was disoriented in time and space. She could have been in the basement or the attic. She could have been herself or someone else.

Still more sensations crowded in against her will: she was confined in a tight space just like this one. A second body pressed against her. She felt small, and felt the smallness of the second body beside her. A cry escaped her and the person beside her shushed her, begging her to be quiet in his tiny voice.

Somewhere above her head, footsteps made their way across the living room, down the hall, and paused directly overhead. There was a loud scraping sound at the basement door—the chair being dragged across the floor.

The basement door creaked open. The footsteps descended the stairs, one at a time. He was taking his time—he clearly knew they were trapped with no escape, and was therefore in no hurry to dispose of them. He moved as if he had all the time in the world.

The footsteps paused at the foot of the stairs, then shuffled across the cement floor. There was a resounding crash as the shelves tipped over. The footsteps changed direction. This time, they headed in the direction of the chest.

Emily was aware of the sound, but she heard the footsteps as if they were ascending the steps of the attic. She was simultaneously torn between the present and the past. She felt her fear, compounded by the fear the children had felt when they had hidden, trapped like rats, in a dark place just like she was.

Emily squeezed her eyes shut tight and thought desperately for anyone—or anything—to help them. She remembered all those weeks ago, when she typed those words on the old typewriter from the attic. Now she was the one who needed help.

The footsteps paused in front of the chest. Emily heard fingernails scrabbling at the handles

She screamed. "Help us! Please help us!"

As the lid was thrown open, Emily saw bright lights fly upward into the face of the intruder. He shouted and stumbled backward.

The basement light blazed on as brightly as the sun. Jesse threw open the door to the secret passage and leapt out, wielding his sledgehammer. He stopped in amazement at the sight of the lights swarming the intruder, whose face was concealed by a black ski mask. The intruder screamed as he clawed his way across the floor towards the open passage door.

The front door upstairs crashed inward and the voice of Sheriff Oglethorpe shouted, "This is the police!"

Emily and Jesse looked up simultaneously. The intruder pulled himself into the secret passage. Jesse looked back and raised the hammer to try and stop him, but he slithered into the wall like a rat into a hole and disappeared from sight. Jesse started to chase after him, but stopped at the sound of Emily's voice.

"Jesse, look!"

The lights around them dissipated, revealing the basement wall for the first time since the lights went out. Painted on the gray cement in dripping red letters were the words,

WE WILL NEVER FORGET.

he snow came down in giant fat flakes, and a smile spread across my face. Snow meant poor visibility, slow emergency response time, and power outages.

Tonight was the night.

As I watched the house on the hill, the lights popped off and the building was plummeted into darkness. That's the problem with old homes: one little incident with inclement weather, and it's back to the Stone Age.

Smoke poured from the chimney, so I knew they weren't in total darkness, which was unfortunate. Ideally one of them would go to check the breaker box (even though it was obviously the storm) and the two would be separated.

They were the only thing that stood in my way, the one thing between me and my fondest prize: the house. If I could only eliminate them, that prize would be mine.

I traipsed across the snowy lawn. I came prepared. I had snow shoes. Their truck was unlocked, naturally. I never met two more gullible, trusting people in my life. I popped the hood and removed their distributor cap.

I made my way to the toolshed. This shed was not like other sheds. It contained a small trapdoor in the floor that went below the earth to a long tunnel leading to the house—into its very walls.

The couple had only been there a few scant weeks, and I was certain they had yet to discover the hidden network of tunnels and passageways running throughout the walls of the house. They seemed flighty, younger than their age would imply—like most of their generation. Bumbling, broke, helpless. Reliant on the charity of others. How fortunate for them that they were related to the old lady of the house. She loved charity.

Until I killed her.

Now I had only to dispose of her hapless progeny and nothing would stand between me and my prize. And what a perfect night for it: cold, snowy, dark. They were from somewhere down south and had likely never seen snow in their lives. They probably didn't even know if they could leave the house when it snowed. They probably thought they would freeze to death if they did.

I switched my headlamp on. I lowered myself through the door in the floor, leaving my lantern in the toolshed. I wanted to have both hands free.

I knew these tunnels like the back of my hand and probably could have navigated them in the dark. I heard something scrabbling in the walls ahead of me and paused. A rat? If it was, it was an awfully big rat. I checked my pocket and assured myself my gun was loaded. Whatever it was, it was no match for me.

I didn't know what room they were in, though it seemed unlikely they'd be in the cold, dark basement during a storm while the power was out. Judging from the smoke that poured from the main chimney, they were most likely in the living room. If I came in through the basement, they'd never hear me coming.

I went through the first door that I came to, a small wooden one that emerged in a corner of the basement. I quickly made my way across the room, glancing from side to side so the light of my headlamp swept over any possible obstacles. I crept up the stairs and turned the doorknob. But when I pushed the door, it was stuck. I rattled the knob and pushed harder.

The door was jammed, as if something was wedged beneath the knob. I cursed under my breath. I could have kicked it open, but I didn't want to alert them to my presence. I wanted the element of surprise on my side.

No matter. There were other ways in. If I couldn't start from the bottom, creeping up to catch them unaware, I'd simply start from the top.

I went back to the passage in the walls and began my ascent. As I made my way to the attic, I congratulated myself on my brilliance. The floors were old and creaky and they might have heard me if I came in through one of the bedrooms upstairs, but who would hear an intruder entering through the attic? Who breaks in through the highest point of the house? I thought again of how valuable the house was to me: not just from a financial perspective, but the way it almost seemed built for me; how it worked for me and did my bidding.

It took me a few tries to get through the trapdoor. I always forgot it was covered with that stupid kid's rug with the trains on it. The old lady bought it for the children. She bought everything for the children. It was as if no one had ever told her that it was okay to live for yourself and no one else.

I made my way downstairs, toward the light of their still-roaring fire. Their dog barked furiously at me, then hid behind the couch. I could have cared less. It wasn't the dog I was interested in. Aside from their cowardly mutt, the living room was empty and I felt a surge of irritation. Who leaves their house during the first blizzard of the season? Idiot out-of-towners.

I resumed my search through the house, determined to find them if I had to check every room, every closet, every nook and cranny. There were many places to hide, but I knew them all.

There was no hiding from me in this house.

But they were nowhere to be found. They were craftier than I originally gave them credit for. I looked out the window. Their truck was still in the driveway. Of course, I had made certain of that earlier. But where could they have gone?

They must have realized I was there. Doubled back behind me. No matter. I'd search again.

The only room I hadn't checked was the basement. I found the chair that had foiled me earlier, wedged beneath the doorknob. There was no way they could be in there. Unless…they knew about the passages inside the walls? I hadn't heard them once, and yet they clearly weren't outside. There was nowhere else for them to be.

I dragged the chair aside and opened the basement door. I descended the stairs, imagining them trapped in the dark. I relished the thought.

Even with my headlamp, it was difficult to see. I stumbled into a set of metal shelves, overturning them with a resounding crash. As I kicked them aside, I thought to myself, *if I were trapped like a rat in the basement, where would I hide?*

There was a warped old wooden chest next to the carpentry bench. It was one of the few pieces of furniture in the basement large enough to conceal a human being. I reached into my pocket for my gun, the cold metal reassuring in my hand.

Just as I went to throw open the chest, everything went wrong.

Massive, hideous, horrible lights engulfed me from out of nowhere: not the overhead light of the basement, which surged on at the same time, but an overwhelming trifecta of bright and inexplicable colors that swirled around me angrily. As the lights surrounded me, I heard their voices: *We know what you did...we know who you are...we will come for you... we will have our revenge.*

*B*lue and red flashing lights lit up the driveway of the old Meade House as uniformed officers circled the property with floodlights. Snow drifted down from the sky. Sheriff Oglethorpe watched from the porch as his officers combed the grounds for any sign of the home invader who'd triggered the homeowner's 911 call. It seemed that the intruder had simply disappeared.

"Folks seem to have a funny habit of vanishing from this place," he said.

"Did you say something, sir?" called one of the officers on the front lawn below him.

"Nothing worth repeating," said the sheriff. He went inside to question the shaken couple about what transpired that night at Meade House.

The EMTs had just finished checking the couple for injuries and were currently bandaging the husband's arm. Sheriff Oglethorpe approached the wife, holding her dog: one of those miniature collie-looking things Oglethorpe thought looked like Lassie, zapped with a shrink ray. She gazed into the fire. He said her name several times before she looked up, startled, to find him hovering over her.

"Are you sure you're all right?" Oglethorpe said. "No concussion or anything?"

Emily was surprised the sheriff seemed genuinely concerned for her welfare. In her previous dealings with him, he'd come across as largely indifferent, almost to the point of cavalier. Perhaps she'd misjudged him.

"Almost thought I'd make it through the rest of my book before a call came in," commented the sheriff. "Should have known there'd be trouble at the old Meade place, eh?" Perhaps not.

"Sheriff," said Emily, "Did they catch the person who did this?"

"Not yet," admitted Oglethorpe, removing his hat. He looked mildly chagrined. "We're still searching the grounds, and we'll let you know when we find 'em. In the meantime, maybe you can tell me what happened here tonight? Give us a better idea of where to look."

"We were by the basement when the power went out," said Emily. "We built a fire in the living room when my husband saw what he thought was the groundskeeper walking towards the toolshed."

"Does this groundskeeper normally come up after hours?"

"Yes, actually. He came up the previous evening to bring us some firewood. He also came up the last time you were here, after the property was vandalized. He was the one who reported it."

"Oh, you mean *Richard*." Oglethorpe was hard-pressed to keep from rolling his eyes. He forgot the man even had a formal title around this place. He seemed like one of those busybodies, always hovering around, waiting to self-importantly deliver some long-winded tale about what he'd witnessed like he was on an episode of *Law and Order*. Sheriff Oglethorpe had found, in recent years, that every potential witness to a crime had seen one too many episodes of *Law and Order*.

"Yes, Richard," she said. "We thought it was him, but—"

"It's not," said Oglethorpe dismissively. "Just saw him wandering around out front, getting in the way. Asking a bunch of pointless questions."

"Oh," said Emily, taken aback by the sheriff's tone. "Well, anyway, um…we thought that it was him, but we couldn't see his face. He was wearing a ski mask, we assumed because of the cold, and he had on snow shoes. He was walking towards the toolshed and Jesse went to ask him if we could borrow the shoes in case we needed to leave the house." Here Emily paused. Now she had no idea what to tell the sheriff and what to withhold. If she told the full story, she'd sound insane. If she didn't, she'd leave out the most obvious hiding place for the intruder, who could still be in the house.

Then again, she wasn't sure she trusted the sheriff. Should she share one of the secrets of the house with him? If he was the person she suspected he was, a person involved in her aunt's disappearance, then the odds were he already knew. Maybe she could tell just how much he knew based on his reaction and how truthful it seemed.

"Yesterday, I discovered a secret way into this house," said Emily abruptly, watching the sheriff's face for clues.

His expression exhibited only surprise. Either he hadn't known, or he was a masterful actor. "Really? What is it?" he asked.

"It's an entire system of tunnels that runs underground, out to the toolshed, and inside the walls," she said. "Sheriff, I think it might be how my aunt was taken out of this house without anybody seeing what happened."

Sheriff Oglethorpe scratched his chin thoughtfully. He had investigated the disappearance of the Emily's aunt the previous year—not just her, but the three children she was fostering and another young woman, all of them missing and now presumed dead. Emily had inherited the house from her aunt, and all its mysteries and secrets with it.

"That could be," he said cautiously, not wanting to give her any ideas. The only thing worse than *Law and Order* witnesses were *CSI* private citizens, fancying themselves detectives. "We'll have to take a look at it. If the person who broke into your home is still here, I'd assume that's where they'd be hiding."

"We think they came in through the toolshed," said Emily. "That's where the outside entrance is."

Sheriff Oglethorpe radioed one of his men to secure the toolshed and asked Emily to show him the entrance to the secret passage.

"There are several," Emily explained. She shoved the couch forward, exposing a small door in the wall. "I believe there's one in most of the rooms of the house."

"Well, I'll be," said the sheriff, leaning forward to peer at the door. He rapped on it with his knuckles, creating a hollow echo.

From inside the walls, something rapped back.

Emily gave a jump and looked at the sheriff. He gave no sign of having heard anything.

"How did you come to find this?" asked the sheriff. "Did your aunt tell you about it?"

This was exactly what she didn't want to get into: at the time of the break-in, she'd gone inside the walls to see if the ghosts who haunted her aunt's home—one of whom, she was certain, was her aunt—would lead her to a clue revealing what happened to them the night they all died. Emily knew that in the state of Florida, it took only two people to certify someone mentally insane and have them committed. She didn't want to find out what the law was here.

"Well," said Emily truthfully, "she sort of let me discover it for myself."

"That sounds like Matilda," muttered the sheriff, still studying the door. "Everything was always a teaching moment with her." He looked up as one of his deputies came through the front door. "Hawkins, get me the skinniest, toughest guy out there you can find. I need someone who can navigate a tight space as quickly as possible."

Hawkins, who had the portly appearance of a man who spent a great deal of time in a parked car, drinking coffee and eating doughnuts, flushed involuntarily. "Yes, sir," he mumbled, going back outside.

Oglethorpe turned back to Emily. "Don't know how anybody survives at this altitude with even a few extra pounds on them," he said pleasantly. "My daddy always told me, 'ain't no fat people in Colorado.'"

Emily smiled politely. Inwardly, she was startled by how casually cruel he was.

A rangy young cop with faint acne scars along his chin appeared at their side. He had the intense, eager expression of a hungry and ambitious cadet with a desire to prove himself.

Oglethorpe nodded at the door in the wall. "Think you can search that, Tapper?"

Tapper gave a brisk nod. "Yes, sir." He immediately crouched and disappeared into the wall.

Oglethorpe looked around irritably. "I don't have anybody else skinny on this squad? What are they feeding them in the cafeteria?" He sighed. "What happened after your husband went to talk to the person he thought was Richard?"

"I thought I heard a noise in the secret passage," said Emily. "I wouldn't have checked on it myself, but I thought it was something harmless, like maybe our dog had gotten in it somehow. I wanted to make sure she wasn't stuck." Emily gave what she hoped was a rueful-sounding laugh. "Of course, she was safely in the living room the whole time."

"Of course," echoed the sheriff, giving no indication of whether he found this plausible.

"I went all the way up to the attic without finding anything, so I exited the passage. I heard a noise behind me, and I realized there was someone else in the passage. I didn't think it was Jesse, because why wouldn't he just use the door? I ran downstairs, running into Jesse on the way, and we went out to the truck, which wouldn't start. I called 911. We came back for our dog, sneaking in through the secret passage using the entrance under the porch. We came out in the basement. By that point, the intruder was downstairs, so we concealed ourselves until you guys got here."

"And they just ran off?" asked the sheriff.

Again, Emily didn't feel comfortable sharing the entire truth. The truth was, when she was hidden inside of an old chest downstairs, she was certain she had experienced the memories and emotions of the children when they had hidden in fear in the house the night they disappeared. And when the intruder opened the chest to attack Emily, it was the ghosts of the children who protected her. The police had arrived at the same time and Jesse tried to attack the invader with a sledgehammer, both of which also contributed to foiling the attack. But Emily felt certain the ghosts had been her primary defenders, and that they had formed a wall between her and the enemy trying to harm her.

Not that she wanted to tell Sheriff Oglethorpe that.

"The intruder found my hiding place right when you came through the door," she said. "I think that's what scared them off."

Sheriff Oglethorpe seemed satisfied with this explanation. "If they were that easily frightened off, it might just be the same people who threw that rock through your window," he said. "Trying to punish you for what they think your aunt did." He frowned, adding, "We haven't questioned the parents of that homeless girl who was living here recently. They would be my first guess."

"Andrea's parents?" Emily stared at him. He couldn't be serious. Emily had questioned Andrea's parents herself days earlier, after Andrea's ghost had contacted her and asked her for help. There was no way they were behind this.

"Vagrants," said Oglethorpe, shaking his head. "Can't stand 'em. The town is crawling with them. There's enough liberals here to feed and shelter them and keep them around. I say, let 'em freeze and starve a few nights and they'll clear right out. Go somewhere warmer. Arizona's not that far if you got a couple feet and a will to use them." He chuckled to himself while Emily looked at him, appalled. Was he really suggesting the entire homeless population walk to Arizona? Just so he didn't have to look at them?

Oglethorpe didn't notice Emily's expression. He was distracted by Tapper's reappearance at his side. Tapper was now lightly coated in plaster and dust.

"Anything, Tapper?"

"Nothing, sir," said Tapper respectfully, at attention. He reminded Emily of a German Shepherd-turned-man.

Oglethorpe turned to Emily. "Well, there you have it." *Have what?* thought Emily. "I'm going to question your husband now. Why don't you make some tea, get warmed up? Power's back on, your heat should be, too."

From where Emily stood, he appeared to have accomplished very little aside from his plan to reduce homelessness by creating a new Trail of Tears. He also told Emily what to do in her own house under the pretense of reassuring her. And while Emily never would have said so, she doubted very much that the rapid decline in the house's temperature had anything to do with either the power outage or the storm.

Emily walked by Jesse on her way to the kitchen, briefly squeezing his hand. He smiled at her as the EMT bandaged his arm and Oglethorpe approached him for another scintillating round of questioning. She disliked leaving him in the hands of the sheriff, but aside from aggressively doing nothing, the sheriff seemed unlikely to cause him any real harm.

In the kitchen, Emily filled the electric kettle with water

and flipped the on switch. As much as she hated to admit Oglethorpe was right about anything, she did want nothing more than a hot cup of tea.

The kitchen door flew open and Emily screamed.

"Oh!" The groundskeeper and maintenance man, Richard, stepped back and covered his mouth. "Emily, I'm so sorry. I saw the police here and I just had to see what happened. I had to make sure that you and your husband were okay. Are you? Is he? What happened? Did someone break in?"

Emily felt overwhelmed and unprepared to deal with Richard after everything that just happened. Against her will, she remembered Sheriff Oglethorpe's earlier reaction and understood just what he meant by the nuisance that was Richard. He meant well. He'd been extremely kind to her and Jesse since they moved into the house, and helpful. He was one of her aunt's only defenders in the face of the town's open contention that she had been the one behind the children's disappearance. Emily was sure he just wanted to make sure they were okay. She also just wanted to drink her tea and go to bed.

"We're fine, Richard," she said, turning back to the kettle. She made sure to only get one cup from the cupboard, lest he get any ideas. She'd get one for Jesse later. After she got rid of Richard. "Someone broke into the house earlier, but they're gone now."

Her back was turned, but his gasp was audible. She rolled her eyes. She seriously doubted Richard could feel more in shock than she did. "No! Someone broke into the house? Did they hurt you guys? Did they take anything?"

"Only my peace of mind," said Emily. "Not that I had much of it left."

"What?" said Richard, looking puzzled. He was none too quick on the uptake, and Emily suspected he was trying to picture what such a possession looked like: was it a piece of jewelry, or an article of woman's clothing?"

"They didn't take anything," Emily elaborated. "And the police scared them away before they could do anything to me or Jesse. Or Widget." She came through the kitchen door at the sound of her name and leaned against Emily's legs. Emily scratched her ears absently.

"Oh, thank goodness," said Richard. "I had the worst déjà vu when I saw those lights. I thought maybe...I thought maybe it was happening all over again."

Emily felt ashamed. She'd forgotten how much Richard had cared about Matilda and how devastated he'd been when she disappeared. She hadn't realized how much he'd grown to care about her and Jesse, and how badly he would feel if something happened to them, too.

"I appreciate it, Richard," she said. "But we're okay, really."

"Good," said Richard, sighing with relief. "I'll just let myself out, then. Let you folks get some rest."

"Good night, Richard," said Emily, watching him leave.

"Good night," he said, pulling the door shut behind him.

WITH RICHARD GONE, she finally felt safe to take out a second mug. She might have appreciated his sympathy, but that didn't mean she wanted him hanging around for another hour.

Emily poured a cup of tea as the kitchen door swung open. Emily glanced up, exhausted but smiling. "I made you—"

"That for me?" Oglethorpe took the mug from her hand. "Ah. Doesn't that just hit the spot."

Emily worked to conceal her annoyance. When would they leave?

Tapper popped through the door. "Do I smell tea?"

Who could smell tea? This seemed to confirm Emily's theory that he transformed back into the K-9 half of his unit after they got back to the station.

The door swung open again. Emily looked up in despair, prepared to see a hungry Hawkins looking for refreshments, but it was Jesse at last.

"Jesse." Emily fairly dissolved in his arms. It had been such a long and terrible night.

"We'll get out of your hair now, folks," said Oglethorpe, miraculously taking a hint. "We've got your statements and if there are any new developments, we'll let you know."

"Do you foresee there being any new developments?" said Jesse dryly.

Emily expected some rote and generic police response about how rarely break-ins were solved.

"It's hard to say," said Sheriff Oglethorpe slowly. "Given this house's history, for your sake, I hope there are."

Emily and Jesse stared after the sheriff as he and his deputies filed out the kitchen door. With everyone gone, the house seemed strangely silent after the chaos of before.

Emily turned to Jesse with a pensive frown.

"Jesse," she said, "did anything about what he just said sound kind of...*threatening* to you?"

Jesse gazed out the door at the sheriff, trudging through the snow to his enormous SUV.

"Only all of it," he said.

*E*mily and Jesse moved from Florida to Colorado with high hopes and a swarm of debt collectors in hot pursuit. Debilitating financial problems had left them unable to renew their lease or even pay their bills, so when Emily found out she inherited the house in Boulder from her mysterious Great-Aunt Matilda, it seemed like a godsend. They would have a place to live and if they fixed it up and sold it, they would have enough money to get out of debt.

Unfortunately, they got far more than they bargained for. Everyone, from the local property management company trying to convince them to sell cheap to vandals damaging the property with rocks inscribed with threatening messages (and Emily wasn't convinced the two were mutually exclusive) seemed to be waging war against the couple's chances at happiness. And that didn't even include the home's previous tenants, who seemed to have remained on the premises—even after death.

Emily barely knew her Aunt Matilda, estranged from Emily's family all her life. She vaguely recalled meeting her at a family reunion once as a small child. She was startled to find herself in her will and had little concept of how she died

—only that she disappeared and was later declared dead in absentia. She and Jesse had been so desperate for a new situation—for something, anything, to come along and save them—that Emily had jumped on the chance without fully considering the potential ramifications. Even if she had, ghosts and murder would not have been her first guess at problems their inherited home might present. Black mold, bad plumbing, or possible roofing issues had been the most they were prepared to deal with.

Now they were stuck there, in the middle of the mountains, with no home to return to and no way to go forward. After they moved in, they discovered that it was not just Matilda who was missing and presumed dead, but the three children she fostered and the assistant who helped her care for them, Cynthia. With each day, it became more and more apparent that they had met a bad end. Emily wasn't sure the person responsible was gone, and after the events of the evening, she felt even more certain that they were still in town and that Emily and Jesse were next on their list.

The next morning when the snow stopped, Emily and Jesse shoveled a crude pathway from the back steps to the truck. As native Floridians, neither of them were particularly adept with a snow shovel. Jesse stayed outside to figure out what was wrong with the truck while Emily went inside to fix coffee. She came out to the back stairs with two steaming black cups.

"Well, it looks like we're gonna need a new distributor cap," he called up to her from the yard.

"Is that normal?" she asked, going down the stairs to join him next to the truck.

"Normal? For your distributor cap to randomly disappear from under the hood? Definitely not," said Jesse, taking the coffee from her. "Somebody took it. Probably the same person who was here last night."

Emily knew she needed to address the fact that they were

in hot water. She would have to present an extremely good argument for remaining in a house subject to break-ins, vandalism, and several murders. It was hard to make that argument even to herself, but after the events of last night, Emily was certain that the ghosts were benevolent. She believed they sought to protect her and Jesse from the outside forces threatening them. She also believed that they were relying on her to help them. Who else would figure out what truly happened the night they disappeared? Not Oglethorpe, that was for sure.

"I guess you want us to get out of here, huh?" she said, figuring it was best to get straight to the point.

"No, actually," he said, taking a sip of the scalding black coffee. "I don't."

"You don't?" Emily was shocked. She'd felt certain he'd have their stuff, Widget, and Emily herself loaded in the truck overnight as they slept. She was surprised to wake up in their bed instead of the cab of a moving truck, halfway back to Florida.

"Here's the thing," he said. "If whoever broke in last night wanted to kill us, they could have. I think that somebody—or more than one somebody—is trying to intimidate us into selling this place cheap and getting out of here, and I'll be damned if anybody's going to rob us out of our best shot at starting a new life."

Emily felt her determination further renewed by Jesse's resolve. "Really?"

"Really. And if, as you say, this…supernatural presence… is benevolent, then I guess we don't need to worry about it. Even though I hate it and it totally freaks me out." Jesse was not one to mince words.

"I think that whoever wants us out of here wants this house," said Emily. "And if we can find out who that is, not only can we stop them, but I have a feeling that this place might not feel so haunted anymore."

"I hope you're right," said Jesse. "What's the plan?"

"I've got to try and get some writing done," said Emily. "I thought moving here would prove inspiring, but I've been so distracted by everything that's going on, I haven't made any progress on my next book. Which certainly isn't doing us any favors financially."

"Well, you definitely have a lot of new material to work with," said Jesse dryly. "If you're considering going in that direction."

"Oh, I am," said Emily. "I'd be a fool not to. I couldn't make this stuff up if I tried." She checked her tote bag for her stainless steel water bottle. Since they moved to Colorado, she never left the house without water. "Worst-case scenario, I can always look up the house," said Emily. "I figure it's been here for a long time. Maybe learning about it will give us an indication of why everyone's so desperate to get their hands on it."

"While you're doing that, I'm going to the automotive store to get a new distributor cap," said Jesse. He looked at the snow with dismay. "Looks like we're walking."

THE GROUND WAS STILL COVERED in snow, but the sun shone so brightly overhead it seemed as though it would melt in a matter of hours. In spite of the cold, Emily found the walk pleasant and scenic. Seeing the steep hills dotted with snow-covered houses was like looking at a postcard while simultaneously being inside of it.

Emily cut down a side street on her way to the library so she wouldn't have to contend with the mob of Christmas shoppers on Pearl Street. She passed two dispensaries, a shop selling alpaca fur jackets, and a store that sold only kites. A glass front building on the corner caught her eye. Stenciled on the glass door were the words Watkins, Taft, and Simms.

Emily paused outside the door. J.R. Watkins was Matilda's lawyer, the one who originally called to tell her she'd inherited the house. Could he tell her anything about Matilda?

Deciding there was no harm if he couldn't, she opened the door and stepped into a small, navy-carpeted reception area populated with antique wooden benches and oil paintings of ships tossed on stormy seas. Fake ferns littered the reception area.

The receptionist sat at the desk, filing his nails. He was smartly dressed in a sweater vest and tie, with a ruler-straight side part in his pale blond hair. The plaque on his desk read Bryce Stevens. He regarded Emily—bundled in her parka, knit hat, and snow boots—as if he thought she might be homeless and took a wrong turn on her way to the shelter.

Emily blushed and cleared her throat. "Um, is J.R. Watkins available?"

"Do you have an appointment?" Bryce asked curiously.

"Well, no. He was my aunt's lawyer, Matilda Meade? I just moved into her house and I had a question about the will. I can make an appointment and come back if that would be better."

Bryce, whose eyes had widened at the name 'Matilda Meade,' waved a dismissive hand in her direction. "No, no, I'll check and ask if he can see you. I know for a fact he doesn't have any appointments until eleven, so I don't see why he wouldn't be able to spare a few minutes." He picked up the phone, hit a couple of buttons, and murmured something into the receiver that Emily couldn't hear. When he hung up, he smiled broadly. "Just take a seat, he'll be with you in five minutes."

Emily settled uncomfortably on a hard, wooden bench. She had the unsettling feeling that someone was watching her and looked up to find Bryce gazing at her avidly with bright, keen eyes.

"The décor in this place is absolutely terrible," he said

THE HAUNTING OF MEADE MANSION

conversationally. "I've been trying to get Jonathan to change it, but he simply refuses." Emily wondered who Jonathan was. Did he mean Watkins?

"He thinks these tacky sailboat paintings and old pieces of wood are the height of chic," continued Bryce. He clearly had strong opinions about the waiting room. "He inherited it from some swarthy old sea captain grandfather and will not get rid of it." He set his nail file carefully at the edge of the desk and asked delicately, without looking up, "So, what do you think of the house?"

Emily had no doubt in her mind that Bryce had heard all about the house and had his own opinions about what happened there. She had no inclination whatsoever to satisfy his morbid curiosity.

"It seems like a nice place so far," she said politely, lying through her teeth. "My husband is fixing it up, doing a few repairs so we can maybe sell it further down the line, unless we decide to stay here for a while."

Bryce gave her a look that indicated he knew she wasn't telling the truth. "Well, I don't know if you realize this," he said in a mock casual tone, "but *everyone* assumes that your aunt is behind what happened up there, the night everyone disappeared? You know, just in case people are rude to you. I thought you should know why. Everyone in town assumes she had something to do with the disappearance of those kids and that's why she disappeared herself." He reached up and ran a hand over his immaculate side part before continuing. "Of course, *I* would never judge anyone based on what someone else did. I just want you to know that if you hear talk, don't even pay any mind. It's just a lot of gossip, I'm sure."

He smiled pleasantly enough at her, but Emily's larger impression was that Bryce very much believed Matilda was responsible and that Emily would be a fool to believe otherwise. Emily was both taken aback and hurt on Matilda's behalf. She had no doubt in her mind that Bryce was one of the people gossiping about Matilda.

"How kind of you," she said frostily. "I'll be sure to keep that in mind."

They were both in position like players in a tense one-act, staring at each other with fake smiles fixed in place, when a door at the back of the room opened.

A stern and imposing man in a three-piece suit emerged and glared at Bryce. "Bryce? What are we discussing out here?" Emily recognized his eloquent voice from the phone from when J.R. Watkins called her in Florida to inform her she had inherited Matilda's house.

Bryce gave a casual little shrug. "Oh, nothing, Jonathan. Matilda's niece is right here, whenever you're ready."

"I can see that, Bryce," said Watkins. His demeanor, when he turned to Emily, was considerably warmer. "Ms. Meade? If you'd like to come back now, I have a few minutes before my first appointment."

Emily passed Bryce's desk and tried to ignore the sensation that he was staring at the back of her head as she walked by. She went through a heavy mahogany door into the office of J.R. Watkins, who closed it firmly behind her.

"Have a seat," he said, indicating a black leather chair across from his massive old antique desk.

"Thank you," said Emily. "I appreciate your taking the time to see me."

"It's no trouble at all," said Watkins, regarding her seriously. "Your aunt was a decent and honest woman who cared about this community. The least I can do is answer any questions you might have. You do, I assume, have questions?"

"Well, yes," said Emily. "I was just wondering, did Matilda mention anything to you about the house, or anything strange? I mean, did she seem nervous or apprehensive about something, like maybe she was afraid?"

"You're wondering if your aunt knew that something bad

was about to happen to her?" Watkins swiveled his chair back and forth, as if the gesture helped him to ruminate on the subject. "I would, too. But to be honest with you, aside from her financial difficulties, she seemed unconcerned that anything might happen to her."

"She was having financial difficulties?"

"Matilda, as you might know, inherited the house from her grandmother upon her passing," said Watkins. "As far as I know, she had no formal education and held no career. She held a variety of jobs, from nanny to daycare aide, but what she really wanted was to create a space for children with nowhere to go. Initially, she took in foster children. Eventually, she took out a loan and applied for the appropriate licenses through the state so that she could make things official, and she created a home for wayward children. Her goal was to place children with loving and supportive families who were willing to adopt them."

"Who would want to hurt somebody who does something that selfless?"

Watkins shrugged, looking troubled. "It's difficult to say. It seems that only a maniac would do such a thing. I think a lot of people want to believe Matilda did it simply because they can't wrap their heads around the notion that someone hurt not only innocent children, but also a human being who was purely kind. They certainly don't want to believe such a person has gone uncaught and unpunished, still living among them. I think it's just easier for them that way."

"Your receptionist said people in town might feel hostile towards me because of Matilda. He said that everyone in town is convinced Matilda did it."

Watkins snorted. "Bryce does love a good horror story. But really, you'd have to talk to the police to be certain of what they found." Emily thought of Sheriff Oglethorpe and inwardly shuddered.

"Could I see a copy of my aunt's will?" Emily asked.

He looked concerned. "I sent it to you by courier shortly after we spoke on the phone. Did you not receive it?"

"We left Florida in kind of a hurry," admitted Emily. "I think we may have just missed it."

"It's not a problem. I can have another sent to you."

"Thank you," Emily said. "And thank you again for your time."

"Of course." Watkins stood and extended his hand. "Any friend of Matilda's is a friend of mine."

Emily left the law office, Bryce's eyes boring holes in the back of her head the whole way. Outside, she inhaled the cold, thin air while she gathered her thoughts.

Matilda had money problems, just like Emily. That didn't make her a murderer. The only reason anyone in the town thought otherwise was to reassure themselves no killer remained in their midst. Whatever happened, Matilda hadn't seen it coming. Emily didn't know if that made it better or worse.

She set off walking. Footsteps and jingling tags indicated someone was walking their dog behind her, up the steep hill that led to the library. Within minutes, she was out of breath. Would she ever adjust to the altitude?

As she leaned over to catch her breath, she heard the footsteps pause. Turning, she was startled to see a dark coat whip around a tall hedge next to the sidewalk and vanish from view, leaving the sidewalk behind her empty.

She was being followed.

15

*E*mily considered resuming her walk to the library as if everything was normal. She was only a short distance away from her destination and it was broad daylight. Just what did whoever was following her plan to do? Emily suspected that it wasn't so much about following her as it was about keeping tabs on her and finding out what she was up to.

Emily went a few more steps before becoming over-whelmed with frustration. She was getting tired of being chased, attacked, and harassed. Just once, she wanted to confront whoever was after her.

She jumped off the sidewalk and ran around the hedge. A woman in a long black overcoat screamed as Emily rushed her.

It was Darla Chinn, one of the property managers at Three Star Properties. She and her partner, Roger Oglethorpe, were after Emily and Jesse to sell them the house, thereby saving Darla and Roger a large pile of money on the property's actual worth. The fact that Roger was the sheriff's brother did little to ease Emily's suspicions.

"Can I help you?" Emily demanded.

Darla fixed her hair and adjusted her coat, her silver bracelets jangling. "You've got quite a set of lungs on you. You certainly gave me a scare."

"Were you following me?" said Emily. She was not about to let her off the hook that easily.

"Yes, I was," said Darla frankly.

Emily was taken aback. She'd expected her to make an excuse of some kind.

"I saw you at the bottom of the hill and rushed after you, but you were walking so quickly, and I was too winded to call your name. It occurred to me when you turned around I might not be the person you most wanted to see, judging by the fact that you've been avoiding my calls."

Emily was disarmed by her candor. She figured this was a common tactic of Darla's. She also felt defensive, like Darla was implying that Emily was the rude one for ignoring her calls rather than Darla being rude for spying on her from the shrubbery.

"We had a break-in," Emily said shortly. "I've had some other things on my mind."

"Oh, no!" Darla gasped. Rather theatrically, Emily thought. "Is everyone okay?"

"We're fine."

Darla shook her head. "If I told Roger once, I've told him a thousand times: that property is cursed. I feel as though your aunt did you a disservice, leaving you stuck with that spook house."

Emily was startled. Spook house? How much did Darla know?

"Run-down and attracts trouble like no place I've ever seen," the property manager continued, and Emily realized it had just been a figure of speech. "Roger believes a house is just a house and that buildings are merely a system of joists and support beams covered in plaster, but I don't agree. I think a house has a soul. And that house?" Darla lowered her voice, as if the house could somehow hear them. "That house has an extremely dark soul."

Emily felt a chill skate up her spine. Either Darla had studied at Juilliard or she really believed what she was telling Emily. Emily found it difficult not to believe her, riddled with agendas as she was.

"What do you mean?" Emily's instincts told her to extricate herself from the situation and beat a hasty retreat, but her curiosity got the better of her. This was the first time since she moved into Matilda's that anyone had addressed how weird the house was. Jesse acknowledged it, just barely, but he hated to address it in any great detail.

"Exactly that. Structures are like people: they have personalities. Some take on the ones of those who inhabit them. If enough dark things happen in one place, that place becomes a dark place." In spite of herself, Emily shivered, and not because of the weather. "Obviously, it would benefit me if you and your husband were to sell to us," Darla added, almost as an afterthought.

Of course it would, Emily thought.

"But to be honest with you, I'd never rent out that property again," Darla continued. "I'd raze it to the ground and start from scratch."

"Okay, well," said Emily. "I'll certainly keep that in mind."

"Please do," said Darla. "Call me when you're ready to talk." She turned and clicked up the street, her high black heels sinking in the thin layer of snow lingering on the sidewalk.

Emily shook her head. What kind of reverse psychology mind trip was that? She should have never given Darla the time of day.

Emily strongly suspected that Darla and her partner—maybe in conjunction with the sheriff, maybe of their own accord—were doing everything in their power to get her and Jesse out of the house. The Three Star representatives knew that if Emily and Jesse felt desperate enough, they would sell cheap and fast just to get out of the situation. To what lengths would Darla and Roger go to ensure that happened? Rocks through their window, painted with threats? And if they'd done something that desperate and illegal, had they also broken into the house? If so, was it just to scare them?

Or had their intentions been more sinister?

IT WAS Emily's first time in the library, and she was instantly reassured by the presence of innumerable books. Emily became a novelist her second year of grad school after publishing a short story collection she wrote for one of her workshops. The book was met with modest success, and it was then that Emily knew she could make a living from her writing.

It was unsurprising, then, that Emily felt the most at home when she was among a large collection of books. In spite of her reservations about Aunt Matilda's place (Emily found she was still unable to think of it as her own), she had been delighted when she and Jesse found the small library located on the first floor. While Emily wanted to find out all she could about the house, she also wanted to get away from it to make another attempt at starting her next novel—this time, ideally, without any ghostly intervention.

As far as public libraries went, this one was pretty spectacular. A massive skylight flooded the first floor with light, and a sweeping staircase spiraled up to the second floor. Beneath the staircase, a fountain burbled pleasantly. Nestled among the long rows of shelves was the occasional solitary chair, facing a massive window that comprised the far wall.

Emily picked the most remote chair she could find, as far as possible from other people. She sat down and looked out the window. The window looked out over trees and a path leading to a footbridge over the creek. It was beautiful and scenic and should have been everything she needed to find inspiration, but it wasn't.

EMILY SIGHED and closed her laptop. She was afraid this would happen. She thought the change of scenery might be enough to jolt her out of her usual slump, but her inability to start a single sentence, let alone an entire novel, seemed to follow her wherever she went.

She reached into her bag. Emily had accessed the catalog online the night before and already had the call numbers she needed to look up the house. Entering the reference section, she selected several tall and heavy tomes detailing the town's history.

It didn't take long to find the passage she hoped she would. In a section dealing specifically with historical homes of the area, Emily found a reprint of an extremely old, sepia-tinged photo. Emily recognized the house immediately. The photograph was dated 1927, but the house looked exactly the same.

Hunched over the book, Emily eagerly read the accompanying paragraph.

THE MEADE RESIDENCE was constructed in 1923 by Hershel Meade, a local entrepreneur-turned-bootlegger throughout the Prohibition era. Meade began as a grocer, selling food and beverages from the successful market he owned several blocks from where the Meade home was later constructed. He and his wife, Delphine, lived in an apartment over the shop. When Prohibition outlawed the couple's most popular item, a home brew perfected in their bathtub, they decided to continue selling it illegally.

They were so successful in the endeavor that Meade had a mansion on the hill built, where they'd have space to continue their successful moonshine trade. While Hershel and Delphine resided there, the house was rumored to have a fully operational speakeasy in the basement, accessible only by a secret password. The couple continued their sale of illegal whiskey until the end of Prohibition. The house sat empty after the death of Hershel, when Delphine moved to a nearby retirement home. Eventually, the property was passed down to a relative and remains a private residence to this day.

So, that explained the tunnel system. Emily imagined dozens of bootleggers scurrying in and out of it like ants in a colony. She wondered if the copious volume of criminal activity resulted in what Darla referred to as the house's "dark soul."

The book had provided a glimpse into the history of the house, but no further insight as to what had happened the night Matilda died and who might be responsible. Frustrated, Emily placed the books back on the shelf and left the library. She walked to the nearest bus stop to catch the SKIP back up Broadway.

Before she boarded, she checked over both shoulders, just to make sure no one was following her home.

EMILY WALKED into the house and threw her keys on the table. Widget ran to the door to greet her. There was no sign of Jesse.

In spite of the fact that no one was home, music drifted from the back of the house.

Had it been a month ago, Emily might have reassured herself that it was Jesse, playing records in the parlor. Even if he wasn't there, she would have assumed he'd forgotten and left it on. Now, Emily knew better.

She knew it was one of the ghosts who haunted the house. They'd started leaving her messages the night she and Jesse moved in. While this notion once terrified her, she now felt reassured by the idea that Matilda's spirit might be trying to contact her. Maybe that meant she was on the right path.

She opened the parlor door, and her gaze fell upon the source of the sound: an old gramophone from the basement that mysteriously appeared in the parlor one night. Everyone —Jesse, Richard, and Emily—had each sworn they hadn't been the one to move it, yet still it was here.

Emily looked around the parlor. Why had Matilda wanted her to come to the parlor? Was there something here she hadn't seen?

Emily avoided the parlor since her first night in the house, when she caught a glimpse of a ghostly woman in the darkened window pane. At the time, Emily attributed it to an overactive imagination and her own reflection. Now, she wasn't so sure.

Emily approached the picture that hung behind the gramophone. It depicted a smiling Matilda, three children— two girls and a boy—and a woman around Emily's age. The woman was the only person in the photograph not smiling. Emily believed this was Cynthia, Matilda's assistant, who vanished the same night that Matilda and the children had.

The photograph fell from the wall and onto the carpeted floor with a muffled thump. Emily leaned over to pick it up. As she straightened, she hit her head on the old telephone table beneath the photograph.

"Ow!" Emily clutched her head with one hand and the photograph in the other. She struggled to her feet, setting the picture on the table. A small drawer in the table had been knocked open by the impact from her skull hitting the underside of it.

Emily pulled the drawer open the rest of the way. In it, she found an address book.

"Is this what you wanted me to find?" Emily said aloud. She was becoming accustomed to this strange form of communication between her and the ghosts. It was oddly reassuring, almost as if it connected her to Matilda in a way she hadn't been in life.

As if in answer to Emily's question, the volume of the music rose. Emily sat down at the telephone table and flipped through the address book.

Like many others in the house, it was yet another relic of a previous time. Emily hadn't known anyone to use an address book since she was a child, but she suspected that Matilda was someone reluctant to adapt to change.

Emily flipped through the book and found many of her family members listed, which surprised her. She assumed Matilda hadn't kept in touch with anybody. Now it seemed silly to think that Matilda hadn't cared where they lived or what they were doing. If Emily had learned anything about Matilda, it was what a caring person she had been.

Emily was moved to see her own name, written out in Matilda's careful penmanship. Next to this was the address of Emily's very first apartment after college. On her birthday that year, Emily had received what looked like a handmade card in a pale blue envelope, wishing her luck at her new job. In the card was tucked a neatly folded hundred-dollar bill. She remembered feeling startled and moved that this woman she'd met only once had thought of her enough to send a card. Had she sent her a thank you card? She hoped so.

Emily flipped to the next page. There was a neon green Post-It stuck to the page. CALL ASAP! Emily flipped the Post-It note up to reveal a business card taped to the page. HAROLD R. WIMBLY, WIMBLY HARDWARE. Emily remembered Jesse making a joke about "old man Wigglesworth who runs the mom-and-pop hardware shop."

Had Matilda ever called him? Or had it been too late?

Emily picked up a long black dialing wand lying next to the rotary phone. With trembling hands, she dialed the number on the card.

16

*A*s she dialed, she tried to figure out what she would say to Harold Wimbly. Obviously, she couldn't announce that the ghost of her aunt had suggested she should give him a ring. But what excuse could she have as a reasonable pretense for asking what Matilda wanted so badly to speak to him about?

"Wimbly Hardware, Harold Wimbly speaking," a pleasant older man's voice answered the phone. Emily felt less worried about coming up with something to say. Mr. Wimbly sounded like a department store Santa Claus, only kinder.

"Hi, Mr. Wimbly," she said. "You don't know me, but I think you knew my great aunt, Matilda. My husband, Jesse, has been buying supplies from you so we can renovate her house."

"Jesse's wife!" Mr. Wimbly sounded delighted. "That boy is such good company. Why, he has me in stitches every time he comes into the store."

Emily thought Jesse might object to being referred to as a boy, but then, Mr. Wimbly sounded about four hundred years old. To Mr. Wimbly, anyone under the age of seventy-five was probably considered a young man in his prime.

"He does have quite the sense of humor," Emily agreed with a smile. Of all the strange and occasionally terrible people they'd met since moving here, Mr. Wimbly sounded like the nicest.

"Indeed. And Matilda's niece! Why, your aunt was one of my favorite people." On the imaginary scoreboard within Emily's mind, she mentally increased the number of people besides her who believed in Matilda's innocence from two to three.

"Thank you, Mr. Wimbly. That's kind of you to say. I was just wondering if you knew my Aunt Matilda was planning to call you and what it might have been about."

"Oh," said Mr. Wimbly, and for the first time since she'd called, he sounded less than benevolent. "*Them.*"

"Who?" asked Emily, startled at the sudden shift in his tone.

"The *property management company*," said Mr. Wimbly, his words dripping with sarcasm. "Them."

"Uh, yes," said Emily. It was easy enough to infer that he was not a fan of Three Star Properties. "They've been pestering me and Jesse for a while now."

"That don't surprise me none," said Mr. Wimbly. "Been after me and the wife to put our place in their hands for the last five years now. Aggressive, bullying. The city of Boulder sits firmly in their palms, driving up the property tax every year. It's gotten so high that those who've lived in their homes all their lives, retired in them, and own them fair and square can barely afford to live in their own houses. Some couldn't afford it and they've been driven out.. And then those *property management* vultures sweep in and make an offer. It's a disease, is what it is. Three Star just wants Boulder to be a rich, elitist town filled with snobs and phonies. They want all the old residents out so they can replace us with them—whaddya call them, the computer people?"

"Tech guys?"

"Yeah, them tech guys. Boulder will be the next San Francisco, mark my words. Burn and bury the real residents of this town and replace us with soulless corporate drones and bloodsucking leeches."

Emily was momentarily speechless. Mr. Wimbly had gotten very dark, very quickly. It was like hearing Mr. Rogers transform into Hannibal Lecter.

"Don't let them get you," Mr. Wimbly said. "Whatever you do, you gotta hang on to that property. We can't let them win."

"No, definitely not," Emily agreed. Partially because she did agree, but mostly because she could see this was expected of her, and to say anything else would bring a swift end to the conversation. Which, come to think of it, might be for the better.

"They'll bribe you, intimidate you, and flat-out lie to you, but you can't let them win! We gotta hold out. We're all that's left of this town, from when it was great, and if they have their way, we'll all be gone."

"Well, we definitely don't want that," said Emily.

"Indeed," said Mr. Wimbly. It was a far more solemn 'indeed' than his earlier one, and Emily saw it as her opportunity to exit the conversation. "Well," she said, "I'll definitely talk this over with Jesse, and we'll be sure to take your advice."

"Oh, I've told him all about those rodents. I bring it up every time he comes in."

No wonder it had been so easy to convince Jesse to stay in the house after the break-in. Emily silently thanked Mr. Wimbly for his propaganda.

"Well, it was nice to talk to you, Mr. Wimbly," said Emily. "I hope you have a wonderful evening."

"You as well," said Mr. Wimbly.

Emily hung up the phone. As usual, it all came back to Three Star. There had to be some way for her to get something substantial on them. There was no way Darla had tailed her in order to be helpful. And something else was bothering her, too—everyone said they'd vanished without a trace. But there was no way two adults and three children disappeared into thin air. It seemed obvious that something terrible happened.

So why were Matilda, Cynthia, and the children written off as missing for so long? Had the person investigating wanted it to look like a missing person's case, rather than a potential homicide, and hidden their bodies? If only she could get her hands on the police report without Oglethorpe finding out.

Emily felt beyond frustrated. For some reason, her eyes kept coming back to rest on the picture hanging on the wall: Matilda, Cynthia, and the kids. Something about it was bothering her, and she couldn't quite figure out what it was. She studied the picture, thinking.

She heard the voice of Andrea through the typewriter. She heard the memories of the younger children that night in the basement. She and Jesse had both seen a shadow gliding wraith-like down the hallway. And she thought she had seen a face in the window their first night here, but the next day dismissed it as her own reflection.

If it was her reflection, and the shadow she followed was Matilda, then where was the ghost of Cynthia Harkness?

LATER THAT DAY, Jesse was in the backyard with Richard, standing over the open hood of the truck.

"Just brought over a distributor cap," Richard said. "I got an old Ford out back I mine for parts."

"Lucky I hadn't bought the part yet," said Jesse. "I spent

most of the day getting stuff to block the passageway and looking at security systems. Old Man Wimbly's gonna give me a deal."

Richard nodded. "That's wise of you. Enhance your security, and no one can breach your fortress."

Jesse gave him an odd look he didn't see.

"Richard," said Emily. "What do you know about Cynthia Harkness?"

"Cynthia Harkness?" Richard scratched his head. "To tell the truth, I never did know too much about her. She was pretty aloof when she worked here, liked to keep to herself. Good with the kids and got along well enough with Matilda, but never really much one for conversation. Why do you ask?"

"I thought I saw her in the parlor, but it turned out to be my reflection," said Emily, shrugging. "It just made me curious. She disappeared with Matilda, but I know so little about her."

Richard looked spooked. "Do you think you saw a ghost?" he asked.

"Why do you ask?" said Emily. She'd never once confided in anyone besides Jesse about what she saw in the house.

"Ghosts are real," said Richard seriously. "People might not believe in them, but just because you don't believe in something doesn't mean it's not real."

"I agree," said Emily. "So, you think I saw a ghost?"

Richard bit his lip, as if debating how much he wanted to say. "It seems to me that if any of them were alive, somebody would have found them by now," he said.

"Do you know why it was considered a Missing Persons case and not a homicide?" asked Emily.

"No bodies, were there? Hard to rule something a homicide if there's no concrete evidence that somebody's been killed."

"But what else could have happened?" Emily asked. "For

that many people to go missing like that, especially children —surely the sheriff at least suspected there was foul play involved."

"If he did, Sheriff Oglethorpe probably hid the evidence before anybody noticed so he wouldn't have to conduct a proper investigation," said Richard.

"Why would he do that?" asked Jesse.

"Oglethorpe likes his job for the power and influence, no other reason. He's just biding his time till he can retire and collect his pension. One more election and he can coast the rest of the way through. Last thing he wants to deal with is a homicide, let alone five."

"You don't like the sheriff, do you?" said Emily, watching him closely.

"What's to like about a man afraid of a hard day's work? You know he's not even in town right now? He's up at his place in Vail, probably sipping hot chocolate in front of his fireplace." Richard shook his head. "I don't understand what's happened to this town," he said, and Emily was reminded of Mr. Wimbly. "Used to be hardworking, decent, honest people. Now it's nothing but moneygrubbers and crooks."

IN THE KITCHEN, once she and Jesse were alone, Emily quickly recapped the day's events: Watkins, Darla, the library, and Mr. Wimbly. She ended with her epiphany in the study.

"It's weird how we keep seeing all these specters—ghosts, whatever you want to call them: a spirit's imprint of their memory here on earth. Andrea spoke to me through the typewriter. I'm pretty sure the shadow we saw was Matilda's. I heard the children in the basement during the break-in. I thought I saw Cynthia's reflection in the window of the parlor, but now I'm not sure. I'm beginning to think I was imagining things."

"But she's dead," said Jesse. "Isn't she?" He glanced around nervously, as if waiting for her to appear.

"That's what I thought," said Emily. "It seemed the most natural and obvious conclusion to assume that everyone who disappeared that night died—where else would they be? People don't just vanish into thin air. We've heard all these ghosts, confined to the house in which we can be pretty sure they were murdered. The only one we haven't seen or heard is Cynthia. Wouldn't she be here, too? We know nothing about her but what we've been told by Richard and the sheriff, which is nothing. The whole thing is just really weird. If she's not here with the others, does that mean she made it out somehow? And if she is alive, she's obviously hiding from someone, or several someones. She's probably terrified."

"If they offed Matilda and the kids but Cynthia somehow escaped, why wouldn't she just pack up and leave town?" asked Jesse. "Why stick around here?"

"Watkins told me they declared death in absentia after months of monitoring them for any signs of life, like bank account activity and phone records," said Emily. "She probably couldn't go anywhere. They would have picked her up immediately. She might be hiding somewhere, like the woods behind the library, pretending to be homeless. She probably *is* homeless now; it's not like she can go home. I'm sure they have people watching her place. If it is really her, we have to find her. She's the only one who can tell us what happened that night."

"Who can she tell?" said Jesse. "It's not like we can go waltzing into the sheriff's office."

"We have to find her before the sheriff gets back from Vail," Emily said. "And if Sheriff Oglethorpe is out of town all weekend, this is our chance to get our hands on that case file."

ugust 23rd, 2003

I CAN'T BELIEVE *this is happening. Grandma Delphine left me the house instead of Chelsea. She told me she knew I would do something meaningful with it. Chelsea is furious, of course.*

The house has not been decorated since Mother moved Grandma Delphine to the home five years ago, and it shows. Unfortunately, even with my modest inheritance, I do not have the means to redecorate it. I will have to make do with what I can find secondhand.

The groundskeeper, Richard, who worked for Grandma Delphine and Grandpa Hershel, has been most helpful with this. He has a number of secondhand items from his family's home, and he volunteered to bring them up to the house. He knows of my dream to create a home for wayward children, and he's already brought over a few things—a toy chest, a jewelry box, an old carousel horse—that once belonged to his sisters.

I only hope my venture is successful and I can create a space

*filled with laughter, love, kindness, and empathy. The kind of space
I never had when I was a child.*

MATILDA GAZED at the old lion's head door knocker before
she turned the key in the lock of the front door. She wanted
to relish the moment that this place—the sanctuary from her
difficult childhood—became hers.

It wasn't that her family had been particularly abusive or
unhappy. As far as she knew, Matilda had been the only
unhappy one among them. But her father spent more time at
work than he did at home, as so many fathers do, and
Matilda rarely saw him. On the occasions she did, he was like
a stranger to her. She felt as though they were passengers on
a train, making polite conversation with one another.

Her mother seemed as though she couldn't stand Matilda
—the way she dressed, her hair, and even her expressions.

"How do you expect to find a husband with that moody
look on your face?" her mother would demand as Matilda
would look up, blinking from whatever book she was reading, still half in another world. "Can't you smile? Be charming? Make jokes? Laugh? It's as if you're indifferent to
everything and everyone around you but your own
interests."

And she was. Matilda didn't see why this was an issue: if
their father could ignore his wife and daughters in favor of
work, why couldn't Matilda ignore her mother and sister in
favor of books? Especially Chelsea. She was maddeningly
superior, judgmental, and constantly criticizing Matilda for
everything she said and did. Matilda wondered how she
would see herself if she weren't constantly reflected in the
hateful mirror of Chelsea's condescension. It was almost as if
she was threatened by Matilda and needed to diminish her in
order to validate Chelsea's own existence, which seemed to

consist of little besides brushing her hair and trying on dresses in front of the mirror.

Matilda mostly hid from her mother and Chelsea, who were predictable in their habits. They were always in the living room, plaiting each other's hair and discussing what dress Chelsea would wear to various school dances and other functions. Meanwhile, Matilda retreated upstairs to her room to read the endless books she checked out from the library. She suspected her father actually knew her much better than he was able to openly express, because for every Christmas and birthday, he always got her a book. He'd get her something long that would require weeks of concentration and attention, something that most people would consider unsuitable for a young girl: *The Fountainhead, Moby Dick, To Kill a Mockingbird.* Chelsea, on the other hand, read only *Nancy Drew.*

"She's a much simpler person than you are," her father said one night when Matilda and Chelsea had a dreadful fight where Chelsea pulled her hair and tore the pages from her favorite book, *The Prince and the Pauper.* Matilda dreamed of finding someone to switch places with so she could live out a different, better life. She pretended she was an orphan, adopted to the wrong family, one that didn't particularly like her and only tolerated her. Like *Jane Eyre.*

Matilda had been relieved to come of age and leave her family behind, though she had no real direction or idea of what she wanted to do. She liked books, but didn't know how to write them. She loved children, but had little desire to teach. She drifted from job to job, working variously as a seamstress, a waitress, a secretary, and finally, a nanny. This was when she felt what she'd heard other people describe as a calling. It was the feeling she got from helping children who weren't her own.

Matilda, who worked for families much wealthier than her own, couldn't believe they didn't want to spend time with their own children. She supposed it reminded her of her own parents, whom she could at least pretend were separated from her by their need to work. The families she worked for, on the other hand, seemingly had everything and still abandoned their children. But it was only after her most recent job at a daycare when she realized what she truly wanted to do.

One of Matilda's favorite children in the daycare had been a precocious and charming boy by the name of Tyler. He loved nothing more than to curl up in the corner with a good book while the other children rambunctiously ran circles around him. One day, Tyler's mother failed to arrive on time. Matilda read with him hours past the regular closing time, hoping to distract him. It was clear that Tyler knew exactly what was happening and, even worse, seemed resigned to the fact. Eventually, his mother showed up reeking of alcohol and cigarettes, as if she'd brought the entire bar in her purse. She shunted Tyler away into the back of a taxi and Matilda never saw him again.

While she was normally reticent and kept to herself, Matilda surprised herself with how fiercely she pestered the daycare's manager, Ann, for information about what happened to Tyler. Ann was initially dismissive of Matilda's questions, telling her it was none of her business and she had no real stake in his life. Nevertheless, she persisted, and Ann eventually relented. She told her that Tyler had been taken away from his mother, an unrepentant alcoholic, and placed in foster care. Matilda was devastated.

What would become of such a bright boy with a promising future, abandoned to the system? She could only hope he found placement with a kind and nurturing family, but there was no way to know that would happen. She had no control and no way of finding him. She would have taken him in herself, had anyone asked her, but of course no one had.

There was, she learned, a whole series of hoops that a well-meaning person had to jump through in order to care for a child not her own, and Matilda was in the midst of this process. She wanted to foster orphans and other children like Tyler with no place to go, thereby ensuring their futures would be happier ones.

This house, she knew, would be fundamental to her goal. She could feel it. She opened the door that led to the foyer and went into the living room, overwhelmed with memories of her grandparents. This was the place she came to get away from her mother and Chelsea when their nagging got to be too much. She'd go to her grandmother's house, where she'd teach her how to make apple dumplings and her grandfather would let her spend hours in the library, poring over his vast collection of books.

Out of habit, Matilda felt herself drifting there now, entering the cozy space with its fireplace and built-in bookshelves. She ran her fingers along the spines of old leather-bound tomes, picturing the worlds that lie within, and was badly startled when someone cleared his throat behind her.

A man who looked to be about Matilda's age stood in the doorway, nervously twisting his cap in his hands.

"I'm awful sorry, ma'am, I didn't mean to startle you," he said. "I was working on fixing that loose stair on the back steps; board's a little rotted through. I used to work for your grandparents, and your grandmother still paid me to come up here every so often after she moved out to keep up the place. I guess she wanted to keep it nice for you."

Matilda was touched. Her grandmother had mentioned the handyman, Richard, a handful of times when Matilda visited her, but it was usually in passing. She didn't realize he still came to the property even after both her grandparents had passed on.

"Richard," she said warmly, shaking his hand. "It's so good to meet you. Thank you for all the work you've done here."

He blushed. "Well, of course. Your grandparents couldn't have been kinder. I was heartbroken when—" he stopped. "I shouldn't be saying that to you about your own family. It must be so hard on you."

"Well, Richard, whenever I feel sad, I tell myself about the long and adventurous lives they led," said Matilda as she examined a book on the shelf more closely: *We Have Always Lived in the Castle* by Shirley Jackson. "I think about how happy they were together, and how happy I was when I was with them. I'm sure we'll be reunited someday."

"That's real nice, ma'am," said Richard. "What do you plan on doing with this big old place in the meantime?"

Matilda was grateful for his tact: he had not asked what she and her nonexistent husband planned to do with it, or if she would have many children to populate the rooms, as the presumptuous and frankly patronizing lawyer had. She would have to replace him at her earliest convenience.

"Well, Richard," she said. "What I'd really like to do is start a home for wayward children. A place for displaced girls and boys to go until they can find a more permanent home."

"Wow," said Richard. "That's awfully selfless of you, ma'am."

"Please call me Matilda," she said.

"Matilda, I got some old kids' stuff at my parents' place I'd be more than happy to bring over for you," he said. "Stuff that belonged to me and my sisters mostly, but certainly nothing anybody would miss."

"That would be wonderful," said Matilda.

"I'll go right after I fix up that step," said Richard. "Won't do to have you falling through the next time you go out the door."

"Thank you, Richard," said Matilda.

Over the next few weeks, Matilda dusted, mopped, and cleaned the dusty old house to its former grandeur. With Richard's help, she cleared the gutters, repaired loose shingles, and painted the walls to brighten up the place. There wasn't much she could do about the floors or some of the uglier light fixtures for the time being, but Wilson Wimbly at the hardware store gave her an extremely good deal on several dozen cans of paint. By the end of the month, Matilda felt like she had a home of her own.

She hung new drapes in the living room to better block the blinding light that flooded that side of the house—especially after a blizzard, when the sun reflected off the snow. Richard's Ford truck pulled into the front yard, and Matilda could see that the flatbed of the pickup was covered with a canvas tarp. She went out to the front porch.

"What have you got there?" she called to Richard as he got out of his truck.

"Well, I know you said the kids' rooms aren't very kid-like," he called back. "So, I wanted to bring you some of those old things I mentioned."

He threw the tarp aside, revealing a wooden toy chest and what looked to be a hand-carved, hand-painted carousel horse. Matilda marveled over the horse until she got to its eyes, beady red rubies set deep in its skull. She shuddered.

"Why are the horse's eyes red?" she asked as Richard hefted it out of the truck and carried it up the stairs. "I mean, it's lovely, of course, just a little…jarring."

Richard paused to examine the horse. "Huh. You know, I never noticed." He carried the horse past her as Matilda contemplated prying its eyes from its head and replacing them with a more benevolent gemstone, like sapphire or topaz.

They arranged the items in the attic after Matilda unfurled a large rug decorated with toy trains she found at a yard sale for next to nothing. They stood back and admired their handiwork.

"It's not much, but it's a pretty good start," said Matilda.

"Are you kidding me?" said Richard. "If I could have had a place like this when I was a kid, I'd have been in paradise."

Matilda flushed with pride. "I just hope this house is the refuge to the children that it always was to me."

EMILY READ Matilda's diary while Jesse drove to the local police station downtown. She had discovered it in the pocket of an old sweater in Matilda's armoire. Emily thought perhaps if she studied it in great detail, it might yield some clue—something mentioned in passing, a stray observation Matilda had made that led to the culprit. Maybe Three Star had threatened her, or she'd seen the sheriff sneaking around the property after hours.

While it was interesting to learn about the house and her life from Matilda's perspective, most of the entries seemed fairly innocuous, detailing her plans to decorate and her musings about the past. On top of this was the fact that Matilda's handwriting was an incredibly old-fashioned cursive which seemed better suited to the Victorian era, making it incredibly taxing and time-consuming to wade through. At the same time, Emily worried that if she skimmed through the journal or started with more recent entries first, she'd miss some important observation or insight. Something Matilda had witnessed or seen without even necessarily realizing it.

"How's the detective work going?" asked Jesse, turning on his blinkers to pull into the parking lot.

Emily sighed. "It's going. I wish her writing was a little more legible, like in capital letters or something. It takes me forever to get through one of her entries."

"Well, keep at it. You're bound to find something in there, right?" Jesse turned off the engine and regarded the squat, one-story tan brick building before them warily. "Are you ready for this?"

"No time like the present, right?" Emily climbed out of the cab of the truck and Jesse did the same. Glancing around the parking lot one last time to make sure Sheriff Oglethorpe's massive black SUV was nowhere to be seen, they headed towards the front doors of the police station.

18

The police station was still and silent as a church, as if there was very little crime to report. When Emily and Jesse approached the front desk, the receptionist there looked pleasantly surprised, as if they were dropping in for tea.

"What can I help you with?" she said.

"We were looking for an incident report for the night of December 11th of last year," said Emily. "Regarding the Meade property. It belonged to my aunt. I just need it for my records."

"Of course," said the receptionist. She reached for a clipboard and a pen, handing them to Emily. "Just fill out your information, your reason for requesting the report, and the fee. I'll have that to you in no time."

Emily filled out the form in the lobby, remarking to Jesse how easy it seemed.

"I thought we'd have to sneak into Oglethorpe's office after the station was closed," she said. "With night vision goggles."

"We're not out of the woods yet," he said. "Oglethorpe could still find out we were here, looking at the report."

"If he ever comes back from Vail," said Emily.

She went back to the desk and delivered the clipboard to the receptionist.

"Just one moment please," she said. "I'll just need to retrieve this from Records and print it out for you."

While they waited, Emily walked around the lobby, pausing in front of a glass case filled with framed newspaper articles and various commendations praising the local police force. Most concerning was one of Sheriff Oglethorpe with the mayor, cutting the ribbon on a brand new natural foods store. KEEP BOULDER GREEN, the headline read.

"Man, is everybody in power here best friends here or what?" said Jesse, coming up behind Emily and looking at the picture.

"Apparently so," said Emily. "Let's just hope we never meet the mayor."

The receptionist returned to her desk with an envelope.

"Here you go," she said. "Is there anything else I can help you with today?"

"No, that's it," said Emily. "Thank you so much."

They waited till they were back in the truck to examine the report. It was written by

Sheriff Oglethorpe.

ON THE NIGHT of December 11th, 2017, I was dispatched to the Meade residence at 734 Redwood Trail. Richard Danforth, a local handyman employed by the homeowner, reported the home's residents missing. This included two adult women, Matilda Meade and Cynthia Harkness, and three children fostered by Ms. Meade: Tricia Mills, Bobby Mills, and Andrea Hayworth. There was no sign of forced entry. Nothing appeared to have been taken from the home. Danforth stated all had been present two days earlier, prior to the storm, when he brought them several bundles of wood. When he returned to check on them and saw no sign of them in the house, *he says he became concerned and alerted the authorities. No sign of foul play. Officers dispatched to Miss Harkness's home at 217 Inverness Lane. The residence was empty, with no sign of forced entry or foul play. Currently presumed missing pending further investigation.*

"THAT'S IT?" cried Emily in dismay. "That's all they found?"

"Either somebody's phoning it in or somebody covered their tracks very well," said Jesse.

"Or both," said Emily bitterly. "I can't believe this. It doesn't even say anything about the blood on the floor."

"If there was any," said Jesse. "Or maybe Sheriff Oglethorpe doesn't want anybody to know what he found."

"We need to find out more about Cynthia," said Emily.

"Do you still think she might be alive?" said Jesse.

"I don't know what to think. I definitely still think it's weird that we know next to nothing about her and nobody who's told us any of these stories seems to know anything about her, either. It's weird that of all the things we've seen and heard in the house, none of them seem to be related to Cynthia. She's like a missing puzzle piece."

"What did Matilda have to say about her in her diary?" asked Jesse, starting the truck and pulling out of the parking lot.

"She mentions her in one of the last entries, when Cynthia started to question her regarding her money problems. Then I went back to the beginning, to when she first got the house. But there is a passage I found from more recently that seems to describe her in more detail."

"What does it say?" asked Jesse.

Emily opened the diary and read aloud.

SEPTEMBER 7*th*

. . .

I'VE FINALLY HAD to acknowledge that I need to find a suitable assistant to help me take care of this place. Richard has been pestering me about it for years. I've taken out an ad in the local paper in the hopes of finding a reliable individual. I can only hope to find someone as passionate as I am about creating a better life for the kids.

THERE WAS a knock at the front door. Matilda hurried from the kitchen to the front entryway. Her imagination hoped for Mary Poppins: a smartly-dressed Englishwoman with a firm sense of discipline balanced by whimsy. The wan and slightly dour-looking girl waiting on the front stoop left much to be desired.

"Come in, come in," said Matilda, inwardly chiding herself for her snap judgement and eager to accommodate the girl in order to make up for her mental rudeness. Hadn't her own mother constantly scolded her for not looking bright and happy enough? Who was she to judge this girl?

"Thank you," said the girl. "I'm Cynthia. It's nice to meet you."

Matilda shook her hand. Contrary to her waifish appearance, Cynthia had a firm handshake. Matilda felt herself warming to the girl. She ushered her into the living room where they sat across the coffee table from one another. Matilda offered Cynthia a cup from her favorite silver tea set.

"Just hot water, please," she said. "With lemon, if you have it."

Matilda thought this rather odd, but who knew what the latest diet craze was among young women Cynthia's age? Matilda herself had once gone a whole week living off nothing but pinto beans and tap water just because her friend Rowena swore by it.

Cynthia crossed her legs primly. She wore a long sheer slip dress under a heavy sky-blue pea coat. Her face was devoid of any make-up. She wore no jewelry. Her stockings were pale, her eyes were pale, and so was her hair. She looked insubstantial enough to disappear at any moment. Matilda felt concerned for her health.

"Would you like something to eat, dear?" she asked kindly. "I have cheese and crackers, or if you haven't eaten dinner, I could offer you a nice steak. Maybe some potatoes. Asparagus. Dessert, if you'd like some."

Cynthia smiled politely, as if used to people attempting to feed her and just as accustomed to politely declining. "That's quite all right. What sort of help are you looking for, with the children?"

"I'm looking for a well-qualified caretaker to assist me with everything from morning to night," said Matilda. "What kind of experience do you have working with kids?"

"I was a nanny in New York for five years after college," said Cynthia. "I have references, of course, if you'd like to contact the family I worked for. I was an Elementary Education major in college, and I planned to teach K-12 when I got out of school. Unfortunately, the job market proved much tougher to navigate than I anticipated. I came back home because I thought the competition would be less, but it seems you can't get anywhere these days without a Master's no matter where you go, doesn't it?"

Matilda smiled, hoping that Cynthia wouldn't sense her discomfort. Matilda had barely finished high school. She found the insufferable boredom of school intolerable. Her teachers assigned her books and then told her what to think about them, and everything else seemed like mindless busy work to keep kids occupied and out of the adults' hair all day so that they could work.

"Well, it sounds like you're highly qualified to work with kids," said Matilda. "Were you looking for something full-time?"

"Oh yes, definitely," said Cynthia firmly. "Ever since my husband left me, I've been struggling to make ends meet."

Matilda was uncertain as to whether or not to pursue this: would she seem empathetic, or merely nosy? To be honest, she was a little uncomfortable that the younger woman was so blunt in the first place.

"Well, there's plenty of work to be had around here," she said briskly. "I'll need help with the children from dawn until dusk. I'd be happy to take you on, if you feel like you're up to the challenge."

Cynthia smiled for the first time since Matilda opened the door.

"I think I can handle it," she said.

"GOD, can anyone in this town afford to eat?" said Emily as she closed the diary.

"I don't know, those property managers look pretty well-fed to me," said Jesse. "It's weird enough that somebody came up here to whack an old lady and a bunch of kids, but why the assistant, too? Was she just in the wrong place at the wrong time?"

"I don't think there's any aspect of this that wasn't premeditated," Emily said. "Whoever did this knew Cynthia was there, too."

"Why would they need her out of the way? If they wanted the house, why not just take out Matilda and the kids?"

"Maybe the blizzard was their only opportunity," said Emily. "The same way they waited till we were trapped to break in. Which makes me even more certain it was the same person. The night they disappeared, Cynthia hadn't left for the night like she would have normally, but there was no better opportunity for them to break in than a night when the power was out and the roads were closed. I don't think they would have cared whether or not she was there. They just needed to ensure that everyone in the house was completely trapped and isolated." Emily thought of how helpless they had been in the house and shuddered.

"But if she did escape, how could she have gotten out?" asked Jesse.

"She might have known about the passage," said Emily. "She'd been here for a year. Andrea said that Cynthia got upset when she opened the closet with the tea towels. There's an entrance there, under the bottom shelf. Maybe she didn't want the kids to find out about it. She probably didn't want them playing in there and getting stuck in the walls."

"Do you think she still has family in the area? Someone we could talk to?" said Jesse.

"The diary mentions an ex-husband," said Emily. "I doubt he'll want to talk about Cynthia if it ended badly and she disappeared, but I suppose it's worth a try."

"It ended badly...then she disappeared..." repeated Jesse slowly. "Do you think her ex-husband could have had anything to do with it?"

"Wouldn't the police have questioned him?" Emily said.

Jesse snorted. "Oglethorpe might have sent him a survey, strongly encouraging him to return it as his leisure." He pulled into the driveway and cut the engine, then glanced at the incident report.

"Her address is in here," he said. "Do you think the ex is still there?"

"It's possible," said Emily dubiously. "You think we should go out there?"

"It seems like the best possible lead."

"But what if he's a murderer? Even if he's not, what's our pretense for questioning him?"

"We'll go up there together in broad daylight. We won't

go inside, even if he asks us in for tea. And as far as pretenses go, we're frustrated that nobody can tell us what happened that night. I'm sure he is, too."

"Okay," said Emily. "As long as we're safe."

"I'm sure it'll be—what's that thing Richard said? The day we moved in? Safe as houses."

"Yeah, and look how well *that* turned out," said Emily.

INVERNESS LANE WAS MORE of a long dirt alley between two streets than an actual lane. It wasn't even labeled, and they passed it several times before realizing it was there. On Inverness, the houses were spread out few and far between until the very end, where a small cluster of trailers was situated around a cul-de-sac.

Emily peered through the windshield of the truck. "Are we sure this is it?"

Jesse parked on a narrow strip of gravel between Cynthia's address and the trailer next door. "You were expecting maybe the Taj Mahal?"

"Do you think her ex-husband's here?" Emily glanced anxiously around their gloomy surroundings. "Lurking in the trees with a baseball bat?"

"Oh man, you have *got* to start writing again. You're doing that thing where you write everything we do out loud. No, there's no way he's lurking around with a baseball bat. Let's go. I want to get our untimely murder over with."

They approached the trailer cautiously. It was dark, and the grass in front was overgrown. They peered in the small windows of the little Airstream. It was pitch dark with no sign of life.

"I don't think there's anyone in here," said Emily.

"Not unless they're hiding under the trailer," said Jesse.

"Oh my god, Jesse, stop," said Emily with a shudder.

"I'm serious. It would be a good hiding place."

"Can I help you?" said a voice behind them.

Emily jumped and screamed simultaneously, turning in the air as she landed to face whoever had just spoken. Her reaction was so strong she scared both Jesse, who gave a scream of horror of his own, and the woman who'd just approached them, who also screamed. She placed a hand to her heart over the flowered housecoat she wore beneath her parka as she stared at Emily, wide-eyed.

"Oh, I'm so sorry," said Emily, embarrassed. "I didn't mean to startle you."

"*I* didn't mean to startle *you*," said the woman in the flowered housecoat. "I just saw you in the yard, looking lost, and I thought you must have the wrong place. I live next door. I'm Theresa Plumber."

"I'm Emily and this is Jesse," said Emily. "I'm sorry again about scaring you. We were looking for anyone related to Cynthia Harkness. Her husband, maybe? I'm not sure who would be here."

"Oh," said Theresa, looking solemn. "Cynthia. No one knows what happened to her, do they? This place has been sitting here empty since she up and vanished. Husband hasn't been around since before she moved in. She came here alone."

"Did you know her? Or anything about her?" Emily asked.

"Cynthia mostly kept to herself. She was real quiet. I offered her coffee and pie a few times, but she always said no. Polite as could be. I got the impression she wasn't too trusting after her divorce. Some people get like that. They get disappointed by somebody, or betrayed, and they just shut right down."

"No one ever bought the land after she disappeared?" asked Jesse.

"Not much to buy, is there? The trailer is all tied up in

probate. The ex-husband is after it, but so is her brother. Big mess, if you ask me."

"It's a trailer," said Jesse in disbelief. "How much is an Airstream going for these days? Five grand?"

"Families are messy," Theresa said wisely. "Some will fight for the sake of fighting."

"Well, thank you so much for your help, Theresa," said Emily. She pulled out one of her cards. "If you think of anything else, please don't hesitate to give me a call."

Theresa studied the card with interest. "A writer, huh? You doin' a book about all this?"

"Something like that," said Emily.

She watched Theresa crunch across the icy gravel back to her own trailer, which had a laundry line stretched between two trees next to a ramshackle shed.

Emily squinted as Theresa disappeared into the trailer, and Jesse turned away to go back to the truck. It looked as if there was a light inside the shed.

"Jesse?" Emily said, taking a few steps towards it. He turned back.

The light flickered out.

19

The light was rapidly fading, and it would soon be pitch black outside. As the sky changed, so did the temperature, beginning its descent from barely tolerable to freezing. It could have been a trick of the light, her imagination, or any other reasonable explanation—but Emily was now hesitant to attribute anything she saw out of place as something that could be easily explained. She'd once tried to rationalize everything, but now she was starting to see that some things existed outside the parameters of what seemed logical or possible.

She thought, what if there's someone out there? What if it was Cynthia?

"What is it?" Jesse asked.

"I thought I saw—" Emily took a few steps towards the shed. "A light, maybe? I'm not sure."

"Think her old man's got himself a man cave back there?" said Jesse.

Of course. The shed was on Theresa's property, not Cynthia's.

"Yeah, it's probably that," said Emily, not believing it even as she said it.

"Should we investigate?" inquired Jesse.

Emily glanced at Theresa's trailer, which she'd disappeared into only moments before.

"She's probably settling in to watch *Wheel of Fortune*," Jesse reassured her, reading her mind.

"I feel weird creeping around Theresa's property," said Emily.

"I'm sure Theresa doesn't necessarily want an allegedly dead person hiding in her shack," said Jesse. "We're probably doing her a favor."

The shack was a crude little lean-to between two tall trees and a wooden stump. It looked like a place to store tools or possibly a snowmobile. They approached it cautiously, as if waiting for someone to come flying out of it at any moment.

"Where's the door?" said Emily, mystified. There didn't appear to be any entrance or exit, and its sides were perfectly smooth.

"Here's a window," said Jesse. "It's hard to see into, though."

Emily circled the shed to where Jesse was standing, peering through a small glass pane. The window was so coated with dust that the only thing visible through it was a small table holding a partially melted candle.

"I don't like this," she said. "Something's weird."

"Maybe Theresa will open it for us," said Jesse.

They went up to the door of Theresa's trailer and knocked. She opened it. She was eating a chicken leg and seemed unsurprised to see them again. On her television in the background, Pat Sajak made a sardonic comment as a contestant leaned over to spin the wheel.

"It's us, again," said Emily. "I mean, um, obviously. I know this sounds really strange, but we were just getting ready to leave and thought we saw someone on your property. In your shed. We just wanted to check on you and make sure you were safe."

Theresa smiled warmly at this. "Well, isn't that nice! But I can tell you right now it's those damn squatters."

"Squatters?" said Jesse.

"They're everywhere. All the ones you don't see in the streets with their signs and the parks with their sleeping bags, they find any space they can and slip in through the cracks. Can't say I blame them. Not that I'm exactly thrilled about it, either." She frowned. She disappeared from the doorway and reappeared with a torch flashlight. "Let's see who's out there this time."

Back at the shack, Theresa slid her hand along the edge of the building. There was a hidden catch on one side, revealing a door that blended in perfectly with the rest of the facade.

"Thought maybe if I hid the opening it would discourage them, but I guess if wishes were horses, then beggars could ride," she mumbled, almost to herself.

"You built this?" asked Jesse, impressed.

"With my own two hands," said Theresa, opening the door and shining her light into the shack.

There was no one there.

There was, however, an old gray blanket in the corner near a stale bread crust next to the table with the candle on it. Emily found herself thinking how easily someone could have slipped out while she and Jesse were knocking on the door of Theresa's trailer.

"I knew it," said Theresa triumphantly, taking in the blanket and old food. "Squatters."

"Right," said Emily. "Squatters."

In the truck on the way back home, Emily stared pensively out the window, thinking over what they'd just seen.

"You think it was her?" Jesse asked. "Cynthia?"

"I don't know what to think anymore," Emily said. "I think there's a strong possibility she's alive, and if so, she's got to be hiding somewhere. She's the only one who knows what happened that night. We have to find her. She's the only one who can tell us the truth about what happened and stop what's happening now."

"What makes you think she's alive?" asked Jesse. "How do you think she got away?"

"If she knew about the passage, then maybe she escaped," said Emily. "If they provide an easy way into the house, then it stands to reason that they also provide an equally convenient way out."

"How can we be sure?" said Jesse.

"We need to be able to tell for certain that she's not in the house," said Emily.

"How?" asked Jesse.

"I think I have an idea," she said.

THE THIRD SECONDHAND store they visited had exactly what Emily wanted, buried in the toys and games aisle.

"I found it!" she exclaimed as she pulled it triumphantly from the shelf filled with old used board games.

"A Ouija board?" said Jesse dubiously. "I don't know about this."

"This seems easiest, for our purposes," said Emily. "Andrea seems to be the only one who uses the typewriter. The younger kids don't seem to be able to communicate that well at all; the only time I heard them was when we were trapped in the basement. And unless you want to see the shadow again—"

"Okay, okay," said Jesse hurriedly. "Let's do it."

Emily stopped in a second aisle to collect a few partially used candles and went to the register.

"Oh man, we're really doing this," mumbled Jesse, eyeing the candles nervously.

"Having a séance?" the checkout girl inquired brightly.

"We're not really serious or anything," said Emily. "Just messing around." In her pursuit of the truth and her quest to clear Matilda's name, she was growing more and more accustomed to telling half-truths and white lies.

"Well, I always say it's nothing to mess with," the girl said solemnly, scanning the game and the candles. "I take the other side very seriously, and I would highly recommend you burn sage and also use a rose quartz."

"Of course," said Emily.

"We don't have that here, but there's a great place off Pearl where you can get all that stuff—it's near that alpaca fur store, you know the one I'm talking about? Next to the gluten-free pizza place."

"I know exactly where that is," said Emily. She had no intention of going there.

"Good. Did you guys bring your own bags? Otherwise, I have to tack on an extra dime."

"We'll just carry them, thank you," said Jesse.

They took their purchases and carried them out to the truck.

"Please explain why you believed we could live here comfortably and happily for the rest of our lives," said Jesse.

"I never said for the rest of our *lives*," said Emily. "It's not like I knew what we were getting into."

"Okay, well, let's just get home for our séance, then," Jesse mumbled, starting the truck. "At least we're not paying rent," said Emily.

"Yeah, but at what cost, though?" Jesse answered as the truck rumbled down the road toward the steep hill toward the house.

THEY PLACED the Ouija board on the living room table and arranged the candles around it in a half circle.

"I've never done this before," said Emily, "so I'm not entirely sure how this is supposed to work."

"And I am?" Jesse surveyed their handiwork. "I mean, this looks pretty terrifying, so I'm guessing we have a pretty good handle on it."

"Maybe we should build a fire," said Emily. "So we can turn the lights out."

"Oh man," said Jesse. "Let's just make this as freaky as possible." Reluctantly, he arranged the logs on the hearth inside of the fireplace. It was only their first month out west, but already their fire-building skills had considerably improved.

Emily lit the candles with a long match from a box in a kitchen drawer while Jesse lit the fire. Widget came in through the dining room, looked at them with her head cocked, then turned and left the room.

"Even the dog thinks this is weird," said Jesse.

"Only because it is," said Emily. "If I knew what we were getting ourselves into, I might have just stayed in Florida and lived in a box. But, as Theresa said—if wishes were horses, then beggars could ride."

"What does that even mean?" asked Jesse.

"Think about it: if you had nothing and no means, but you could wish for whatever you wanted, then you wouldn't have to ask anyone for anything."

"Oh. I get it," he said.

"Are you stalling?" asked Emily.

"Absolutely," said Jesse.

"I know it's a little unsettling," said Emily, and Jesse's eyebrows practically rose right off his face at her choice of words. "Okay, *highly* unsettling, but I really believe that Matilda and the children want to protect us. I believe we can help them. And I think that Cynthia's alive and this may be the key to finding her."

"Okay," said Jesse, resigned. "Let's do this."

Emily placed the planchette on the board and read off the back of the box. "Okay, so apparently, we just rest our fingertips on the planchette and then focus on a question. We can ask it out loud, but we also need to focus on it with our minds for the information to be revealed." They placed their fingertips on the little wooden triangle.

"What are we asking first?" asked Jesse.

"I think we need to establish how many presences are in the house," said Emily. "Confirm whether there are four or five." She paused. "How many of you are here?" she asked.

Emily closed her eyes as she tried to fix the question in her mind. She was unsure how much time had passed before she felt it, just beneath her fingertips: movement.

"It's moving," whispered Jesse.

She opened her eyes to see Jesse, wide-eyed, leaning over the table. The little planchette glided across the board.

"Are you moving it?" asked Emily.

"No," he said. "Are you?"

Emily shook her head and bit her lip.

They stared as the planchette slid to the numbers at the bottom of the board: 4.

"Oh, man. This is so weird," Jesse moaned.

Emily was now intently fixed upon the board and barely aware of his discomfort. "Is Cynthia Harkness here with us?" she asked.

The planchette glided up to the upper right side of the board: NO.

"Can you tell us where she is?" Emily asked excitedly.

The planchette hovered, as if uncertain, then went back to NO.

"Oh," said Emily, disappointed.

"If they can't leave the house, there's no way for them to know," said Jesse.

"Is she still alive?" Emily asked.

Again, the planchette seemed uncertain.

"They probably can't know that for sure, either," said Jesse.

"Did she get away? The night everyone disappeared?"

The planchette paused, as if deciding something. Then it slid up to the upper left part of the board, landing on YES.

"Is this Matilda?" asked Jesse.

The planchette, moving much more quickly now, as if excited, immediately slid to YES.

"What happened the night you died?"

The planchette skated so quickly between the letters it seemed to spell out the word all at once: M, U, R, D, E, R.

It had been obvious all along, but having it confirmed filled Emily with dread. Tears formed in her eyes for this kind and selfless person who gave so much. "I'm so sorry," she said. "I promise that we'll do whatever we can do to help you."

The planchette raced over the letters once more: D, A, N—

"Dan? Was that who killed you?" Jesse asked eagerly.

"Dan? Who's Dan?" said Emily.

—G, E, R.

"Dan Ger?" said Jesse. "Does he work for Three Star?"

"No, she's saying 'danger,'" said Emily. "Matilda, are we in danger?"

The planchette raced to YES, then began spelling out another word: DELPHINE. Emily stared at the name: Matilda's grandmother and Emily's great-great-grandmother.

"Is she here, too?" asked Jesse.

The planchette slid to NO. Then it went back down to the numbers: 1,9,2,7.

"1927," said Emily. "That's the year the photo was taken in the book I found in the library. But what does it mean?"

A knock sounded at the front door.

The planchette slid to the bottom of the board: GOOD-BYE.

"Good-bye," whispered Emily.

"If that's Richard..." Jesse shook his head as he got up to answer the door. "I swear, that guy has like the worst timing ever."

She heard Jesse's voice change as he opened the door. "Oh," he said. "It's you." He couldn't have sounded less enthusiastic if it had been his mother-in-law. Emily went to the front door to see who it was.

It was Sheriff Oglethorpe.

Emily felt herself tense. She thought of the words on the Ouija board: DANGER. Was this who Matilda meant?

"How are you folks doing tonight?" asked the sheriff with a pleasant smile.

"Fine," said Emily cautiously. "How are you?"

"I'm about as well as can be, thank you. Just got back from the mountains. It's beautiful up there," he said with his wide wolf's grin.

"I've heard," said Jesse.

Emily couldn't shake the fear that the sheriff had learned of their request for the police report and this was the reason for his unexpected visit.

"What can we do for you, Sheriff?" asked Emily. She tried to sound calm, as if they had nothing to hide.

"It's more about what I can do for you," said the sheriff, tipping his hat genially.

"For us?" said Jesse curiously.

"I just wanted to make sure you folks felt safe and there's been no further activity on your property," he said. "I just got back and hadn't heard anything, but since I haven't been here for a couple days, I wanted to come by and check on you folks. Make sure you were okay."

"We're okay," said Emily with a forced little smile. She wanted more than anything for him to leave.

"Glad to hear it," he said, winking at her. She felt a little sick. What kind of cat-and-mouse game was he playing?

"Anything suspicious happens, please don't hesitate to let me know."

"We will," said Emily, thinking *go away go away go away go away.* "Thank you so much for stopping by."

The sheriff smiled. "Y'all take care now," he said, adding, "Be safe." He turned and strode down the steps to the waiting darkness, crunching down the gravel driveway to his unseen SUV.

"Campaigning," muttered Jesse under his breath. "What a swell guy."

He shut the door, and Emily was unable to control the overwhelming wave of thoughts that crashed over her brain: Was the sheriff sincere, or was it a veiled threat?

Was he the danger Matilda had warned them about?

*W*ith Sheriff Oglethorpe back in town and showing up randomly at their house, Emily felt that time was of the essence.

"We've got to find Cynthia," she told Jesse in front of the roaring fireplace. Neither of them wanted to let it die in the wake of the chilling events of the evening. "She's alive, I'm sure of it. I think she was hiding in that shed behind Theresa's trailer. I think she's out there somewhere."

"Why not go to someone for help?" asked Jesse. "Why not come to us?"

"For all she knows, we'll just turn her over to the sheriff," said Emily. "She doesn't know whose side we're on. If someone came out of the woods talking about conspiracies and showed up at your house, you'd call the cops. That's probably what she thinks we're going to do."

"How can we find her, though?" said Jesse. "She's obviously pretty good at hiding."

"She had to have some connection with somebody in town besides Matilda," said Emily. "She didn't just materialize out of nowhere. In the journal, she tells Matilda she came 'home' to Colorado. Where was home for her?"

"Was Harkness her name? Or was that her ex-husband's name?" asked Jesse.

"I didn't even think of that." Emily buried her face in her hands. "Now do you get why I didn't want to change my name? It's like she no longer exists."

"Maybe she changed it back," suggested Jesse. "If she hated the guy, why hang on to a bad memory?"

"Let's look her up," said Emily. "If it's her name, we'll find her family. If it's the ex's name, maybe we'll find him."

They opened Emily's laptop and searched for Cynthia Harkness. The first thing that came up was a series of newspaper articles about the disappearance. Most of them quoted Sheriff Oglethorpe, who always seemed to subtly imply that Matilda had most likely taken the children.

"He told me that was stuff the town was making up," said Emily indignantly. "Yeah, making it up because he said it first. What a liar."

"Are you surprised?" said Jesse. "Wait! Do you see this?"

Emily leaned closer to the screen, squinting.

At the bottom of one of the last articles they'd opened was the line *Cynthia Harkness's husband, Ray Harkness, was unavailable for comment.*

"Ray Harkness!" she said. "That's it!"

"What if he's in Dallas?" asked Jesse.

"Don't even say that," said Emily, typing his name.

There were three local Ray Harknesses. The fourth was a moderately successful comic book artist who lived in Australia. Of the remaining three, one was a child, posing in a Little League uniform; one was a local musician named Stevie Ray Harkness, who appeared to be a woman; and finally, a glowering, beetle-browed man named Ray Harkness appeared at the bottom of the page, where he sold insurance in Thornton.

"Man, his SEO game is terrible," said Jesse.

"I bet you this is him," said Emily.

"Why, cause he looks like a jerk?" asked Jesse.

"Well, I mean, yeah," said Emily.

"What do we do? Email him? Call him? He doesn't look like he spends a lot of time on social media. Should we maybe use LinkedIn? I bet he's on there *all* the time."

"No way," said Emily. "What will we say? 'Hi, we'd like to ask you about your dead wife who we think is possibly still alive?' There's no way a guy like that is getting back to us. This isn't Theresa Plumber we're dealing with here."

"He looks like that guy in *Rear Window*," Jesse observed, studying Ray Harkness's picture. "That dude who offs his wife and hides her in the garden."

"We'll have to ambush him," said Emily. "At his office. We'll make an appointment to buy some insurance—"

"Probably should do that anyway," Jesse murmured. "Under the circumstances."

"—and while we're there, we'll bring up the fact that we live in this house, which is bound to get a reaction out of him —unless he's a robot—and then we'll ask him about Cynthia."

"You do realize," said Jesse, "that this is like, the worst plan ever, right? Trapped in a small office under false pretenses with this weirdo who might have had his wife taken out?"

"I admit, some things could go wrong," said Emily. "But unless you have a better plan…"

THE RIDE to Thornton the next day was a brief one, just under thirty minutes. The highway was surrounded on both sides was endless prairie with mountains in the distance. Emily would have thought it was pretty, if it hadn't reminded her of how isolated she felt here.

She and Jesse stopped short of wearing actual disguises, but they didn't want to appear entirely recognizable, either. Jesse wore his only suit, a pair of fake glasses, and a side part in his normally unruly hair. Emily wore a conservative pencil skirt with a long blazer and matronly shoes. She found a pair of reading glasses in an upstairs drawer that she had to wear on the tip of her nose so they wouldn't affect her vision. She styled her hair in a granny bun.

"You look like Old Maid," said Jesse. "Like from the card game?"

"You look like an insurance salesman," she said. "We're supposed to be buying insurance, not selling it."

"How am I supposed to know what people wear to buy insurance?" said Jesse. "I've never done it before."

"Neither have I," said Emily. "I guess I just figured people in insurance offices dress pretty conservatively."

"Well, in that case, maybe we'll blend in."

They didn't. The secretary who greeted them, young and dressed in jeans ("casual Friday," Jesse muttered to Emily upon seeing her) regarded them curiously when they came in. All the insurance salespeople wore black, gray, or navy, and Emily and Jesse's matching brown business casual made them look like they were in a 70s caper about a stolen briefcase.

The secretary, however, was cordial enough to hide her concern over their odd appearances. "Mr. Harkness will see you now," she said pleasantly, removing a pen from her messy bun to write something in the appointment book on her desk. "Down the hall, third door from the left."

Emily and Jesse skulked nervously down the hallway in their strange attire, hoping Ray Harkness wouldn't see through their ridiculous disguises.

They were in luck. Ray Harkness barely looked at them at all. For a salesman, he wasn't very charismatic. Dark circles under his eyes suggested he hadn't been sleeping well, possibly for months or even years. His dark suit was rumpled, as if he either hadn't taken the time to press it or didn't own an iron in the first place. His comb over was hardly convincing, and he sounded like he had sinus problems. Emily couldn't help but stare when they sat down. He looked like he could barely get out of bed, let alone plan a murder. Or several.

"What can I do for you folks today?" he said tiredly. His smile was thin and seemed like an afterthought.

"We wanted to buy some insurance," said Jesse.

"Well, you've come to the right place for that," said Harkness. "What kind? Life? Health? Homeowners? Property and casualty? Long-term care? Ideally, you're looking for homeowners' insurance, because that's what I sell. If you need life insurance, I can send you across the hall, to Perkins."

"Oh no, we specifically wanted to meet with you regarding your home insurance policies," said Emily. "I just inherited a property from my aunt. Unfortunately, I learned after the fact that she let quite a few things lapse, financially speaking."

"Inheritances," said Harkness, shaking his head. "They're a real double-edged sword, let me tell you. You might think you're getting valuable property, then you discover the person who left it to you had a bank lien and a reverse mortgage. So it's not even your house at all. And to *not* have home or property insurance in an area this dry? Practically criminal."

"Um, yes," said Emily, who understood only half of what he was saying. "So my aunt, Matilda Meade—"

Harkness went chalk white, as if all the blood spontaneously drained from his face. Emily was used to the negative effect her aunt's name had on people, since so many seemed to assume she was a kidnapper, murderer, or both. But she could never have anticipated the dramatic effect it would have on Cynthia's ex-husband.

"Did you say Matilda Meade?" demanded Harkness. It was clear he was badly shaken as he reached for his coffee mug with a trembling hand.

"I did," said Emily, acting bewildered. "I'm sorry, did you know her?"

Harkness reached for a handkerchief he'd tucked sloppily into the front pocket of his suit jacket, dangling out like a limp sock. He mopped his brow. He was sweating profusely. "I apologize, but I don't think I can sell you this policy. If you'd like to reschedule with Mollie at the front, Edwards down the hall is really exceptional—"

"Are you all right?" Jesse interrupted Harkness before he could attempt to get rid of them. "Do you need a glass of water? Let me get you a glass of water." He jumped up and ran from the office before Harkness could protest, leaving him no choice but to deal with Emily.

"Did I upset you?" asked Emily, feigning worry. "I know there are terrible rumors about my aunt, but I can assure you, they aren't true. That's why we came all the way out here for insurance. No one in town would sell to us." Emily made sure to let her voice quaver and catch a bit at the end.

"I'm very sorry," said Harkness, still sweating profusely. "I wish that I could be the one to help you, I truly do, it's just—I have a very personal...*connection* to your home, and I just wouldn't feel right about it. Really, it would unsettle me greatly."

"Wait," said Emily, as if something were just occurring to her. "You're not related to...Cynthia Harkness, are you?"

Ray Harkness looked at her with open devastation on his face. For the first time, Emily felt guilty about the charade they were imposing on this poor man. Then she remembered Matilda, and it strengthened her resolve.

"She was my wife," said Harkness, and it appeared to be all he could do not to break down in tears. "We had some issues and we were separated, but I loved her very much. I always thought we'd work it out. I tried to forget myself in my work, but we only grew more distant. And then she... disappeared." He broke off with a choked little sob. It seemed that he hadn't spoken on the subject for a long time, if ever, and once he started, he could no more prevent the words from coming out than he could stop a torrential downpour.

"So you don't know what happened, either?" said Emily gently. "I know, it's a terrible burden."

"Of course it's a burden!" Harkness burst out. "And I mean no disrespect to you, but I have to say, I very much blame your aunt for what happened."

"Why?" Emily didn't have to feign her bewilderment. She couldn't understand why everyone was so eager to scapegoat Matilda. Sheriff Oglethorpe used her as a fall guy and the townspeople believed him, but what was Ray Harkness's agenda?

"Cynthia and I spoke once, by phone, shortly before she disappeared," said Harkness. "And she was so worried about money, but of course too proud to accept any help from me —we were still married! I don't see what difference it would have made, but she was stubborn. She told me how that woman concealed all kinds of things from her—about the house, her financial situation. Cynthia's checks bounced constantly. She was barely getting by. You ask me," said Hawkins, narrowing his eyes, "I think she sold those kids and got rid of Cynthia to keep her quiet about it."

Emily was shocked. It was the first time she heard someone make such an open accusation about Matilda to Emily's face.

"Yes, I do," Harkness repeated, defiant at the expression on her face. "I'd testify to it in any court of law. I think she's out there somewhere, in hiding, with whatever money she got, while Cynthia—" All his audacity left him like air leaking out of a balloon and he slumped over his desk, suddenly defeated. Emily watched with horror as he buried his face in his arms and sobbed.

Jesse reappeared at the doorway, fake glasses askance, clutching a tiny paper cone of water. He looked from Harkness, still weeping, to Emily, watching him as her tiny reading glasses nearly fell from the tip of her nose.

"Uh…is everything all right in here?" Jesse asked.

"Um, I think we'd better go," said Emily.

She jumped to her feet without saying anything to Harkness—at this point, it didn't seem like there was much left to be said—and Jesse gently set the water cup on his desk, which promptly tipped over and spilled.

"Oops," he said, slowly backing away from the desk while Harkness cried. He eyed the spill as if determining how to best clean it up.

"Come on!" Emily grabbed his arm and pulled him from the office. They hurried by Mollie in reception, who called after them, "Did you need to make another appointment?" and then, leaning further over her desk, "Do you need me to validate your parking?"

They ran to the truck outside and peeled out of the parking lot.

"What did you say to him?" Jesse demanded as he practically stripped his gears flying off the entrance ramp onto the highway. "He went from normal to sobbing baby in the five minutes I was gone."

"Nothing! Well, I mean, first I asked him if I had upset him, then I told him that the rumors weren't true, then I lied and said no one in town would sell us insurance, and he was our only hope."

"That's pretty dirty," Jesse said admiringly. "And then he cried?"

"No, then I asked him if he was related to Cynthia. He got really mad and kind of scary, going off on this tirade about how Matilda was crooked and screwing her over. *Then* he cried."

"Because he was so mad?" asked Jesse.

"No, I think he just misses Cynthia. He said he loved her and he blamed Matilda for her disappearance. He thinks she kidnapped the kids and murdered Cynthia to keep her quiet. I was getting a little bit worried he was going to do something crazy, but then he just lost it. I feel bad for the guy."

"Well, at least we can rule out Harkness as a suspect," said Jesse. "Which only leaves us with the rest of the town."

They exited the highway and coasted down the hill when Emily saw a black BMW with tinted windows parked at the end of the lane that led up to their house.

"Jesse, stop right here," said Emily. "I think someone's here."

"While we're not?" said Jesse. "How convenient."

Jesse pulled the truck into a nearby copse and cut the engine. They crossed the lawn and approached the house, scanning it for any signs of the most recent invaders. Emily tugged on the sleeve of Jesse's suit jacket and pointed.

The front window was opening from the inside.

*J*esse tugged Emily behind the forsythia bush in the front yard and they crouched down, watching as the window slid open and revealed a set of dangling legs, clad in pressed gray trousers: Roger Oglethorpe. The legs were followed by the rest of Oglethorpe's body as he dropped to the porch, then reached back for the person inside. Darla Chinn appeared only slightly more gracefully, straddling the windowsill in her charcoal skirt while Roger offered her his hand.

"Aw," said Jesse sarcastically from the bush. "He's being chivalrous."

Emily pulled out her phone and filmed the pair as they exited the house. She didn't think having evidence of this would do much good where the sheriff was concerned, but at least it was proof that the property managers were up to no good.

Darla held his hand and dropped neatly to the porch below in a highly practiced fashion, as if it wasn't the first time the two had executed this particular maneuver. She dusted off her skirt, and they scurried down the front steps past the bush and down the lane to their car.

Jesse's fists were balled and his shoulders were tense as he and Emily exited the bush and stared after the retreating figures of the Three Star Properties team.

"I want to chase them, but I don't even know what I would do when I caught up with them," he said through clenched teeth. "Punch them? So they could get me thrown in jail and then kidnap you and get their greedy little mitts on the house?"

"I've confronted Darla before," said Emily with a sigh. "Somehow she made it seem like my fault. If we confront them now, they'll just come up with some excuse about how they were supposedly stopping by to chat about the house and thought they smelled smoke or something. Something obviously ridiculous and contrived that we'd still have no way of arguing with or proving otherwise."

"There has to be something we can do!" Jesse pounded his fist on the porch railing as they walked to the front door. "They just can't break in like this and get away with it!"

"I'd suggest we take this video to the police, but I have a feeling it wouldn't do much good," said Emily.

Jesse reached for the door and Emily rested her hand over his, stopping him.

"Jesse, wait," she said. "What if they left something for us?"

"Like what?" he asked. "Do you think there's a bomb?"

"Widget!" said Emily. She ran inside.

The little dog scampered across the wooden floor, paws sliding, and leapt into Emily's arms. She was so relieved to find Widget unharmed that she didn't realize anything was wrong until she looked up to see Jesse staring at the wall in shock.

Spray painted over the couch in enormous letters were the words:

LAST CHANCE
GET OUT NOW

JESSE SIGHED. "I just painted in here," he said.

RICHARD SCRATCHED his head over a steaming cup of tea. "Never known them to outright vandalize property, but it doesn't surprise me," he said darkly, shaking his head as he stared at the writing on the wall. "They're devils. Always after Matilda to sell to them. She made it abundantly clear it was never going to happen. Maybe they think if they lean on you enough, you'll cave."

"Richard, you mentioned when we moved in that you thought that Three Star might have something to do with the disappearance of Matilda and the kids," said Emily. "And Cynthia, of course. Do you think they were behind it?"

"Yes, I most certainly do," said Richard. "With that Roger being brother to the sheriff, they can get away with whatever they want to, can't they?"

"So, you think they're capable of violence?" Jesse clarified.

"I think they'll resort to anything if it means more money for them," said Richard. "Money makes people do terrible, crazy things. Money, and also love. You look at most murders you see on TV or read about, it's hardly ever just strangers fighting at random. It's always about something. Something people want but can't have."

"Well," said Jesse glumly, "I guess I'll get to repainting in here."

"I'll help you," said Richard. "Got a nice shade of off-white in the back of my truck."

"Thank you, Richard," said Emily gratefully.

Emily took Richard's mug and went to the kitchen. The

refrigerator was woefully empty. Their recent hijinks hadn't left much time to go to the store.

Emily grabbed a canvas bag from the pantry, clipped Widget's leash to her collar, and went out the back door.

IN SPITE OF THE COLD, Emily felt the awe she always did when she left the house and saw the mountains right across the street. In spite of their troubles, it was truly beautiful here. Emily could only imagine what their lives would be like if they hadn't had to deal with the drama that came with inheriting Matilda's house.

Emily walked into town. It was the day of the farmers' market, and she thought it might be nice to buy something she could cook. They'd been eating an ill-advised amount of take-out, and Emily thought that a home-cooked meal could contribute some sense of normalcy to their currently upside-down lives.

The park was crowded with weekend shoppers. She browsed the various tents, studying their offerings. She walked by a tent near the teahouse and stopped. It was filled with art, not food, but something about the art looked familiar.

Emily walked back to the tent and stared at the paintings for sale: a ship on a storm-tossed sea, a dead ringer for the ones in J.R. Watkins' office. A family portrait: one of a family Emily had never seen, but something about the style it was painted in reminded her very much of the painting hanging over the fireplace in the living room.

"Can I help you?" A short bald man with a pleasant voice and a pointed goatee approached Emily in the tent. His eyes were shielded from the winter sun with steam-punk goggles.

"Oh, hello," she said. "Can you tell me who painted these paintings?"

"I did," he said, looking pleased. "Nolan Sawyer's the name. Do you like them?"

"Oh, yes, they're lovely," she said. "I've been seeing them all over town. My lawyer has a few in his office."

"Watkins!" He fairly lit up at the name. "Great guy. I do work for him all the time. That assistant of his comes to pick up my work, always with a look on his face like he smelled something bad. He doesn't seem to like it too much, but who cares about him, right?" He laughed. "Where else have you seen my work?"

Emily hesitated. She had grown so tired of fielding the reaction to Matilda around town. After the Ray Harkness episode, she didn't know if she could handle another outburst. But maybe he knew something.

"Well, there's a painting in my aunt's house that I think you might have done," she began cautiously. "Matilda Meade, and the children she took care of."

"Oh, yes, Matilda," he said solemnly. He didn't react the way Emily feared he would: with shock, horror, disgust, or wild accusations. He spoke in the hushed, near reverential tone of those who don't wish to speak ill of the dead. "I remember her well. Nice lady. Well, seemed like it, anyway. Who knows what to believe? She had a very lovely picture she commissioned me to paint for her home, so I did."

Emily thought of the picture hanging above the telephone table behind the old gramophone in the parlor. "That picture...there was another person in it, wasn't there? A woman?"

"Indeed there was. I remember every picture I'm given to paint, because I stare at them for so long, you know? There was another woman in the photo, about your age, I'd say, but your aunt asked me not to include her in the final portrait."

"Did she say why?" asked Emily.

Nolan shrugged. "Nothing specific. She just said the

woman wouldn't be working for her for much longer, so there was no sense including her in the painting."

A sea of questions flooded Emily's mind: was Cynthia planning to leave? Had she given Matilda her notice? Was Matilda planning on firing her? Or maybe even...something worse? Against her will, Emily remembered the words of Ray Harkness: *I think she sold those kids and got rid of Cynthia to keep her quiet about it.*

"Actually," he said, holding up a finger as if just remembering something. "I have something for you."

Emily felt bewildered. What could he possibly have for her? She'd only just met him.

"Your aunt commissioned another piece from me," he said, rummaging through a nearby box under one of the folding tables in his tent. "About a month before she disappeared. She was very proud of the house. You could almost say she was obsessed with it. She asked me to do this one of when the house was first built." He found what he was looking for and handed Emily a small square wrapped carefully in tissue paper. Emily unwrapped the paper and looked at the small painting inside.

It was a replica of the picture from the book in the library, the house as it had looked in 1927. *Meade House, 1927* was painted in miniscule letters in the corner of the painting.

"Oh, it's beautiful," said Emily.

"I never got a chance to give it to her," he said. "I finished it the night before she disappeared. It was very sad. I'd never had a patron go missing like that. I didn't know what to do with it, and I didn't feel right just throwing it away. I feel like it's only right that you have it."

"Thank you so much," said Emily. She reached into her canvas tote bag. "How much would you like for it?"

He shook his head. "You don't owe me anything. Matilda already paid for it. I think she'd want you to have it, don't you?"

Emily looked at the painting again before wrapping it carefully in the tissue paper and tucking it carefully into her bag. "Yes, I think she would like that."

She smiled at Nolan a little sadly and offered him her hand. He shook it.

"Thank you again," she said. "I appreciate it."

"Of course," he said. "You seem like a very nice person." Emily couldn't help but wonder if this indicated that he assumed Matilda hadn't been. She pushed aside this troubling thought as she waved good-bye to him and headed out of the park. Widget trotted along beside her, straining her leash in the direction of the occasional squirrel. She was so preoccupied by her thoughts, she was all the way back at the house before she realized she'd forgotten to buy anything for dinner.

She could hear Jesse and Richard in the living room, painting over the latest round of graffiti defiling their home. She went into the parlor and took the picture off the wall, studying it: Matilda, the kids, Cynthia. Matilda and the children looked happy enough, but Cynthia looked serious, as if concerned the camera might steal her soul. What had caused Cynthia's plan to leave? Was their parting amicable or was it, as Ray Harkness implied, the result of something more sinister?

Emily reached into the drawer of the telephone table where she'd placed Matilda's journal for safekeeping. Opening it to where she'd last left off—when Matilda hired Cynthia to work for her at the house—she began to read.

SEPTEMBER 28th

I MUST ADMIT, Richard was right: I badly needed help running the house and taking care of the children. My mother always said I was too stubborn for my own good and my father told me I didn't know when—or how—to ask for help, even if I needed it.

Cynthia has been a dream. She's a superb cook and can always calm the children down no matter what the situation. While she doesn't come off as affectionate or approachable at first, I think the children respect her sternness. Her habitually taciturn nature leaves them uncertain as to what her boundaries are, so they're hesitant to test her. To be perfectly honest, I feel the same way. I'm careful never to press her regarding her personal life or question her too intensely about anything. She doesn't seem to like it and I can't risk losing her. I'm beginning to think she should take over this place someday. I'm getting older and I have no children of my own to leave it to, so who better than Cynthia?

I brought up the idea the other day in passing, in a casual sort of way, to see what she thought of the suggestion. She was preparing supper, much to the children's relief (my menu consisted largely of chicken nuggets, Spaghetti-Os, grilled cheese, and tomato soup on rotation). Her back was to me, so I couldn't see her expression when I said how much she'd turned things around and that I hoped she wasn't planning on leaving anytime soon.

She gave a non-committal shrug and said, "Oh no, I'm planning to be here for a while." I think she may have smiled, but I couldn't tell. I hope so. I don't know what I would do without Cynthia.

 ctober 14*th*

IT'S GETTING WORSE. *I really thought I could keep this place afloat between the loan I took out from the bank and all my credit cards, but I've used all the money I borrowed and am getting dangerously close to going over the limit on all my credit lines, with no real way to pay my monthly balances. Even with the money from the state for the children, there's upkeep on the house to be done, and most of the money goes to feeding and clothing everyone, anyway. I sometimes worry that I'm in over my head. No, that's not true: I always worry that I'm in over my head, and not just worry, I'm certain of it. What will I do if I lose this place? Where will the children go? I can't imagine the guilt and shame I would feel. No one in my family will be surprised. And I can't imagine how disappointed Grandpa Hershel and Grandma Delphine would be if they were here to see that I lost the fruit of their life's labors: the most valuable prize they owned, which they entrusted to me.*

Worst of all, I can barely afford to pay Cynthia. Her check bounced again, and while she acted patient and forgiving, I could

tell she was both troubled and annoyed. Cynthia has enough prob-
lems of her own without being subject to mine.

I made another excuse, which she seemed to accept for the time
being, but how much longer can I conceal what's happening? And
what will happen if she finds out how deep in the hole I really am?
I can't afford to lose good help, but I can't afford to keep it.

EMILY SET THE JOURNAL DOWN, disturbed. It painted the portrait of an increasingly desperate person who might resort to things they wouldn't have ordinarily. Was Emily wrong? Was Matilda who the townspeople said she was? And if Matilda was the villain, what did her ghost want from Emily?

23

---

*E*mily was starting to doubt her conviction that Matilda was innocent. Her diary depicted her as a desperate woman surrounded by people who had grown to depend on her, all of whom would have nothing if she failed. That kind of pressure had to weigh heavily on a person. Most of the town thought she was guilty of something terrible. The sheriff, compromised though he undoubtedly was, refused to even acknowledge the possibility that it might have been someone outside the house and was adamantly convinced that Matilda was the one responsible.

Emily had moved across the country to a strange place where she had no friends or family besides Jesse and Widget. As Richard said, money made people desperate. How desperate had Matilda been? Especially with Cynthia leaving? Had Matilda done something to try and keep her there?

Emily reached into her bag and pulled out the portrait Nolan Sawyer gave her at the farmers' market. She carefully unwrapped the tissue paper and held the painting on her lap. This house had been a refuge for Matilda and the physical embodiment of her family history. Would she have gone to any means to keep it?

MEADE HOUSE, 1927. For some reason, Emily's eyes were continually drawn to the words in the corner of the picture. There was something familiar about it, something important. It had also been the caption under the photograph in the book she found in the library, the same photograph Matilda had used to commission this painting. But there was something else—

"The Ouija board!" exclaimed Emily.

During her séance with Jesse, the planchette spelled out a final cryptic message before Matilda had vanished when Sheriff Oglethorpe knocked on the door. Matilda spelled out DELPHINE 1927. Delphine was Emily's great-great-grandmother who had owned the house originally. Combined with the date the picture was taken, it would make the ideal password to Matilda's computer. Emily found the laptop the night of the blizzard but had yet to figure out Matilda's password. What if it was Delphine 1927?

Emily hurried into the library where she'd left Matilda's laptop. She hit the power button and waited, biting her lip. She had a feeling this was the combination of words that would grant her access to another source of evidence Matilda left behind, and now the momentary suspense created by Matilda's slow old laptop was agonizing. At last, the password screen came up and Emily quickly entered *delphine1927.* The password she entered was incorrect.

"No!" She'd been so sure. She tried again: DELPHINE1927. This, too, failed. Emily visualized the Ouija board. It contained letters, numbers, and a few words—hello, good-bye, yes, and no—but certainly not a full QWERTY keyboard and no special characters. Emily typed *Delphine_1927,* and Matilda's desktop promptly emerged.

"Yes!" Emily was starting to feel like she could have entertained a second career as a fledgling detective.

Most of Matilda's hard drive seemed to be taken up by pictures and videos of the children she'd taken care of over the years: not just Andrea, Tricia, and Bobby, but dozens of others. They all looked content, clean, happy, and safe. There were pictures of Richard in the garden with the children. There were pictures of Matilda with them on their birthdays and holidays. Emily felt guilty for doubting her. But what had happened to Cynthia?

Emily clicked on a folder marked PERSONAL_DOCS. In it was a document labeled LAST WILL AND TESTAMEN-T_OCTOBER 2017. This correlated with the most recent entry in Matilda's diary. Emily scanned the contents of the will: she was still named as the one to inherit the house, but only in the event that Cynthia Harkness was unable or unwilling to accept it.

Emily was shocked. She couldn't fully articulate why. Matilda mentioned leaving everything to Cynthia in the diary, so why did this come as a surprise? Emily guessed it was because if it made anybody a suspect, it was Emily herself. According to this version of the will, the only thing standing between the house and Emily was Cynthia. Of course, she and Jesse hadn't even known the house existed, who Cynthia was, and were barely aware of Matilda's existence, but anyone looking in from the outside wouldn't have known that. Emily was surprised Sheriff Oglethorpe had never questioned her about this. Unless he had never seen it.

Emily was beyond confused. Matilda had named Cynthia the beneficiary in her will and only weeks later had her taken out of a painting and told the artist Cynthia was leaving. Another few weeks later, everyone in the house vanished. What took place in the interval?

Emily took the diary from her pocket. She had only two entries left. There had to be something conclusive contained within those final pages.

November 21st

. . .

THE SITUATION HAS ESCALATED in only a few short weeks. I missed all of the credit card payments again last month. I was only able to make my payment on the bank loan by selling off several pieces of antique furniture. I hope no one notices they're gone. I unplugged the phone to keep the collection agents at bay during the day when Cynthia is here, so she won't become even more suspicious than she already is.

Worst of all, the Three Star rats, as if somehow sensing my distress, have taken to ambushing me in public spaces all over town. They keep bringing up how much the property is worth, talking about how I could retire to Miami and move somewhere warm. Why struggle? they ask me, and it seems like a fair question. But what would happen to the children?

And what will happen to the children if I can't take better care of them than their parents would have? Wasn't the whole point to give them a better chance than they would have had otherwise? What was the point if I can't even do that?

I know that this is the time I should consider swallowing my pride in order to ask for help, but who can I ask? I haven't spoken to my sister in years, and I barely know her daughter or anyone in my extended family. Who is there to ask for help? Richard is certainly hardly any better off than I am. I'm supposed to be the one paying him, not the other way around.

Maybe I should sell the house? I'd have to find a safe place for the children to go first, but maybe it's time to stop being so stubborn and put others ahead of myself for a change.

DECEMBER 1ST

CYNTHIA CONFRONTED me about my recent financial difficulties, just as I feared she would. We were in the parlor and I tried to hush her; sound always did carry so freely through the house. It was late evening and the children were in bed, but she was so angry, practically yelling, and I didn't want them to wake up and realize that something was wrong.

She wanted to know why her checks kept bouncing. I made up the usual excuse: banking errors, whatever I could think of. This time, she didn't accept my reasons so freely.

"No one makes that many mistakes, Matilda," she said. "I know there's something else going on. Why can't you just be honest about it? You know I have problems of my own. Can't you see that you're making it worse?"

I felt terrible. She was right, of course. I'd been lying to her for far too long. I broke down and told her the truth: I was broke, in debt, with no way of recouping my losses. I'd never learned to work and save or had a head for business. I'd gotten in over my head and hid it, and now the situation seemed irreversible.

"Why didn't you tell me?" she asked. "I'm extremely organized. I could have helped you untangle this mess you've gotten us in. I still can, if you'll let me."

Now I felt especially bad, because at this point, I'd already resigned myself to having to let Cynthia go after we found homes for the children so I could begin the long, terrible, and shameful process of dealing with Three Star. A property this large, in this location? They'd surely divide it into as many units as they could and then charge students some astronomical sum to live in them. They'll pay me a fraction of what they'd make, but what other choice did I have?

Cynthia was furious. How could I sell out this way? I'd done nothing but badmouth these people the entire time she worked for me, vowing I would never sell, and now, just like that, I was giving in? When was I planning to tell her? Was she just going to walk up to the house one day and see a FOR SALE sign on the lawn and then realize she was out of a job?

I realized at that point how selfish I had been and what a compromising position I'd put her in. On the surface, she seemed to accept my apology, stating that she knew that I was scared, but it was still not an excuse to lie to her and manipulate her all these months. She was right. She was short with me as she gathered her things and did not say good-bye when she left.

There's no point in leaving her my "empire" because there will be nothing left of it. I wonder now if it wouldn't be better for everyone involved if I wasn't here anymore, either. I could leave the house to family and ensure that the vultures never got their greedy mitts on it. The children would be in better hands with anyone other than me. Cynthia would find a better employer in someone else.

I just don't know what to do anymore.

IT WAS the last entry in Matilda's diary, and it was dated ten days before they disappeared. Matilda had clearly been filled with despair. She sounded like she was on the brink of doing something desperate. But while it seemed she might consider harming herself, there was nothing in the entry to indicate she would ever harm the children, or Cynthia. If anything, she seemed overwhelmed with remorse for the position she had put them in.

Emily heard Jesse talking to Richard in the kitchen, followed by the sound of the door closing. She went out to see Jesse, splattered with paint, brewing a fresh pot of coffee.

"Well, that was tedious," he said. "An afternoon of painting combined with Richard's stories about his childhood. Apparently, he caught a lot of frogs in his day."

Emily almost smiled in spite of the heavy thoughts now weighing on her. "I got into Matilda's computer, finally," she said, pouring a cup of coffee. "And I finished the diary. It turns out Matilda originally left the house to Cynthia, but they started arguing about money. Matilda was keeping a lot from her."

Jesse's jaw dropped. He ran a hand through his hair, accidentally leaving a bright streak of paint in it. "Wait, this place was originally supposed to go to her? And she, what, wrote her out of the will?"

"In her diary, she said there was no point in leaving her empire to Cynthia if there was no way to keep it going."

Jesse snorted. "Her empire, sure. It's clearly done us wonders. Do you think she knew? That Matilda wrote her out of the will?"

"I'm not sure she knew she was in it in the first place," said Emily. "Matilda hinted that she would leave it to her, but I don't think she ever told her anything definitive. It seems like Cynthia was even a little dismissive of the idea. Maybe because she already knew about the money problems, or at least suspected. It would have been like inheriting a sinking ship."

"Was that will that you found the most up-to-date copy?"

"I'm not sure. The lawyer promised me he'd send me one, but it hasn't arrived. He doesn't have the greatest help," she added, remembering his assistant Bryce's cold-blooded interrogation about what really happened at the house.

Jesse bit his lip. "We need to see that will," he said. "We should have demanded it and memorized it before we even came here. It's weird that he hasn't sent it to you. Do you think maybe he's in on it?"

Emily was startled. Watkins seemed like a pretty unassuming figure to her. Unless it was an act. "You think he's working with Oglethorpe and Three Star?"

"I always thought it was weird that Cynthia disappeared the same night as Matilda and the kids," he said. "Why bother with the assistant? Why not just get the old lady who won't cooperate with you out of the way and whoever else is in the house? Maybe they knew they'd have to get rid of Cynthia, too. But who would have told them something like that? Who would have had access to that information?"

"Only someone with access to the will," said Emily,

remembering the benevolent, paternal air Watkins adopted with her so shortly after snapping at Bryce. It seemed a little two-faced. "And they'd know they'd have to get rid of us as well."

"I don't want you going back to Watkins," said Jesse. "I think it would be safer if I went this time."

"What about Three Star?" said Emily. "We need to know if Matilda talked to them about selling the house before she disappeared. If she had, they would have had no reason to get rid of her, knowing they were about to get their hands on the house, anyway."

Jesse shook his head. "I don't know. I don't want you going near those people again until this is resolved."

"Jess, it's the middle of the day, broad daylight, during business hours. The office is packed with their little property minions. I feel like they'd be hard-pressed to do anything now. I'll just tell them I'm on my way to discuss selling the house. That way, it will be in their best interest to keep me alive as long as possible."

"Okay," he said grudgingly. "I'll go talk to the lawyer. But you have to text me every fifteen minutes until we meet back at the house so I know nothing's gone wrong."

Emily agreed and set the timer on her phone. They went out to the truck, and Jesse drove down the hill and into town. Three Star, quite naturally, was located in one of the biggest houses on the block. The business was on a quiet side street inside of what had once been a rambling old Victorian, freshly painted and restored to look modern.

"How much do you want to bet that used to be some-one's house?" asked Jesse, looking at it through the windshield.

"They're probably still chained up in the basement," said Emily as she opened the passenger side door.

"Be careful," Jesse cautioned her.

"You too," she said.

"I think I can handle one elderly lawyer," he said with a rakish grin.

Jesse pulled away from the curb and the truck rumbled up the street. Emily stood on the sidewalk, staring up at the bright blue house with no little trepidation. She went up the front steps of the porch and pushed open the bright red door.

"*E*mily! As I live and breathe! At long last, you're finally here." Darla Chinn swept over to Emily the moment she stepped over the threshold of the doorway. Emily expected an over-the-top reception, but this was slightly absurd even by Darla's standards.

Darla's long red coat whipped around her like a cape. Emily repressed her urge to turn around and run out the door the way she came.

"We're so glad you've finally come to see us," gushed Darla. "Instead of the other way around."

Emily flashed on the memory of them crawling out of the living room window, fresh graffiti in their wake, and forced down a surge of anger. Was she really going to be this blatant? Although for all Emily knew, maybe they thought their little break-in wasn't as obvious as it had been. She glanced around for Roger Oglethorpe.

"Roger's out showing a property," Darla said. Not for the first time, Emily wondered if Darla had the ability to read minds. "But I'd be happy to sit down with you and discuss your options. Right this way, please."

Emily followed Darla down a long hallway into a large

and opulently-decorated space that looked like it had once been a living room. A vast and imposing mahogany desk sat across from the doorway. In front of the massive desk was a tiny swivel chair. The set-up seemed designed to make the person meeting with Darla feel small.

"Can I sit behind the desk?" Emily asked Darla as she ushered Emily over to the swivel chair.

"Oh, Emily!" Darla laughed loudly. "That's what I love about you. Your sense of humor." She pulled the tiny chair out for Emily. The phone in Darla's coat pocket vibrated. She pulled it out and glanced at the screen.

"Excuse me, Emily. I just have something I need to attend to for just a moment, and then I'll be right back with you. Please feel free to help yourself to coffee or water and any of the snacks in that basket on the table. Be right back!" Darla swept out of the room, her long red coat streaming behind her.

Emily got up from her small swivel chair and went over to the coffeemaker. The room was freezing cold, and she wanted something hot to hold more than she wanted caffeine. She poured herself a cup of coffee and texted Jesse *all good*. He texted her back a thumbs up.

She went over to the window with her coffee and discovered the source of the frigid temperature. The window was open just enough to gradually let in the cold air from outside. This, Emily speculated, was another tactic of Darla's to make anyone she met with as uncomfortable as possible and therefore more likely to agree to whatever she wanted. Emily marveled at Darla's cunning. Had she worked as an interrogator prior to entering property management?

Emily was struggling to close the window when she heard voices. One of them was clearly Darla; the other, while muffled, sounded like Roger. Where were the voices coming from?

She stopped trying to close the window and instead

pushed it open farther. Their voices drifted out the open window from the room adjacent. Emily leaned out her window and strained to hear them, but could only catch about every other word. She pushed the window the rest of the way open and climbed out, carefully lowering herself to the ground. If they could climb in and out of her windows, she figured it was only fair that she climb out of theirs.

On the ground, she crouched down low and snuck beneath their open window.

"I told you it would work!" Roger's voice was triumphant. "Of course they don't want to deal with the situation. That crazy old bat left them a murder house in the middle of nowhere, and now they're getting threats on a weekly basis— I guarantee you they'll want to sell. They probably don't even care how much they get at this point."

"As I've told you repeatedly, I think they might be just a little bit shrewder than you give them credit for," said Darla. "If they were that hapless and stupid, they would have sold to us the first week they were here. I have a hard time believing that your little rock-through-the-window trick and some paint on the wall convinced them to give up that easily, let alone if they weren't even bothered by the prospect of living in that graveyard in the first place. I'm sure they're going to want to negotiate the price, not just throw it into our laps."

"So? Let them. Who cares if we spend a few extra thousand bucks on this one? It's not the house I'm after, it's the land."

Emily looked up, surprised. This was the first she'd heard about this.

"We can rent it out to that marijuana farmer for some exorbitant sum, funnel half the proceeds back into my brother's campaign to ensure he gets re-elected, and all these little vandalism complaints homeowners have been making will continue to get swept under the rug. Once we finish driving out these long-time hold-outs, we'll really start to see a profit."

"I don't think you should rent that house to anyone, Roger," said Darla. "If I told you once, I told you a thousand times. There's something wrong with that place. They've never found the bodies. They're probably hidden in the walls."

Emily thought of the secret passage in the house and felt an overwhelming wave of nausea at those words.

"They're not in the *walls*," said Roger, sounding exasperated. "They would have found them by now. There would have been a smell or something. They're probably not even there. I'm sure whoever murdered them did us the additional favor of carrying them off into the mountains and dumping them somewhere up there."

"Roger!" Darla sounded pained. "Please don't refer to those poor people getting murdered as 'doing us a favor.' I'm all for breaking a few eggs if it means making an omelet, but I would never condone purposely harming anyone."

"Well, neither would I, obviously. I'm just saying the fact that someone did has proved extremely convenient," said Roger.

"Convenient or not, we still have to deal with the current tenants," said Darla. "Can't your brother do something about them? Lock them up for unpaid parking tickets or whatever?"

"How big of a cut do you want him to get? Do you want to make it even bigger? He already downplayed what could have been a massive murder investigation into a Missing Persons case so we could rent out that sad pile of bricks once we get our hands on it. He went to a lot of trouble to prevent that from becoming a massive media circus. I'm not about to ask for another favor after that. Can't you do anything yourself?"

"Okay, okay! I was *joking*. I have one of them in my office.

Ideally by now, she's half frozen and ready to sell. Call me in five minutes and interrupt our meeting. The longer she shivers, the sooner she'll want this to be done."

Emily shook her head, marveling at Darla's audacity. How did she know Emily wouldn't just get up and leave? She'd obviously been successfully bullying people for a very long time.

Emily decided not to go back into Three Star. Let Darla try to figure out where she'd gone. She imagined the frustration on her face when she came flapping back into the room to find it empty.

Emily walked around the side of the building back out to the sidewalk, taking out her phone to call Jesse. If what she heard was true, they were behind the vandalism and the break-ins, but they'd had nothing to do with the murders. The only thing the sheriff was covering for were their attempts to intimidate homeowners by damaging their property.

In spite of what she'd heard, it seemed hard to believe that Three Star and the sheriff had nothing to do with Matilda, Cynthia, and the children's disappearance. They might have purposely tried to downplay it, framing Matilda and saying it was kidnapping so future renters and buyers wouldn't purposely steer clear of living in, as Roger put it, a murder house. But if what Roger and Darla said was true, they'd had nothing to do with the actual murders.

And if it wasn't Three Star and the sheriff, then who was it?

JESSE OPENED the door to J.R. Watkins's office. The rug was so thick it muffled the sound of his footsteps. There were a lot of ugly paintings of boats and a bunch of fake plants. His phone went off in his pocket and he checked it: Emily. *All good*, she texted him. He texted her back a thumbs up.

There was no one at the desk in the reception area, which made Jesse nervous. Was he the only other person in the building besides Watkins?

"Can I help you?"

Jesse jumped about ten feet in the air. He turned to see a tall, dapper, silver-haired man in a nicely pressed suit standing behind him at the door. The man held a brown paper bag that smelled like cheeseburgers. He regarded Jesse curiously.

"Oh—yeah—sorry—I mean, my name is Jesse, and my wife and I just inherited the old Meade place? The one at the top of the hill."

"Oh, Emily's husband." Watkins closed the front door behind him. "Come in, come in. I'm just eating lunch, but I have no appointments until two, if you'd like to sit down for a few minutes."

He was, as Emily described him, extremely accommodating. Maybe too accommodating. What if he had Jesse right where he wanted him and there was no way out? Jesse discreetly checked the office for a fire exit and saw none.

"What can I help you with?" Watkins surveyed Jesse from behind his desk. He sounded politely inquisitive.

"We still haven't received a copy of the will," said Jesse, figuring he might as well get straight to the point. He was pretty sure he could take Watkins in a fight, unless he had a gun, in which case Jesse was pretty sure he could fit through the window. "Frankly, I'm getting a little annoyed. I don't see what's so difficult about getting this document. Unless you have some reason for not giving it to us." He looked at Watkins, openly challenging him.

Watkins looked embarrassed.

"I am so sorry," he said, wiping his hands with a brown paper napkin. "It seems that Bryce hasn't been following up with my most recent requests. I'll get it for you now."

Jesse was surprised. Of all the reactions he'd prepared for, this wasn't one of them. Could it really be this easy? He craned his neck to make sure Watkins wasn't reaching for something other than files in the filing cabinet, like a pistol.

Watkins removed a thick folder and went to the copy machine on the far side of the room. "I really do apologize," he said over his shoulder. "It's so hard to find good help these days. I keep Bryce on because he does do his job, for the most part, and because the prospect of replacing him and having to interview another dozen people for the job is too ghastly to contemplate."

"No worries," said Jesse, feeling it was best to act amicably until Watkins gave him a good reason not to. "We just found something kind of strange the other day, and we wanted to follow up on it."

"Oh?" said Watkins, his face illuminated by the glow of the copier. "What did you find?"

"Emily found Matilda's old laptop with a version of the will naming Cynthia Harkness as the inheritor of the house," said Jesse, watching Watkins for a reaction.

"Oh yes," Watkins said regretfully without turning around. "That whole mess."

"What whole mess?" said Jesse.

Watkins turned and began neatly stacking the documents into a manila folder. "They were business partners, you see. And, if I'm not mistaken, friends. Matilda had always expressed a certain fondness for the girl. Wanted her to take over after she retired. But when her money problems got the better of her, she thought it was best if the house went to family. She knew there was no way to continue what she'd started."

"Did Cynthia know about this?" asked Jesse.

"As far as I know, she never told her," said Watkins. "Cynthia was always quite reserved. I don't think Matilda was even sure if she'd want the house, let alone the responsibility of carrying on the home in her absence. She told me Cynthia was planning to leave, and she wished to change the will so that your wife would inherit the house. To the best of my knowledge, their parting was amicable." He finished neatly stacking the papers in the folder and closed it. "Would you like me to place this in an envelope for you, so it doesn't get creased?" He smiled.

"No, it's all good, I'd like to look it over right away," said Jesse, distracted by his phone. Not by a text or a call, but the absence of either one. It had been over fifteen minutes since Emily's last text, and he was worried.

"Certainly," said Watkins. "Is there anything else I can do for you today?"

"Nope, I think we're good," said Jesse, taking the folder from Watkins. He got up and pulled out his phone, checking for a message from Emily. When he didn't see one, he scrolled through his recent calls and hit her number as he left the office.

Watkins waited until he heard the front door open and shut before he picked up the phone. He hit number one on his speed dial.

"It's me, Watkins," he said into the phone. "He's on the move. And he has the will."

25

$\mathcal{E}$mily's phone vibrated as she left the Three Star office. She reached for the phone, realizing she'd forgotten to text Jesse at the appointed time. He was probably worried sick.

"Are you okay?" was the first thing he said when she answered the phone.

"I'm okay, sorry I didn't text you," she said. "I got caught up eavesdropping on Roger and Darla."

"What did the dynamic duo have to say this time?"

"They didn't do it," said Emily. "They threw the rock through our window and painted the wall, but they didn't do anything to Matilda, Cynthia, or the kids. They didn't know I was listening, so they had no reason to lie."

"The lawyer finally gave me the will," said Jesse. "I have it with me now."

"What does it say?"

"Haven't looked yet. On my way back to the truck."

"Can you meet me at the coffee shop on the corner from where you dropped me off?" asked Emily. "I don't want to hang around Three Star. I snuck out the window."

"Way to go, Nancy Drew." Emily could hear the smile in Jesse's voice. "Yeah, I'll meet you there."

"Okay, see you soon."

"See you soon."

Emily turned the corner and went into the coffee shop, relieved by the immediate warmth. A fire crackled in a fireplace in the corner. An acoustic guitarist sat on a stool on a makeshift stage, strumming a folk song. Emily went to the counter and ordered a chai. She was studying the various pastries in the glass front case when someone behind her said her name. "Emily?"

Emily turned to see Theresa Plumber standing next to her in line. "Oh, Theresa. How are you?"

"I'm well, thank you," said Theresa. "You know, it was the oddest thing. When I left my place, I saw lights on in Cynthia's trailer. I thought of you, because you were asking about her. I knocked on the door and the light immediately went out. I thought maybe it was the squatters, but that place is locked up pretty tight and they don't have a key."

Emily's mind immediately went to Cynthia, possibly hiding in the trailer. "What time was this?" she asked Theresa.

"Right before I left to come here," said Theresa. "Couldn't have been more than twenty minutes ago."

Emily's mind cycled quickly through the various possibilities: call Jesse, who was on his way here, and go to Cynthia's. Wait for him to get here and possibly miss Cynthia. Leave immediately and meet him there. She knew he wouldn't like this, but he'd probably do the same thing in her position. She pulled out her phone and called him. No answer.

Emily looked at her phone, beyond frustrated. She had just talked to him! How had he gotten that far from his phone in the ten minutes since she spoke to him last? Should she wait for him? But what if she missed finding Cynthia? Jesse knew where she lived; he could meet Emily there. He wouldn't be happy about it, but better to ask forgiveness than permission.

"Theresa," she said, "would you be willing to take me to Cynthia's? I really think she might be there, hiding, and I want to help her."

"You really think it's her?" asked Theresa. "And we could be the ones to find her? Do you think there might be a reward?"

Emily thought this largely beside the point, but saw her opening and took it. "Oh, there's definitely a reward," she said. "I met Cynthia's ex-husband a few days ago in Thornton, and he mentioned he'd set aside money for anyone with any information leading to her whereabouts or the whereabouts of the person responsible for taking her." She was getting exceptionally good at lying, although she preferred to think of it as a gift for fiction.

"Well, let's get going then," said Theresa.

Emily asked for her chai to go as she tried calling Jesse one more time. No answer. Now Emily was getting worried. Where was he, and what was he doing that he wasn't picking up the phone?

Theresa's car was a forest green Subaru Outback, the unofficial car of half the state. Emily texted Jesse as she climbed into the passenger seat. *Going back to Cynthia's with Theresa, think she's definitely there, meet me at her place?? Call me when you get this.*

Theresa and Cynthia's neighborhood was only a short distance away, and Emily was relieved at how quickly they arrived in the heavily wooded dead-end street. Theresa parked in the front yard. Emily got out and approached Cynthia's darkened trailer. She knocked on the front door. No response.

"Cynthia?" she called. "Cynthia, if you're there and you can hear me, please open the door. I'm here to help. Cynthia?"

Theresa came up behind her as she pounded on the door. "You know, I think Cynthia might have hidden a spare out here somewhere," said Theresa. "She asked me to water her plants one time while she was away, and she left the spare under a little planter shaped like a turtle. Not sure if she kept it there all the time, or if it was just for me to use when she was out of town. Never thought to check for it after she disappeared."

Emily stepped back from the door and looked down at the dry, dead branches on the ground, seeing nothing. "What did you say it was under?"

"A turtle, a little ceramic turtle. With big eyes, like a cartoon."

Emily poked through the branches with a long stick, uncovering a muddy ceramic statue that looked like it might have once been a turtle. She turned it over with the stick, and there on the frostbitten ground was a dull metal key.

Emily grabbed the key from the ground and put it in the lock. She turned the key and pushed the door inward. The stale smell of must hit her in the face and she coughed.

"Is she in there?" asked Theresa from the front stoop.

"I'm not sure," said Emily. "I can't see anything."

The inside of the trailer was pitch black. Emily groped along the wall for a switch and found none. Fumbling in her pocket for her phone, she switched on the flashlight app and shined the bright light around the living room.

There was a sagging couch in the corner with a warped wooden table in front of it. On the table was a mug. Emily shined her light onto the dark liquid inside of it. It looked like tea. She reached her hand out and grasped the mug: still warm.

Emily immediately shined her light towards the narrow hallway. There was a narrow door set in one side and a closed door at the end. She knocked on the first door in the hallway, calling "Cynthia?" There was no response. Emily pushed open the door, revealing an empty bathroom.

She held the light higher and went down the hallway. Was Cynthia behind the second closed door? Or was it someone else?

"Theresa?" she called over her shoulder to reassure herself there was still someone else there.

"Just a minute," said Theresa. Emily heard the sound of someone fumbling through the dark. "I can't see anything out here."

Emily shined the light against the closed door and cautiously pushed it open. She shined her light in every corner: a simple twin bed, a nightstand, a lamp on the bedside table. There was no one in the room.

"She's not in here," she called to Theresa, turning back to the door. It was closed. Puzzled, Emily went over to the door and tugged. It was stuck.

"Theresa?" she called. "Theresa, are you out there? I can't get out."

Emily heard footsteps, followed by the sound of the front door opening then closing. In the darkness, in the small confined space, there was the definitive click of a front door lock. Emily had left the key in the door.

"Theresa? Theresa! Let me out!" Emily frantically yanked on the door. It felt like someone had tied the knob to something. Emily pulled violently on the flimsy wooden door, which opened just slightly enough to reveal a thin wedge of the hallway. She shined her phone's light in the crack and saw a length of rope tied to the handle of the bedroom, with the other end tied to the handle of the bathroom door.

"Damn it!" Emily kicked the door in frustration. Why would Theresa lock her in? She tried Jesse again. He still wasn't answering.

Emily shined her light on the wood-paneled walls of the trailer's bedroom. Above the bed was a narrow window.

Emily studied it, quickly calculating her odds of fitting through. She jumped on the bed and shoved it open, knocking the screen out with an impatient fist. She pulled herself through the window, grunting with the effort of squeezing herself through the narrow frame. For a precarious instant she hung, suspended several feet above the ground, before dropping into a narrow bank of dirty snow beneath the window's frame.

Emily struggled to her feet, brushing mud, snow, and leaves off herself. She ran around the side of the trailer to the front yard.

Theresa's car was gone.

Jesse walked back to the truck, parked in a narrow alley behind the law office. He carried the folder containing Matilda's will under one arm. The lawyer seemed polite enough, but something about him had given him the creeps. The sun slipped rapidly from view. The temperature dropped as darkness fell.

Jesse climbed into the truck and studied the folder: should he wait to meet Emily at the coffee shop, or scan the contents briefly now and look at it more in depth once he got there? Curiosity got the better of him, and he opened the folder and flipped through the pages.

It was the most recent draft of the will: the last one, Jesse assumed, before the night Matilda disappeared. There was no mention of Cynthia anywhere in its pages.

A black Town Car with dark tinted windows pulled into the narrow alley behind the law office. The car loomed large in the rearview mirror of Jesse's truck. Jesse, immersed in the will, took no notice of it.

Jesse found the page which dictated the house would be left to Emily. Beneath this was an additional line, and Jesse squinted as he read: *if, in the event, my closest living family does*

*not wish to claim the property or cannot be found, I hereby desig-
nate an alternate inheritor of the property.* Jesse flipped the page
and stared at it in shock.

The car pulled up behind Jesse's truck, boxing him in. The
driver got out, swinging a crowbar in one hand and pulling
on a thick black ski mask.

Jesse looked up with a frightened yell as the driver's side
door of the truck flew open. He barely had time to react as he
was yanked from the truck and thrown to the ground. He
threw his arms over his face as the crowbar whistled through
the air, striking his skull and knocking him out cold.

A second masked figure emerged from the car and helped
the first drag Jesse down the alley. They threw him into the
waiting back seat of the Town Car. One slammed the door
and got back into the car while the other climbed behind the
wheel of Jesse's truck.

They glided silently out of the alley, one after the other,
and disappeared up the street.

STRANDED in the middle of a dark neighborhood on a dead-
end road, Emily had never felt more helpless. She reached for
her phone to try calling Jesse again. Her pocket was empty.

"No!" Emily ran back around the trailer and peered at the
ground below the window. Either it had fallen outside while
she wiggled through the window, or it had fallen out in the
bedroom while she was still inside. Either way, it was dark
and getting darker, and nearly impossible to see. The
window was high enough above her head from the outside of
the trailer that getting back into it seemed like an impossi-
bility without a ladder, and Emily was sure Theresa took the
key to the front door with her. She ran to the front to check.
The key was gone.

Faced with the prospect of wasting endless minutes
searching for a phone she might never find, Emily remem-

bered how short of a drive it had been from the town to Cynthia's trailer. She ran up the narrow dirt street to where it intersected with the main road and headed down the hill towards the light of town. Had Jesse gotten her message? Was he on his way here? Or had his phone died? Was he in town looking for her, frantic? She kept going until she reached her destination.

Emily finally opened the door to the coffee shop, the bright light and warmth washing over her like a benediction. Her lungs burned from running even a short distance at this altitude. She huffed and puffed her way to the counter before slumping over it, barely able to get out words. The barista looked at her with alarm.

"Have you seen—a man—with a beard, and—he would have been wearing—a bright yellow shirt, and a— green jacket," Emily wheezed.

The barista filled a cup with water and set it on the counter in front of Emily. She quickly chugged the water.

"No, I haven't seen anyone who looks like that," said the barista. "Are you okay?"

Emily nodded and threw the cup in the trash. Jesse hadn't been here yet. He already had the will when he called, so he wasn't at Watkins's office. Had he gotten her message and gone straight to Cynthia's? What if Theresa or whoever locked her in Cynthia's trailer was there waiting for him? If he got there and she wasn't there, would he look for her at home?

Emily decided that her best bet, with no way of reaching Jesse or knowing where he was, would be to walk up the hill toward home. She could use the landline to try Jesse again until he answered. It was less than ideal, but she had no better solution. It was certainly preferable to returning to Cynthia's trailer and running into lunatic Theresa trying to lock her up again.

In her first stroke of luck all evening, a bus pulled up

outside just as she passed the stop. Emily fished two crumpled ones out of her coat pocket and boarded the bus. She was still dizzy from running to town, and the light on board felt too bright.

The bus let her off at the corner only a brief walk from the house. Emily was relieved to see lights on in the window and the truck parked out front. Jesse was home. His phone had died, probably as soon as he left the law office. Everything would be okay.

Emily opened the front door and leaned over as Widget ran up to her, wagging her little tail excitedly and barking. "Hey, girl, where's Jesse? Where's he at, huh?" Widget turned and dashed out of the room, still barking.

"Jesse?" she called. There was no answer.

Frowning, Emily went through the foyer and into the living room, where Widget incessantly barked. As Emily crossed the doorway, she looked up in horror at the words written on the wall.

Someone had taken a leaf out of Darla and Roger's book, and covered the living room wall in dripping, blood-red letters. Emily thought randomly of the hours Jesse spent repainting the wall, and the memory was like a knife to her heart.

GIVE UP THE HOUSE
OR YOU'LL NEVER SEE HIM AGAIN

26

*C*ynthia Harkness gazed out the window as the blizzard raged outside. It was perfect timing. She'd been waiting for this opportunity for months, and at last—it was here. She could finally put an end to this charade. She could finally cease pretending to be a wise and loving caregiver, happily employed by a philanthropic savior. Cynthia didn't see Matilda Meade as a savior any more than Cynthia viewed herself as an earnest caregiver. She considered Matilda an aging dunce, but a dunce very much in possession of the thing Cynthia wanted most in the world: this house.

Cynthia placed a sandwich on the table for the children to share. The youngest two were a brother and sister named Bobby and Tricia, and the oldest was a girl named Andrea. It was difficult to conceal her anticipation at never having to cook or clean for them again. It wasn't that they were particularly annoying or bratty; if anything, they reminded Cynthia of her own childhood—destitute and helpless. In a way, this was even worse than if she'd had to put up with terrible children. It also served to affirm her determination to carry out the plan. She'd never go back to that existence again.

The power went out. The kitchen was plummeted into darkness. Matilda uttered a startled "oh!" as the youngest children screamed. Andrea murmured words of comfort and consolation in an attempt to soothe them. In the darkness, Cynthia smiled.

It was time.

"There's nothing to worry about, it's just an outage," said Matilda reassuringly.

That's what you think, Cynthia thought with a private surge of glee.

The children, who struck Cynthia as high-strung on the best of occasions, were reacting poorly to the sudden absence of light. Tricia started crying. Cynthia thought of how relieved she'd be never to hear that sound again.

"Cynthia, take this flashlight," said Matilda.

Cynthia felt a surge of annoyance at the way the old woman bossed her around. It pained her to play the hunched servant, bending at Matilda's beck and call. She bore it by reminding herself she was only biding her time. Now she thought, *the time has come.*

"I'll go to the fuse box and see if I can get it back on or if it went out with the storm. If it's the storm, I'll have to get the backup generator. Take the children upstairs to the attic."

Take the children upstairs to the attic, Cynthia inwardly mocked Matilda's bossy, take-charge tone to herself. The only thing that woman was fit to run were her stockings. Aloud, she said only, "Come on, everyone. We'll just go upstairs and wait for the storm to pass. It will be over before you know it."

Cynthia turned the flashlight on. She took Bobby's hand and led him along, looking pointedly over her shoulder at Andrea. Andrea took Tricia's hand, mirroring Cynthia, and meekly followed as Cynthia went upstairs. Cynthia didn't have to say a word to control Andrea. It was as if she could sense Cynthia's will and immediately did her bidding, no

questions asked. Perhaps the girl sensed what the conse-
quences would be if she ever defied Cynthia.

As they marched upstairs in an orderly line, she almost
felt a little sorry for them. The words *sitting ducks* came to
mind.

Once they were upstairs, Cynthia firmly closed the attic
door. Andrea sat on the rug in the middle of the room.
Bobby and Tricia huddled together on the toy chest. Tricia
asked when the storm would be over.

"It's hard to say, dear," said Cynthia. "But it's almost
morning now, and when the sun comes up, the snow will
melt and the power will come back on. In the meantime,
we're all here together. Everything will be fine."

She told them it would be fine, but she didn't mean it. It
wouldn't be, of course. Things, in Cynthia's experience,
rarely ever were. She didn't see why their childhood should
be any different from hers.

No sooner had she uttered these false words than a
scream downstairs, followed by a crash, alerted Cynthia that
the plan was fully underway.

"What happened?" Bobby cried.

"I'm sure it's nothing," said Cynthia. "Maybe Matilda fell.
I'll go check on her."

She instructed Andrea to keep an eye on the younger
children. Cynthia found that one of the few things that made
her situation tolerable was passing her more strenuous
responsibilities to Andrea. The girl was ridiculously eager to
please and practically worshiped Cynthia. If she told Andrea
to jump out the window, she probably would have done it.
Cynthia considered this briefly before dismissing the notion.
Better that she wouldn't be the one to end up with blood on
her hands.

Cynthia locked the attic door behind her so they couldn't
escape. She stood on the landing of the attic stairs, looking
down into the darkness below. She could hear the faint

sounds of a scuffle coming from the first floor. She shined the flashlight on the stairs and headed for the kitchen.

The sight that met her eyes couldn't have pleased her more. Her sister, Theresa, stood over Matilda, who was tied up in a kitchen chair with a piece of duct tape over her mouth. Matilda's eyes widened when she saw Cynthia. She made a sound as if to warn her.

Cynthia glanced casually over at Theresa, then went to the sink and filled a glass of water from the tap. Matilda's expression shifted from fearful concern to confusion.

"I see you've met my sister," Cynthia said conversationally, as if the three of them were out to lunch. "Turns out, tonight *I* have someone to assist *me*. Isn't that wonderful?"

Matilda regarded her with horror. Cynthia let the flashlight play over her face, enjoying her expression of betrayal, shock, and terror. Cynthia had imagined this moment many times over the last few months: every time Matilda ordered her to do the dishes or the laundry or prepare the meals or asked her, "What are the children doing, Cynthia?" She thought about it while she bit back her acid replies—*I don't know, Matilda. Why don't you go check?*—and dutifully shuffled around, performing her tasks as ordered (or delegating them to Andrea). She'd been waiting a long time for this.

"I assume you've realized that we're not here tonight to make your life easier, as would normally be the case," said Cynthia. "I'm afraid we're here to make it much, much harder. But don't worry, the house will be well taken care of." She glanced up at the ceiling in the direction of the attic. "I can't say the same of its current occupants, but don't worry: you'll all be together."

Silent tears slipped down Matilda's cheeks, and Cynthia could practically read the older woman's mind: *how could I not have seen—but the children—what will she do?* She knew Matilda well at this point. Well enough to predict her every thought and move.

"Can we get this over with?" Theresa demanded. "I'm missing all my shows."

Matilda tried to yell but could only emit a series of muffled grunts. She tried to loosen her bindings, but Theresa had made them too tight. At least she was good for something.

Cynthia watched Matilda's struggle. A slow smile spread across her face.

"Don't worry, Matilda," she said. "I promise, this won't hurt a bit."

*E*mily stared at the writing on the wall with a mounting sense of horror. The words were painted with bright red dripping paint. It looked like blood on the wall.

GIVE UP THE HOUSE
OR YOU'LL NEVER SEE HIM AGAIN

JESSE WAS GONE. And unless Emily relinquished the house, she might never see him again. But how was she supposed to give an entire house away? And who was she supposed to give it to?

These were the thoughts swirling through Emily's brain when her phone rang. Across the screen was the name Jesse. Relief flooded her being and she answered the phone.

"Jess?" she said. "Are you okay?"

"I'm afraid Jesse can't come to the phone right now," said a cold female voice. "He's feeling a little...indisposed."

"Who is this?" Emily felt a chill wash over her that had nothing to do with the cold. The voice sounded like pure evil. Was it Theresa? Had she been the one to lock Emily in Cynthia's trailer, keeping her from meeting Jesse, so she could kidnap him? Even as she thought this, Emily had a deeper sense that she'd been terribly wrong about one important thing, and the truth was on the other end of the line.

"Oh, you don't know?" the voice asked mockingly. "You've been so eager to find me all this time, haven't you? I would think you'd have been expecting this call, Emily."

"Cynthia?" said Emily slowly. "Cynthia Harkness?"

"Who else?" Cynthia sounded exasperated. "You know, anybody else would have put this together ages ago, Emily. Four people dead in a house and only one gets out? The math would suggest the responsible party was the only one who got away."

"I thought you needed help," said Emily. Even as she said the words, she felt a rising shame at her own naïveté: how could she believe this woman had ever needed her help? She'd been playing her all along.

"Oh, but I do!" Cynthia sounded almost pleasant. "I need your help with one very major thing: I need that house of yours. I need you to sign over the deed, and then disappear." Cynthia paused. "Not literally, of course. If I were just going to kill you both, there'd be little incentive for you to do what I want. And if you don't do what I want, Jesse dies. If you do, I'll let the two of you go. How does that sound?"

"How do I know you won't just kill us as soon as I give you the deed?" asked Emily.

"That's an excellent question!" Cynthia sounded down-right jovial. Emily thought, *this person is completely insane.*

"I'm glad you're finally thinking logically," continued Cynthia. "How about this: You give me the deed, and I'll give you Jesse and a reasonable payoff to keep your mouths shut.

That way, you'll be accessories after the fact. And we all know what happens to accessories to a crime. So, if you get any funny ideas about going to the cops, you'll go to jail. And speaking of the cops," said Cynthia as her voice changed from borderline pleasant to downright menacing. "If you call them regarding anything I just said, you will never see Jesse again. Understood?"

"I understand," said Emily. What else could she say? "How am I supposed to get the deed and change it?"

"I suggest you pay a visit to our little friend J.R. Watkins," said Cynthia. "I think you'll find him surpris-ingly…cooperative." Cynthia laughed. It was an unpleasant sound, like the aural equivalent of milk gone sour. "Once you have—and believe me, I'll know when you have—I'll contact you with further instructions. Any other questions?"

"I want to talk to Jesse," said Emily. "I need to hear his voice. I need to know that he's okay."

"Jesse is currently unconscious and can't come to the phone," said Cynthia. "I'm afraid you'll just have to take my word for it." She disconnected the call.

Emily stared at her phone, paralyzed with speechless horror. How could she have been so wrong? How could she get Jesse back? What if it was already too late?

She immediately dialed Watkins's office.

"Watkins, Simms, and Taft," said the voice of J.R. Watkins's receptionist, Bryce Stevens. "How may I direct your call?"

Emily struggled to harness her emotions. She had to conceal the fact that anything was wrong. "Um, could I speak to Mr. Watkins, please?"

"Mr. Watkins is currently out of the office," said Bryce pleasantly. How could anyone sound normal when Jesse's life was at risk? Emily felt like the world was ending. "May I take a message?"

"No, no message, could you just tell me when he'll be back, please?"

"He's out to lunch," said Bryce. "He should be back in an hour."

"Thank you." Emily hung up the phone. She paced frantically through the first level of the house as she tried to organize her thoughts, which were in total disarray. She felt like a snow globe someone had shaken and thrown to the ground, smashing it to smithereens. An hour? What if Jesse didn't have an hour? What if he—

Emily came to an abrupt halt when she realized she was about to run smack into a closed door. The door was at the end of the first floor hallway, next to the library. It was one Emily never opened. She knew it had belonged to the youngest children, Tricia and Bobby, and the fact that they would never live in it again was too painful to contemplate. Their lives had been cut short before they even had a chance to live them.

Emily thought of Cynthia and her cold voice on the phone, laughing like it was all a joke. A surge of hatred flowed through her as she thought of all the lives Cynthia had destroyed. Not only had she cut off three futures, eliminating all the brightness and promise they could have brought to the world, but she ended the life of a woman who had wanted only to provide a future to countless other children. And for what? Money? Property? Emily had problems of her own and had struggled because of them, but she never would have considered hurting anyone a solution for them.

The door in front of Emily drifted open, as if pushed by an unseen pair of hands. Emily looked up, startled from her dark and upsetting thoughts. She hesitated at the threshold before crossing over.

"Hello?" she called to the empty room. "Is there anyone here?"

As if in response, the curtains fluttered and a breeze

drifted through the room. Emily glanced around the room and saw that both windows were firmly shut. She hesitantly entered the bedroom as if guided by unseen hands.

She gazed around the walls, painted bright blue. The curtains were brightly patterned: dinosaurs on one window, unicorns on the other. Two narrow twin beds were separated by an antique night table. The drawer of the table was ajar and rattled as the breeze picked up and then abruptly ceased.

Emily went to the drawer and pulled it the rest of the way open. It was stacked with childish drawings rendered in crayon. She pulled them out and flipped through them, one by one.

The first few pictures were of dinosaurs and butterflies like the ones on the curtains. Beneath these were pictures of ballerinas and fire trucks, followed by animals and birds. Towards the bottom of the stack, the pictures changed.

There was a smiling stick figure depicting an older woman in glasses, whom Emily assumed was Matilda. She was joined by a girl with long hair—maybe Andrea. They stood in front of a bright blue house under a smiling yellow sun and next to a giant daffodil bigger than both the woman and the girl. Emily smiled as her eyes roved over the page.

She stopped smiling when she saw the figure in the corner. Off to the side, unsmiling, was a taller woman whose only distinguishing characteristics were red eyes and dripping fangs. Apparently, the children hadn't thought too highly of Cynthia. What had they seen about her that Matilda hadn't?

There was a loud knock at the kitchen door. Emily screamed and dropped the drawings. Her nerves were shot. She jumped to her feet, but the door blew shut.

"Hey!" Emily went to the door and rattled the knob. It was stuck. "Let me out!" She could have sworn she heard whispering, though there was no one present. In the past,

Emily would have attributed it to a combination of stress and an overactive imagination, if she hadn't known better by now. "I have to get Jesse, open the—"

The door sprang open as if on Emily's command. Emily would have assumed the children had listened to her but Richard, the property's handyman, stood on the other side of the door. He stared at her in confusion. "Did you say you were stuck? The door wasn't locked. I just opened it. Your back door wasn't locked, either." His tone turned reproving. "You shouldn't be leaving any of your doors unlocked after everything that's happened."

Emily felt deeply conflicted at the sight of Richard. Cynthia said not to tell the police and most likely meant anyone else for that matter, but how could she possibly know if Emily said something to Richard? As far as Emily knew, he was the only person in town who'd known Cynthia before she disappeared. Maybe he would know where to look for her.

"Richard, I need to tell you something," said Emily. Would he believe her? "Cynthia Harkness is alive, and she has Jesse. She told me if I went to the cops, she would murder him. I have to transfer the deed to the house to Cynthia and bring it to her. Do you have any idea where she might be?"

Richard's expression was simultaneously shocked and appalled. "She's alive? How can that be? I thought she disappeared, too."

"I think she pretended to," said Emily bitterly, imagining it. "I think she killed Matilda and the kids and hid their bodies so she could fake her own death, too. All to get her hands on this house. What I still don't understand is why. But there's no time to answer that question. We have to get to Jesse before it's too late."

"Of course." Richard ran a hand over his face, looking overwhelmed. "There's nothing more important in the world than your family, even a house. Don't worry, we'll find him and get him back. I don't know where she could have him at, though. The only place I ever knew Cynthia to live was in that little trailer at the edge of town."

Emily shook her head as a wave of abject helplessness washed over her. "I was just there. Her neighbor locked me in, I think to keep me distracted until they could take Jesse."

"Son of a gun." Richard looked like he was thinking hard. "Well, what are you supposed to do once you transfer the deed? Is she just going to show up?"

"She said she'd call me with further instructions," said Emily. "I'm waiting for Matilda's lawyer to get back to his office now."

"I'll take you there," said Richard determinedly. "And then we'll find out what she wants and where she's at and we'll go get Jesse back, okay? You folks have been nothing but kind to me and if there's anything I can do to help you, I will."

"Thank you, Richard." Emily felt awash with a mingled combination of gratitude and shame at all the times she'd dismissed Richard as a nuisance. She hadn't realized how reassuring he could be until she had no one left to turn to.

As Richard drove into town towards the law offices of Watkins, Taft, and Simms, Emily tried to piece together where she had gone so terribly wrong. She originally assumed that the disappearance of Matilda, the children, and Cynthia had been the result of the scheming and conniving property management company who repeatedly visited Emily and Jesse, trying to convince them to sell the house. One of the managers, Roger Oglethorpe, was the sheriff's brother. It seemed like an obvious conclusion to draw: the two were operating in collusion to get rid of Matilda, cover it up, and convince Emily to sell the house for cheap. Roger had already indulged in vandalism and destruction of property, throwing rocks through the window with ominous and threatening messages, in order to try and intimidate Emily and Jesse into unloading the house for less than it was worth. Who knew what lengths they would go to?

Now Emily realized the enemy was already within the walls all along. It had been Cynthia who betrayed Matilda; Cynthia who would stop at nothing to get her hands on Matilda's house. How long had Cynthia schemed to get rid of Matilda and the children? What kind of person went to such lengths just to get their hands on a house that didn't belong to them?

"Did you ever notice anything strange about Cynthia?" Emily asked Richard. "Anything at all?"

"I noticed she seemed like kind of a loner," said Richard. "You know what I mean? Never wanted to be sociable or stay and chat. She just came in and did her job and that was it. Never even seemed to like the children all that much, though they seemed to respect her well enough. But I guess maybe they were just afraid, if she is what you say she is."

Emily wondered what Cynthia might have done to make the children afraid. She shuddered. "She never said anything to you? About Matilda, or the house?"

"Not a thing." Richard gazed through the windshield at the setting sun. "From what you've told me, it sounds like Cynthia Harkness was a snake in the grass. I never would have guessed she was anything but what she pretended to be."

A snake in the grass. It made a terrible kind of sense, Emily supposed. It would have accounted for why Matilda never realized there was anything wrong with Cynthia until it was too late. Even from beyond her presumed grave, Cynthia had managed to fool Emily—who'd never once met the woman— that she was a hapless victim of circumstances.

The truck pulled to a stop. Emily looked up to see the lawyer's office outside the passenger side window. She had been so lost in thought she hadn't even realized they'd arrived at their destination. Now, she felt a nameless dread at getting out and confronting a new person with only the narrow hope that it might result in getting Jesse back.

Richard, as if sensing her distress, looked over at her reassuringly. "I'll be right here, waiting for you in the parking lot. If you get scared, just call me." Richard patted the front pocket of his jacket, which Emily assumed contained his phone.

"Okay," said Emily in a small voice. She got out of the truck and closed the door behind her, then made the long walk up a sidewalk to the bright red door of J.R. Watkins's office.

Inside the office, the scene was nightmarishly familiar. Nothing had changed about the setting, from the navy carpeting to the sailboats. But now, instead of being here to get answers, Emily was here to save Jesse's life. Her heart pounded wildly in her ribcage. One wrong move could cost Emily everything she had.

"Hello," said Bryce Stevens, smiling up at her from behind his desk. Perfectly innocuously, Emily was sure, but she couldn't stop herself from interpreting his expression as a menacing smirk. "What can I do for you today?"

"I need to see Mr. Watkins, please," said Emily. She was barely able to speak above a whisper. Her knees shook and she felt like she might pass out at any moment.

"Of course," said Bryce, looking concerned. He picked up the phone. "Just have a seat. I'll get you a cup of water in just a moment. You look like you're about to fall over."

Emily sank into a seat in the waiting area as Bryce mumbled something into the phone. He hung up and jumped up. "He'll be right with you," said Bryce, rushing around the desk and over to the water cooler. "You just hold still while I get this for you."

Emily was slumped in the chair with her head in her

hands. She glanced up as a cup of water materialized in front of her face.

"Oh. Thank you," she said, accepting it. Even as she took the water, she stared at it: should she drink it? Was Watkins in on it? Was Bryce? Who could she trust?

"Of course," said Bryce, watching her expectantly. "This altitude can get the better of you even if you've lived here your whole life," he added confidentially. "I once passed out after having a glass of wine or two at a party. Can you imagine?"

Just then, the door to the inner sanctum of Watkins's office swung inward. Watkins appeared, imposing and paternal as always. His presence saved Emily the trouble of having to decide whether to drink the water, and she tossed its contents into a nearby plant as Bryce glanced up at Watkins.

"Hello, Emily," rumbled Watkins. "What can I do for you today?"

"I need to talk to you about my aunt's will," said Emily.

Bryce perked up visibly at the words. He was fascinated by the gory history of the house, and Emily was sure he would be more than intrigued to learn the reason behind Emily's visit today.

Watkins nodded, looking solemn. "I see. I don't have anything left on my plate today, so why don't you come on in?"

Emily went into Watkins's office, Bryce watching her curiously as she went. She sank into the large red leather wingback chair in front of his desk.

"What can I help you with?" Watkins watched her impassively from behind his desk. His face was impossible to read.

"I need to change the deed to the house," Emily said in a rush. How would she explain that she needed to change the deed to be in the name of a woman presumed dead? Cynthia had set her an impossible task.

Watkins chuckled. Emily stared at him. Of all the reactions she'd expected, this wasn't one of them.

"Getting to be a bit much for you, huh?" he said benevolently. "I understand. I wouldn't want to be saddled with that monstrosity, either. I think you're making a wise decision."

Why was he agreeing with her as if this was a reasonable thing? Emily thought of Jesse's words before he went to see the lawyer—the last place Emily knew him to be before he disappeared. *Do you think maybe he's in on it?* Jesse had asked. What if he was right?

Emily watched Watkins behind his desk. He seemed the picture of a stately and trustworthy attorney: his suit neatly pressed, his hair perfectly combed with not a strand out of place. But what kind of lawyer was so casual about changing the deed to a house? Unless he already knew why she was changing it and whose name she was putting it in.

Before she got here, Emily's greatest fear had been how he might react to what she was about to say and how she would explain without compromising the precarious nature of her position. Cynthia had already told her not to tell anyone or something bad would happen to Jesse, which Emily had already violated by enlisting Richard's help. How would she explain to Watkins that she wanted to change the deed by putting it in the name of a dead woman?

But now, sitting in front of Watkins, she realized there was an even darker possibility: that Watkins would have no reaction at all. If he acquiesced with little inquiry, Emily would know that he was in on it, too. She would be alone in a room with one of the people behind Jesse's disappearance.

Watkins was the very first person she'd ever spoken to in this town, over the phone when she and Jesse were still safely ensconced in their sunny apartment in Florida. Had he been manipulating her for a darker purpose than she could have ever imagined? Maybe it was Watkins who lured her out here in the first place when he called her about the will.

"I want to put the house in Cynthia Harkness's name," said Emily, almost defiantly. His reaction would tell her everything.

He acted as if she told him she was planning a stroll in the park after their meeting.

"Certainly," he said in the same pleasant tone Bryce had greeted her with in the office. Emily felt like she was going insane.

"Survivor's guilt can be a powerful thing," said Watkins ruminatively, opening and closing the drawers of his desk. Emily watched him, every muscle in her body tensed. He found what he was looking for and set it on his desk. It was nothing but a harmless-looking folder. He opened it and paged through the documents within.

"Of course, Miss Harkness hasn't been officially declared dead yet, though once she does, the house will most likely go to her next of kin," Watkins continued. "I can see that the rumors asserting Matilda's responsibility in the disappearance of Cynthia Harkness and the children have affected you strongly. I commend your decision to transfer the home to her as a sort of restitution and acknowledgment of what happened."

Watkins regarded her with approval as Emily stared at him in mingled shock and fear. Was he pretending that Matilda had killed Cynthia, when it was the other way around? And as such, she deserved the house as a final payment? Did he actually believe that? Emily had heard the term *gaslight* before, but she had never truly understood what it meant until this moment.

"I can see you're distraught," he said sympathetically. "Why don't I just go ahead and prepare the paperwork for you? I can have it ready for you by the morning."

"I need it done immediately," said Emily.

"If you're concerned about any interested parties," said

Watkins with a raise of an eyebrow, "I'd be happy to inform them on your behalf that the proceedings are under way."

Emily felt a mounting sense of horror as she looked at Watkins. From the surface, his assurances were wholly innocuous: he could mean he would get in contact with Cynthia's estranged husband, Ray Harkness. Or he could mean something much more obvious and sinister—that he would be the one to pass the information along to Cynthia that the ball was rolling.

"Okay," said Emily. "You do that."

"Oh, I will," said Watkins, smiling broadly. He stood and opened the door for her. J.R. Watkins was a perfect gentleman through and through. "You take care now, Emily. And be safe."

As frightened and terrorized as Emily felt, it took everything she had not to slap him on her way out.

"*D*id you get it?" asked Richard. "The deed?"

"He said he'd take care of it," said Emily dully. "He also said he'd inform 'any interested parties.'"

"What?" Richard stared at her, eyes agog. "Does that mean he's working with Cynthia?"

"I guess so," said Emily. "If he is, we'll know when she gets in touch with me. She told me that once I had the deed switched, she'd contact me with instructions of where to get Jesse."

Richard nodded. "Why don't I drop you off at the house until you hear back from her?" he said soothingly. "I'll swing by my place and get ready. As soon as she contacts you, you let me know and I'll be here in a flash. We'll go get Jesse back, mark my words. Don't you worry about that."

As reassured as Emily was by his words, she thought it might be due to the simple fact that she wanted so badly to believe him. He smiled kindly at her as he pulled up to the house and she got out of the truck.

"Call as soon as you hear," he said.

Emily nodded as she closed the door and watched as Richard drove off. She had never felt more alone in her life.

She let herself through the front door. The cold washed over her in waves. Her feelings of dread intensified upon confronting the empty house. What if she never saw Jesse again?

Well, not entirely empty. Widget ran into the living room as Emily entered. She leaned over and picked her up, burying her face into Widget's soft fur. Tears pricked Emily's eyes and spilled over as she remembered the first Christmas she ever spent with Jesse. It was when he gave her Widget.

Emily set Widget down gently and wrapped her sweater around her more tightly. The house was frigid, even colder than it was outside. Emily checked the thermostat, puzzled to see that it read seventy-five. It felt like it was twenty degrees in here.

Emily decided to build a fire while she waited for Cynthia's instructions. There was obviously something wrong with the heater and given the circumstances, she felt like it was beyond her to determine what was wrong with it, let alone fix it.

She went out the kitchen door and down the back steps to the wood pile under the stairs. Something was amiss. She glanced around, paranoid. The wood pile had shifted several feet to the left and lay in a jumble of logs when it was normally neatly stacked and organized. The door in the wall had drifted open, as if pushed by an unseen hand.

Emily stared at the door, paralyzed with fear. Had Cynthia returned for her? Was she waiting in the walls of the house?

As Emily gazed into the darkness of the tunnel just beyond the door, a pinprick of light flared in the abyss and hovered there like a lightning bug. The small gold light hung suspended in the doorway and Emily, as if drawn along an invisible string, drifted closer. The feeling she got from the appearance of the light was not one of worry or fear, but a benevolent sense of reassurance and comfort.

"Hello?" She pushed the door open wider. The light drifted along the passage ahead of her. Emily followed it. "Where are we going?" she asked.

It wasn't that she expected a response, exactly; the ghosts had never verbally communicated with her and she didn't expect them to start now. For some reason, Emily didn't think they could. Something about the boundaries of space and time and death seemed to stand between them and the living in a way that precluded casual conversation.

Emily was surprised when the light paused and flashed three times. She looked over and saw that they were in front of the door that led to the basement.

Emily pushed the door inward, hesitating at the threshold. Thoughts of Cynthia lurking in a corner weighed heavily on her mind. The light glided ahead of her into the basement, as if reassuring her there was nothing to be afraid of. It paused in the corner and grew brighter, until the space beneath it was illuminated. Emily saw a cardboard box on the floor, its flaps neatly folded under one another. She reached up and pulled the chain above her head, flooding the basement with harsh white light. The small gold light remained until Emily opened the box. Then it faded from view.

There was a pile of carefully stacked books in the box that Emily quickly realized were photo albums. She lifted the one on top. As she carefully turned the laminated pages, she saw picture after picture of Matilda and the kids, but more often than not, just the kids. And not only Andrea, Tricia, and Bobby: these photographs spanned many years. The earliest ones at the beginning of the album were taken on film and had the quality of old postcards. Some were Polaroids. The newer ones had been taken digitally and were printed on shiny white photographic paper.

In all of them, the children portrayed were smiling and happy. Some were playing outside—tag, hopscotch, baseball, soccer. They were blowing bubbles and proudly holding up drawings or cookies they baked. On the last page of the album was an envelope beginning to yellow at the edges. Emily carefully pulled it from the album, careful not to tear the delicate paper.

She opened the envelope. Inside was a handwritten note and two photographs. The first was of an older man, holding two small children. The second was a school picture of a young boy with a brown bowl cut. She unfolded the note and read the carefully-printed block letters.

DEAR MATILDA,

I just want to thank you, as I do every birthday and always will, for what you have given me. You gave me the opportunity for a good life by providing me with shelter and safety when I otherwise would have had none. I had no home and no family when I came to live with you. I remember how afraid I was. After a while, it was as if I had always lived there. It came to feel like home. The bad memories faded. I got to play like other kids and go to school. I thought about what I would be when I grew up, instead of whether or not I would eat that day.

This is the first picture I ever had of myself, taken when I came to live with you. The other photograph is of my sons.

I now have two children and a family of my own. I trace the beginnings of this happiness back to the time I spent with you and the sanctuary you provided. I am sure that without it, none of these things would be possible. With it, all things are possible.

WITH LOVE AND GRATITUDE ALWAYS,
   Timothy McFadden

TEARS WELLED up in Emily's eyes and threatened to spill over onto her cheeks as she read the letter. She thought of how many lives Matilda had changed. She realized in that moment how much this house meant to Matilda and how important it had been to her to help the kids who lived in it. It made what Cynthia had done seem a thousand times more heinous than it already did.

As Emily folded the letter up and returned it to its envelope, a new and powerful resolve rose up in her: not only would she get Jesse back, but she would make sure that Cynthia Harkness never hurt anyone again.

As if Cynthia could hear her from whatever dark and evil lair she inhabited, Emily's phone chimed. The text said it was from Jesse. Emily opened it grimly.

COME TO THIS ADDRESS TO COLLECT YOUR REWARD, the message said. There was a shared location beneath the text. Underneath this was a photo of Jesse. He was tied up, gagged, and blindfolded. Emily gave a strangled cry. Her hands shook as she called Richard. "She gave me the address." Emily could barely get the words out. "And she sent me pictures of Jesse. He's tied up and gagged someplace. I'm afraid they hurt him, or worse." She couldn't bring herself to vocalize her greatest fear.

"How does she know we won't take the pictures to the police? It's evidence!"

"Richard, we *can't!* If we go to the police, she'll kill Jesse. We have to do this ourselves." Emily took a deep breath. "Do you own a gun?" she asked.

"As a matter of fact," he said slowly, "I own several. What did you have in mind?"

"I think we need to protect ourselves," said Emily. "I don't believe that anyone capable of what Cynthia Harkness has done plans to keep her word. And I have no intention of going in there without a few tricks up my sleeve."

Cynthia adjusted her oversized black sunglasses and pulled the brim of her straw hat low over her eyes. After the massive blizzard she'd left behind, life in the Caymans was truly a beach. Ray had been thrilled when she finally appealed to him for help: he'd been pushing money on her for months, likely out of the hope that if she accepted his aid, it would lead to their reconciliation, and she'd finally accepted. She made several vague and unspecified references to terrible hardship imposed on her by Matilda, which would ideally serve to cast further doubt on the woman's character after Cynthia disappeared—at least, as far as Ray Harkness was concerned.

Cynthia took a sip of her Mai Tai as she contemplated these past few months. Matilda Meade had been easy to impress. During her brief interview, Cynthia had to do little more than tell the woman about her experience as a nanny in New York, which Cynthia could tell impressed Matilda. As if there was something more glamorous about cleaning up after rich New York brats than cleaning up after poor brats locally. Cynthia claimed her husband left her, when it was quite the other way around, which she figured would earn sympathy points with lonely old spinster Matilda.

Once she had the job, it was only a matter of time and working out the details. Cynthia figured that if she got herself into Matilda's good graces and stayed there for long enough, the older woman—who seemed to have no family to speak of, at least not one that she ever talked about—was bound to consider Cynthia the closest person to her. Matilda frequently confided in Cynthia how worried she was about what would happen to the children if anything happened to her. Cynthia knew that Matilda would want someone to keep things going in her absence.

Having to play the thoughtful caregiver had been quite the arduous task. Cynthia disliked children and always had. The nannying job in New York had been the most well-paying gig she could find as an inexperienced undergrad, and the kids were so zonked out on psych meds she barely had to do anything, anyway.

The kids Matilda cared for were different: needy and insistent. She couldn't turn around without one of the younger kids wanting to color with her or have a book read to them or sing songs. Cynthia dutifully complied so as not to blow her cover, but she sometimes felt that while Matilda seemed blind to Cynthia's true nature, the children saw through it. They never really fully seemed to trust her. Although that certainly hadn't stopped them from asking her for things.

Then there was the older one, Andrea. Andrea was different. She never seemed to ask for anything at all. Watchful and silent, she seemed to appear out of nowhere and followed Cynthia like a shadow, which drove her insane. The girl was curious and naturally inquisitive, which was massively inconvenient for Cynthia's purposes. She was always poking her little nose where it didn't belong.

Cynthia caught her rummaging through a hallway closet

on the first floor one morning and immediately yelled at her to get away. The girl looked mortified and ran off to her room, where she hid for the rest of the day. Unbeknownst to her, Andrea had been troublingly close to discovering what Cynthia had long ago realized was the most important and useful secret of the house: the hidden network of passages that ran through the walls with concealed entrances in numerous rooms throughout the house.

She also suspected the girl was prone to eavesdropping on her infrequent though heated exchanges with Matilda over money. Cynthia tried her best to keep her temper in check; she was, after all, predicating her plan on Matilda's sense of loyalty and love, but Cynthia still had to eat, didn't she? Matilda was terrible at math, awful at keeping track of anything more complex than checking the mail, and seemed bereft of any organizational skills whatsoever. Half the time she seemed little aware of what month it was, let alone what day. One day in particular, Cynthia had been unable to bite her tongue. Short of going to Ray and begging for scraps, which she had no intention of doing, Matilda was Cynthia's sole source of income. And half the time, Matilda either forgot to pay her or seemed irrationally convinced she already had. On the rare occasions she did remember to pay Cynthia, the checks bounced. This was both humiliating and inconvenient.

Matilda always made up some excuse as to why: they'd over-drafted her account taking out too much for the elec-tric, someone must have added an extra zero by mistake, can you imagine? Cynthia could not. After three straight days of polite inquiries and subtle reminders, Cynthia finally had to resort to flat-out refusing to work if Matilda didn't explain why her checks kept bouncing.

"Didn't I just pay you?" said Matilda, sounding annoyed. Not even absent-minded and confused, but actually irritable about it!

Cynthia lost her temper. Not *really*, of course; if she'd lost her actual temper she would have had a body to dispose of much sooner than she'd originally planned. But she did lose her temper more openly than the sweet persona she'd cultivated these long months ever would have.

"No one makes that many mistakes over so many months, Matilda," she said. "I know there's something else going on. Why can't you just be honest about it? You know I have problems of my own. Can't you see that you're making it worse?"

Matilda flushed. She looked horribly embarrassed, which gratified Cynthia. Good. Let Miss Martyr display a rare moment of humility for once. Matilda confessed the obvious: she'd concocted this orphanage fantasy with no realistic plan or awareness of how much it would actually cost, and now she was in over her head and saddled with debt.

Cynthia was exasperated. Who conjured up a pipe dream of running a home for wayward kids without bothering to find out the bottom line? Matilda might have inherited a property worth a great deal of money, but Matilda herself was worth little to nothing. Cynthia estimated her net worth to be somewhere in the neighborhood of twenty-five dollars and some change. She had no savings, no IRA, no CDs, and her sole assets seemed to consist of the house and a broken-down Dodge Dart out back by the shed.

Cynthia, who was often left unattended in the house when the brats were down for their nap and Andrea was off staring into space or whatever it was that girl did all day, had done her homework. She'd searched every drawer and filing cabinet, every nook and cranny. Matilda was not one for either locks or security. Anyone could have robbed her blind at any given moment, and she probably wouldn't have noticed. Not for several days, at least.

"Why didn't you tell me?" Cynthia asked her. "I'm an extremely organized person, Matilda. I could have helped you untangle this mess you've gotten us in. I still can, if you'll let me."

Matilda sighed. "It's too late," she said, and a chill of horror skated up Cynthia's spine. What did she mean, too late? What had the old bat gone and done now? Were her months of research and hard work about to go swirling down the tubes because Matilda had catapulted herself into debt and tried to hide it (badly)?

As it turned out, this was exactly the case. Matilda confessed she was planning to finally cave and sell out to those pushy property managers, Darla and Roger. Cynthia had closed the door in their faces on more than one occasion. They were almost as determined as Cynthia was to get their mitts on the house, although certainly not willing to go to the same lengths, Cynthia felt sure. Of course, Matilda had buckled and caved to the first people to push her into doing so. How unsurprising.

At this point, Cynthia had scarcely been able to contain herself. All the patient planning, all the meticulous care, all this time spent coloring and holding inane conversations about unicorns and dragons—all for nothing. She'd be back to square one. Probably even worse, considering Matilda seemed unable to pay her at all at this point.

"How can you sell out like this?" Cynthia had demanded. Perhaps she could appeal to the woman's earlier righteous indignation she'd always exhibited at the prospect of selling to the property managers. "You've done nothing but bad mouth them the entire time I've worked for you, saying how you'd never sell, and now you're just giving in, just like that? When were you planning to tell me? Was I just going to walk up to the house one day and see the For Sale sign on the lawn? Was that how I was going to find out I was out of a job?"

Matilda stuttered some incoherent apology about how selfish she'd been and the terrible position she'd put Cynthia in. Cynthia had long noted Matilda's remarkable gift for stating the obvious. She was livid that Matilda had shown no sign of relenting, and multiple alarm bells were going off in her head. She'd have to act quickly, before it was too late.

Cynthia mumbled something meant to be somewhat reassuring but probably wasn't, as Matilda remained thoroughly distraught. Cynthia said something about how she understood her fear, but it hadn't entitled her to be dishonest and manipulative. She might as well have been talking about herself, and the irony didn't escape her. Typically, she tried to hold up a mirror for Matilda to see the self-sacrificing martyr she was obviously trying so desperately to be, but things were rapidly spiraling out of control and Cynthia's mask was starting to slip.

Cynthia left the house immediately. She grabbed her purse and didn't bother saying good-bye to Matilda when she left. No sense in maintaining any pretense now. If things had spun as wildly out of control as Matilda claimed, the plan would have to be stepped up immediately. With any luck, Matilda would be out of the picture in a matter of days.

As soon as she left, she called Watkins to make sure she was still the beneficiary named in the will. Who knew how long that would last? If Matilda was thinking of selling out to the property managers, it would only be a matter of time before she paid a visit to Watkins to change their arrangement. The plan would have to be implemented immediately.

It was now or never.

ONCE CYNTHIA GOT RID of them all, it was like a tremendous weight off her shoulders. No more having to act the martyr: Cynthia, the eternal caregiver. Cynthia, the Mary Poppins of Matilda's Home for Wayward Children. Pretending to be like Matilda in order to gain her favor had been exhausting, but now it was over. She'd never have to deal with any of it again.

Cynthia polished off her Mai Tai and sighed with bliss. Watkins had taken care of everything. All she had to do was wait.

And what a place to wait this was. Cynthia was surrounded by surf, sand, and the sound of children's voices would soon become a distant memory.

Her phone rang. Cynthia squinted lazily at the screen. What now?

"Hello?" she said, glancing up as the poolside server returned. "Yes, I'll have another, please. What? *What?* No, not you—I said, I'll take another. No, not *you*! I'm talking to the server. Yes, thank you. And you—what did you just say to me?"

Cynthia sat up in her deck chair, feeling as though someone had just thrown a bucket of cold ice water on her hot skin. "What do you mean, she has a *great niece*? What *is* that, even? Who leaves their only asset to their great niece? Does every person in this woman's family hate her that much? I thought she didn't have family! That was the entire *point!*"

Cynthia listened for a few minutes while she tried to keep her previous Mai Tais down. Her gut was suddenly churning horribly. She thought everything was taken care of, and now it seemed that everything was going to slip through her fingers, yet again. Why did this keep happening? Would nothing go her way?

"Yes, I'll be there as soon as I can get there. What? I don't know! The first flight I can get, obviously. How did this happen? Why didn't Watkins catch this? That idiot. What do you mean, she did it the day before? Why didn't he call us immediately? That's the dumbest excuse I've ever heard! Who cares if his in-laws showed up unannounced? Do you know how many *surprise visits* Ray's mother made? That's no reason to forget there are millions of dollars on the line! Listen, I have to go. I'll call you when I get to the airport."

Cynthia disconnected the call, and it took everything she had not to hurl her phone into the pool. A niece. Matilda had a niece. *She left the house to her niece.*

Cynthia swung her legs over the side of the deck chair and lurched unsteadily to her feet. She practically ran across the hot cement, nearly colliding with the server, who was returning with her drink.

"Give me that. Charge it to the room. Thanks."

Cynthia tossed the drink back in a few gulps, which was probably unadvisable under the circumstances, but who knew how long it would be until she'd get another Mai Tai? She took one last wistful look around the gorgeous pool deck and the infinity pool that seemed to disappear right into the endlessly blue ocean. Then she retreated into the dark air-conditioned catacomb of her room.

She'd just have to book a flight immediately, that was all. And when she got back, she'd deal with this little hiccup, the same way she dealt with Matilda.

She'd already gotten rid of four people, what was one more?

Cynthia regarded her old trailer with dismayed revulsion. She thought she'd never be back here again. After the Caymans, this seemed like a long way to fall.

She dumped her bag inside and opened the window in the back bedroom to air the place out. She couldn't stay here, of course; she was supposed to be dead, after all. She'd have to go to Theresa's: the only thing worse than this. Cynthia sighed with despair.

How many more people would get in her way? Would this be it, or would more of Matilda's relatives appear out of the woodwork when she got rid of this one? What if they were like the brooms in *Fantasia*, and just kept multiplying the harder she tried to get rid of them?

Cynthia told herself firmly not to think that way. She couldn't afford to, this late in the game. She would just have to see it through: eliminate the latest opposition, and the rest would fall into place.

She took one last look of revulsion around the tiny prison she once thought she'd never again call home before she turned the light out and pulled the door shut firmly behind her.

CYNTHIA STOOD in the dark yard outside of the house. She'd parked the next block over and snuck onto the property to see what she was up against.

The night was cold, and she raised the collar of her jacket as she stared into the parlor window. It was bright and warm inside, and a woman just a few years shy of Cynthia's age leaned over to study the picture that hung on the wall over the telephone table. She was the only thing that stood between Cynthia and her final goal: the niece. Oh, excuse her: *great* niece. Whatever that even meant.

The niece looked up, glancing at the window. She looked startled. Cynthia quickly ducked out of sight and crawled under the window out of her eye line. She didn't think she could be seen outside in the dark with all the lights on inside the house, but maybe she had been wrong. No matter. It changed nothing.

Perhaps she'd simply think she saw a ghost.

---

*R*ichard told Emily he kept a shotgun behind the seat of his truck and a forty-five in the glove compartment. Emily found she was not especially surprised to learn that Richard was armed. She could easily picture him shooting at raccoons for getting into his garbage. She realized she was unable to imagine Richard's house, because she'd never seen it.

"Richard, where do you live, anyway?" she asked him as they walked from the house to his truck. "This whole time we've known you, we never asked you anything about yourself."

"I live up in the mountains," said Richard. He opened the passenger side door for her, and Emily climbed in. "I know exactly where that address is: it's in the middle of nowhere. They certainly picked a spot, all right."

Emily imagined going into a dark place in the middle of nowhere with a murderer and expecting to emerge unscathed. "I don't know. Maybe we should call the cops. How would she know? I just have a bad feeling about all of this."

"Do you really want to take that risk?" Richard asked.

Emily thought of the picture of Jesse and shook her head. "No, no I don't."

"All right, then." Richard put the truck into drive and pulled away from the house. "Let's hit the road."

Emily stared out the window as Richard drove out of town to the steep streets that led into the mountains. She thought of Jesse and whether or not he was okay. What would they find when they arrived? Was there any way for them to make it out of this alive?

RICHARD PULLED the truck to a stop at the bottom of a steep hill. Just barely visible among the trees was a steep, narrow trail. The mailbox at the bottom displayed the numbers of the address Cynthia had sent Emily.

"You go up first," said Richard. "I'll wait down here for a few minutes, so they see you and think you're alone, then follow."

Emily hesitated before getting out. "What if she already killed Jesse? What if she's waiting till I get there to kill me as soon as she sees me?"

"If she did that, how would she get the house?" said Richard reasonably.

"Okay." Emily took a deep breath and then put her hand on the door.

"Wait." Richard reached into his glove compartment and handed her his forty-five. Emily had never held a gun in her life. "Have you ever fired one of these before?"

"No," Emily admitted.

"Then only use it if you have to," said Richard. He showed her how to hold it and how to pull the hammer back. "Once you do that, keep your finger off the trigger till you're ready to fire."

"Okay," said Emily. She concealed the gun in the waist-band of her jeans beneath her jacket and got out of the truck, closing the door behind her as quietly as she could without looking back. She felt certain if she so much as looked at Richard again, she would lose her nerve and become paralyzed, unable to leave the truck. Only the thought of Jesse kept her moving forward.

The light was rapidly fading, and Emily could barely make out the steep rocky trail among the trees, but she was reluctant to shine a light and alert whoever might be at the top of the hill, waiting for her.

Emily climbed the trail until the sky was black with night and she was out of breath and winded. Just when she was beginning to wonder if this was all a set up and Cynthia had simply lured her up here to kill her in the woods, she reached a plateau. She could just barely make out the silhouette of an aging wooden structure. It looked like an old log cabin built by hand. The building looked like it had weathered many a storm.

There were no lights on inside, at least none that Emily could see. She approached the front door cautiously and knocked.

"Keep your hands where I can see them."

Emily felt a cold metal muzzle press into the back of her neck and froze. She hadn't heard anyone behind her. Had she been waiting on the porch for her to arrive?

"I said put your hands where I can see them! That's it. Nice and high," the voice continued. It was a couple octaves lower than the voice on the phone, but familiar nonetheless.

"Theresa?" said Emily, confused.

The muzzle immediately jabbed her in the neck again and Emily regretted saying anything at all. "You were expecting maybe Bugs Bunny?" said Theresa. "Open the door. It's unlocked."

Emily turned the knob and pushed the door in with an ominous creak.

"Walk," Theresa ordered her. "*Slowly*."

Emily squinted into the darkness, trying not to trip as she looked around to see if Jesse was there. She couldn't see more than a foot in front of her face.

The footsteps behind her paused briefly and a light in the room switched on. The living room was illuminated. Its bent wood chairs were empty and Jesse was nowhere to be seen.

"Where's Jesse?" Emily demanded.

"Pipe down, and maybe I'll tell you," said Theresa. "Sit in that chair and keep your hands on your head. Good."

Emily obediently sat in the chair Theresa indicated with her hands placed on the top of her head. She glanced around the room frantically, her eyes sweeping the room and taking inventory: there was a fireplace and a rug in front of the hearth, but no Jesse.

"What did you do with him?" she said, her voice breaking.

Theresa came around from behind her and sat in the chair across from Emily's. She kept her gun trained on Emily's face.

Theresa rolled her eyes. "He's fine. I got him tied up in the back and gagged. You can see him in a minute. Do you have the deed?"

Emily was mad enough to spit. Part of her didn't believe Jesse was alive and wished Theresa would just shoot her and get it over with. "No, I don't have the deed yet. It's a process; it has to be transferred."

"I know that!" snapped Theresa. "I'm not stupid."

Emily had concluded a number of contradictory opinions regarding Theresa's intelligence, but her gun was still aimed at Emily's head, so she remained silent.

"Did you talk to the lawyer?" Theresa demanded. "Watkins? What'd he say?"

"He said he was taking care of it," said Emily. "I want to see Jesse."

Theresa snorted. "I don't think you're in any position to be making demands, do you?" She took out her phone, scrolled through it briefly, and tapped one of her contacts. "Hello? I've got her here. Did you talk to him? Well, why didn't anyone tell *me*? No one tells me anything. Fine."

Theresa hung up and sighed huffily. "Looks like you're telling the truth." Emily wondered briefly if she would shoot her on the spot. "According to my instructions, it's time for a little reunion." Theresa stood, with the gun still trained on Emily, and approached her as she reached into her coat pocket. Emily flinched. Theresa took out a large roll of duct tape and wound it around Emily's wrists and then her ankles. "Just so you don't get any funny ideas." Theresa left the room, disappearing through a darkened doorway, and Emily stared after her, both hopeful and terrified.

She strained at her restraints, but Theresa had wrapped the duct tape too tightly. She shifted around to see if she could still reach the gun at her hip. It was just out of reach.

There was a scuffling sound in the hallway off the dark doorway and Emily looked up in fear. Theresa came back through the doorway, pushing Jesse in front of her. He was gagged and badly beaten, his hands tied. Theresa kept the gun aimed at the back of his head.

"Jesse!" Emily tried to get up and immediately fell.

Theresa rolled her eyes. She shoved Jesse onto the couch and then grabbed Emily by her hair, dragging her across the floor as Emily yelled in pain. She tossed her on the couch next to Jesse.

"Jesse, are you okay?" Emily asked him breathlessly.

He looked terrible. One eye was swollen shut, his lip was cut, and his face was purple with dark bruises. He looked at her with his one good eye and made a series of frantic, muffled noises.

"What did you do?" Emily wanted to throw herself from the couch onto Theresa, but she knew it wouldn't do either her or Jesse any good.

"What did *I* do? I didn't even touch him," said Theresa dismissively. "I don't do any of that stuff. I'm not the one who worked him over, so quit looking at me like I'm the devil himself. Not like you're going to do anything about it, anyway."

Jesse was still trying to say something to Emily until Theresa turned the gun on him. He stopped.

"That's better," she said, narrowing her eyes. "You just keep quiet over there till we get through this. Then you can run that gob of yours all you want."

"Why are you doing this?" asked Emily. "Who are we to you? How do you know Cynthia? How do we know you're not going to kill us?"

Theresa shrugged. "You don't. I guess you'll just have to hope for the best." She laughed loudly, as if they were a sitcom she found amusing. "As for why, I thought that would be obvious. For the money, of course. Which reminds me." She frowned as if thinking hard, then reached under her chair and withdrew a small flight bag. "I'm going to leave this here for you, and then I'm going to go. By the time you get loose or get anyone up here, we'll be long gone, the house will be ours, and either you can take the money and live happily ever after with your mouths shut, or you can try to get the house back and tell the sheriff all about who the bad guys are, and then we'll come back and kill you. It's pretty simple, right?"

"You're just going to leave us here?" said Emily, staring at Theresa. "We'll freeze to death."

"I'll build you a fire first," said Theresa. She sounded insulted, as if Emily had called her character into question. "I don't need some hiker stumbling across your dead frozen popsicle bodies all tied up in the spring. Think I'm stupid? And if you're dumb enough not to be able to get out of a little bit of duct tape in time not to starve to death, that's your own fault." Theresa turned and started piling logs in the hearth. "I'll make sure it's a nice big one. That should give you a little bit of time, don't you think?"

"Theresa," Emily said, the wheels in her mind turning. Theresa didn't sound nearly as crazy as Cynthia had when she called her on Jesse's phone. Maybe Emily could reason with her. "What are you getting out of this? What is Cynthia doing for you?"

Theresa shook her head, pursing her lips. "It's not about what Cynthia's doing for me, it's about what I do for Cynthia. She figures out everything and takes care of things, and I just do what I'm told. Same way it's always been, same way it will always be."

"Yeah, but how do you know she'll follow through?" Emily asked. "What if she's lying to you?"

Theresa frowned. "Well, she has to, doesn't she?" she said. "That's what family's for."

Emily studied Theresa's profile as she arranged the logs: pale like Cynthia, but with a light smattering of freckles across her upturned nose, long pale hair that caught in a wild snarl down her back. The resemblance to the woman in the photo that hung in Matilda's parlor was faint but unmistakable. "You're sisters?"

"Unfortunately. I can't say we like each other much, but we're definitely stuck with each other." Now that her duty was nearly done, she didn't seem to mind chatting with Emily like an old friend. She sat back on her heels and surveyed the fireplace. "This looks pretty good. Sun will come up by the time this goes out, so you'll just have to work yourselves loose by sunset tomorrow."

"Are you really going to let us go?" asked Emily. "Meaning, we'll never see or hear from either of you, ever again?"

Theresa looked at her, puzzled. "Well I mean, yeah, why would you? You take the money. You keep your mouths shut. Everyone lives happily ever after. End of story."

"But you killed Matilda," said Emily. "And the kids. What's to stop you from killing us?"

Theresa's eyes clouded over. "I told you. I didn't do any of that. I don't hurt people, I just do what I'm told. Nobody wants to explain why you two are dead or missing on top of that old lady and those kids, okay? We just want the house, free and clear, and we want you to be alive to answer a few phone calls if anybody gets curious or suspicious, and that's it." Her expression cleared as she turned back to the fireplace. She doused the rolled-up newspaper underneath a log with lighter fluid and lit it with a long match from a box on the hearth. "There you go! Let there be light." Theresa watched the fire glowing with a happy expression.

Emily stared at her. It was like talking to a child. She didn't sound like a lunatic, but she seemed no better acquainted with reality than Cynthia. Emily concluded that Theresa not only did whatever she was told, but she also believed whatever she was told.

Theresa got up and gave a bored stretch, as if this much work was more taxing than what she was accustomed to.

"I'll just go lock up so the bears don't get in and eat the two of you, and that's the last you'll see of me," she said. "I have to be across town to get all the fancy stuff out of the house while we wait for the legal stuff to go through. Hope you weren't too attached to any of it." She laughed, then turned and disappeared through the doorway.

Emily turned to Jesse and whispered as softly as she could manage. "I have a gun in the waistband of my jeans. If we can just get loose, we can get to it. Richard brought me here and he should be on his way up. If we can just—" Emily shrugged her coat off and tilted her hip toward Jesse, revealing the gun.

Jesse just shook his head at her, his one good eye wide. He made a series of muffled sounds, then looked in the direction Theresa disappeared and stopped. He wiggled across the couch to Emily and immediately began tugging at her duct tape bonds with his bound hands.

"What is it? Wait, hold still. Maybe I can get that off with my teeth." Emily leaned forward and tried to pull the edge of the duct tape over his mouth without biting him, but it was stuck in his beard.

"Oh, I'm sorry, am I interrupting something?" Theresa came back in the room and cackled loudly as she saw them. "Making a valiant start, I see. It's going to be awhile though, just so you know. There's one thing I'm good at, it's duct tape." She walked past them toward the front door. Emily heard a long creak and a click.

"Jess, I don't think she's coming back," said Emily. "Richard should be here any—"

There was another long, loud creak from the front door, and Emily thought wildly that Theresa had come back, she was going back on her word and returning to kill them. Emily reached for the gun, thinking that if she could only separate her hands just enough to hold it, she could defend them. Next to her, every muscle in Jesse's body seemed to tense.

"Oh my," said a voice behind them. "What did they do to you folks?"

Emily sagged against the couch with relief. Richard. She turned to see him standing in the middle of the living room, regarding them with wide eyes. He looked from the two of them, tied up on the couch, to the bag of money in front of the fireplace, taking it in.

"It was Theresa," Emily said. "She's Cynthia's sister, they've been in it together from the beginning. Them and Watkins. Richard, please untie us, hurry! She said she was leaving us here, but I'm afraid she might come back."

Richard approached them on the couch. Emily held out her hands. "Do you have a knife or something to cut the tape with?"

Richard walked right past her and sat in the chair Theresa had only recently vacated.

"Richard?" said Emily. "What are you doing?"

She glanced over at Jesse, who sat stock still, watching Richard with an expression of dread. She looked back at him. "Richard?"

He smiled. He reached into his pocket and pulled out a pair of black gloves. He pulled them on slowly, one at a time.

"I'm sorry, Emily," said Richard. "I'd like to let you go. I really would. But I'm not going to be able to do that. Not now. Not later." He looked into the fire and continued to smile, as if they were at a pleasant neighborhood gathering. He turned to look at them again. His smile was broad and insane.

"Not ever," he said.

o...not Richard...not our only ally.

Emily stared at Richard and thought these words of denial in her mind. But even as she thought them, when she regarded Richard's mad stare, she knew that it was true.

Looking back, she thought of how ever since they had arrived at the house, Richard always seemed to appear, with uncanny timing, immediately after something had gone wrong. How convenient it must have been for him. He had access to the house at all times. He worked there long before Emily and Jesse ever got there, or even Matilda. He must have known about the tunnels. Emily thought of how many times she'd been in the house alone with him and felt sick.

Richard took out his gun and rested it on his knee. "My sisters would rather we kept you alive. They think you'll take a payoff and vouch for them, that you'll publicly reinforce this story that you transferred the deed of your own free will. But I know better. You're honest people. I don't think you could do that, even if you wanted to. I don't need you to put one of our names on the deed in order to get the house. And your husband here probably knows this from the way he's looking at me, but Matilda named someone else in the will when she changed it from Cynthia to you—in case you didn't want it. An old, falling-down house in the middle of nowhere from a woman you never met who your family didn't like? In the likely event you didn't want it, she wanted it to go to someone she knew and trusted. She wanted it to go to me. So you see, I don't need you around to make sure I get the house. If anything, I just need you to disappear. Just like Matilda and those kids."

"People are going to ask questions, Richard," said Emily, her heart pounding. He no longer seemed like good old easygoing Richard, like someone she could reason with. But she had to try.

"Getting rid of Matilda and the children and making it look like it was her fault is one thing," said Emily. "But to do the same to us, ensuring that you get the house, don't you think that's going to be a little more than suspicious? People are not going to believe that we went missing out of nowhere, or that Matilda came back from the dead, murdered us, and then disappeared again. And that you, coincidentally, just happen to get everything."

"Oglethorpe doesn't care whether or not you go missing," said Richard dismissively. "He doesn't want that kind of scandal in his town. He'll cover it up, like he covered it up last time. Otherwise, he'll have every reporter from every news outlet in the country, running their twenty-four-hour cycles, making him look worse and worse with every second that ticks by while he fails to come up with answers. And he'll never find them. We covered our tracks too well for that."

Emily realized something important as he spoke, something she had missed: Richard was smart. Only an intelligent mind could execute something of this scope, and his aw-gee-shucks routine was probably nothing more than that. A routine. And how thoroughly he had fooled her with it.

"But why, Richard?" Emily asked. "What did any of us ever do to you?" It wasn't that she thought beseeching him would do any good. She only hoped that if she kept him talking long enough, it would buy them a little bit more time. Maybe in the interval she could come up with a plan. She didn't know how she would convey it to Jesse without Richard noticing, but she would find a way.

"You didn't do anything," said Richard, smiling as if they were simply exchanging pleasantries while in line at the bank. "That's kind of the point, isn't it? I was invisible to you. Richard, the local yokel; Richard, the help."

Emily thought of how transformed he was before her, how very different from the person she'd once thought.

"I was nobody," he continued. "I was a nobody my whole life. My father was a nobody. His father was a nobody. All a bunch of nobodys, going all the way back. Is it so wrong, for a man to want to be somebody?" Richard looked into the fire, the light dancing on the glass of his spectacles. It made him look even more insane. His voice was distant now, as if he was in the place he was remembering.

"My father worked for Matilda's father, did you know that? I'm sure you didn't. He did the same menial, thankless tasks that I did. He performed his drudgery with pride. He thought that as long as a man had a job, any job was honorable, as long as you took it seriously and did it well. He thought I should be proud to do the same things that he did. He had me working at his knee when I was barely old enough to spell. I never even had a choice…"

RICHARD'S FATHER, Henry Danforth, brought Richard up to "the big house" (as he called it) for the first time when he was a child. It was one of Richard's earliest memories. He introduced them to Matilda's grandparents and told them he would work for them one day, too. Richard was embarrassed. Even at a young age, something about the idea of working for two people as what was, in his mind, a servant, bothered him. But he said nothing. He resented his father even then, but only ever in his mind.

His sisters were jealous. They wanted to go up to the big house, too, but their father refused. He said it was no kind of work for young ladies. For a while, Richard tried to make a game of it: pulling weeds and raking leaves; painting alongside of his father. But he couldn't get past the lingering suspicion that all this meant was that he had to work twice—once here, and once at home, where all the same chores were waiting for him. He seethed at the unfairness of it. It went on like this for several years, until Richard turned sixteen and decided he would run away. He would live his own life and be his own man, and nobody could ever make a servant of him again.

When he turned thirteen, his father started paying him for his help at the big house—now that he was old enough to make a real difference, rather than "one more thing" Henry had to "look after." Richard thought with silent fury of how his father made it sound like even taking away his childhood had somehow been a burden on the older man.

His mistake, Richard thought smugly to himself in his room at night as he hid his earnings under a loose floorboard beneath his bed, was thinking that Richard would just spend the money: baseball cards, sodas, candy, model airplanes. Richard's father never imagined he'd devote every red cent towards getting away from their family, which was the only thing Richard intended to do. He'd run away and never see or talk to any of them again. He couldn't wait. He lay awake at night in bed, his young back hurting from pulling weeds or hauling around furniture much too heavy for his skinny adolescent arms, and he would dream.

He dreamed about beaches, distant shores where waves crashed and lifeguards blew their whistles. Maybe he could become a lifeguard and save a beautiful girl in a string bikini from drowning. He'd live in a beach shack he built himself where he'd fish and eat crabs. It would never snow. He dreamed about the rodeo, riding a bucking bronco like a real cowboy and living off the land in Texas. He'd start out as a ranch hand and one day have his own ranch. He dreamed about Europe, which he didn't know too much about outside of Social Studies. He'd ride a bike with a basket through the French countryside and eat baguettes. He'd go to London and look at the Royal Guard and try to get them to react before he went to Piccadilly Circus to ride the Ferris wheel and eat peanuts while he listened to the chimes of Big Ben.

Two things interfered with his plan. The first was Cynthia. She saw him one afternoon, hiding his money beneath the loose floorboard in his bedroom. Cynthia was always spying on everyone. She'd spy on Theresa until she caught her doing something she shouldn't, then she'd use the information to blackmail the younger girl into doing her chores. She spied on all the neighbors, gathering information about them just in case she ever got a chance to use it. She spied on Richard, but he was acutely aware of this and usually much too wary to ever do anything of importance when he knew she might be around.

But on this particular night, he was in a hurry and got careless. His friends were walking to a baseball game at the high school and he didn't want to be left behind. He didn't want to bring all his earnings with him; he was too afraid of losing them. It was the worst thing he could think of. It would mean losing his ticket to freedom.

He turned to leave and there was Cynthia, leaning in the doorway, watching him. She smiled slowly. She knew the leverage she'd just won.

"So," she said, sidling over and sitting on his bed. Cynthia hated that he got a room to himself and didn't have to share because he was the only boy. She resented him for this, among an endless litany of other privileges she assigned him, in her mind, as the only son in a family of daughters. She was probably even irked he was going to the baseball game without her, even though he had worked all day and she hadn't. "I see you've started yourself a little savings account, Richie Rich."

Richard was silent. He knew by now that to implore Cynthia would only provoke her further. Your best option was to just wait, find out what she wanted, and how much it would cost you.

"Tell you what," said Cynthia, as if she were doing him a favor. "We'll keep this our little secret, just between us, if you'll give me a little bit every now and then, just to tide me over."

"How much is a little bit?" asked Richard, already dreading the answer.

The smile immediately vanished from Cynthia's face and she held her hand out with a scowl. "Twenty bucks."

Twenty dollars! He was lucky if he made that in a week. Even though his dad was giving him a little bit of money now, it was still exactly that: a little bit.

He'd never considered hurting Cynthia before, but for the first time, he thought very seriously about it. If she kept things up at this rate, he'd be broke by the end of the summer, and he'd never get out of here and away from them.

"It's that, or fork it all over to Dad," she said. She pronounced *Dad* the way other people said *scurvy* or *gout*. Richard resented his father, but Cynthia loathed him. She hated being the daughter of a servant, and she thought her mother's unspoken devotion to her husband, regardless of his station, was pathetic beyond belief.

Silently, Richard withdrew the money from his hiding place and handed it to Cynthia.

"Thanks a bunch!" She smiled broadly and tucked the bill

in the back pocket of her blue jeans before sauntering out of the room.

Richard changed his hiding place often so she couldn't come back and steal everything from him later, as he knew she was wont to do, because who could he tell? He'd been pretending all along to spend the money on other things, like going to movies he never actually saw. He knew she would steal from him bit by bit whenever she felt like it. But of course, just hiding the money made little difference, as she could still demand it from him whenever she felt like it: always threatening to drop the bomb at dinner that Richard was hoarding money for himself even as his father occasionally skipped dinner so the rest of them could have seconds and little Theresa's too-small shoes no longer fit and their mother's clothes were threadbare.

The second thing that happened to dash Richard's hopes of escape forever, or at least for a very long time, was that his father had a heart attack shortly after Richard's fifteenth birthday. Henry was working in the garden on a bright spring day, clear and cold, when he suddenly keeled over in the garden. Richard was terrified. Only partly for his father, but mostly, he later realized, for himself—for he realized even in that moment what would become of him if his father never rose again. He'd become the sole caretaker of his entire family's well-being, and he'd never know a moment's peace again.

He ran up to the big house and rushed inside, yelling at the top of his voice. He was normally very shy and reserved when he went in the house, and that was only ever to fix something or clean. But his panic had driven away all the usual thoughts of tact and reservation.

At first, Richard's pleas were met with silence: the house was empty. He panicked as he looked for the phone. He ran smack into the inside help, a maid by the name of Henrietta, who called the ambulance that saved Henry's life.

His father lived, but was unable to return to work for months while he recovered. From then on, by some unspoken agreement among every member of the family but Richard, it was assumed that Richard would continue working at the big house and keep the family afloat. And not just Richard: if they'd tried to make him do that, placing the full burden of their interests on his young shoulders, he would have run away right then and there no matter what. But his mother took on work as a seamstress, and his sisters baby-sat and shoplifted to contribute. Their parents knew about the baby-sitting but not, of course, the shoplifting.

Richard still considered running. But one day, Cynthia told him her idea. She summoned him and Theresa to her secret fort in the woods. Richard was never allowed in it and didn't even know where it was, which he suspected was Cynthia's way of punishing him for getting his own room. He only knew it existed from Cynthia and Theresa's whispered conversations and prolonged disappearances. But on this particular day, Cynthia made an exception. Even Richard was permitted to enter her secret headquarters.

The fort was extremely cunning, Richard thought, not even just for a girl—Cynthia, while one of the most terrible aspects of his life, was shrewder than any boy he knew. He wasn't surprised her fort was a super villain's dream.

Pages from comic books decorated the crude walls of the lean-to, comprised mostly of branches found in the woods. Richard looked closer and felt unsurprised to see many of the pages came from his own collection. There was a hidden stash of snacks, many of them things that went missing from the house almost immediately, on the rare occasions their mother could afford to splurge at the store. There were also things Richard didn't recognize, which he assumed Cynthia had stolen. As it transpired, he was right.

"I've been taking food from the big house for years now," Cynthia told them, opening a cupcake wrapped in plastic and shoveling almost the entire thing in her mouth. Theresa watched, fascinated. Cynthia ignored her. She didn't offer her or Richard one. "It's easy like you wouldn't believe. I sneak in, I take whatever I want, and then I sneak right back out again."

"How?" said Richard. He knew the house better than Cynthia, and he'd never once seen his sister there.

"You don't *know*?" Cynthia looked at him, aghast. Or, more likely, pretending to be, just to get under his skin. "But you've worked there for *so long*! I thought for sure you'd have found it by now."

"Found what," said Richard shortly. He was getting irritable. He was missing the pick-up game in the park, his back was hurting him, and he would have very much liked a cupcake, which Cynthia clearly wasn't going to offer him. "There's nothing to find up there but china and doilies."

"I disagree," said Cynthia. "There's a lot more in that place than china and doilies. And some of that stuff is worth a whole lotta money."

Richard furrowed his brow. "We can't just steal from the big house. They'll think it was Dad, or Henrietta. Or me. We'll all get fired. Are you stupid? You're lucky they haven't caught you stealing food."

Cynthia waved a hand airily, dismissing his claims. "I've never been caught, and I never will be. I never take enough for them to notice. I just take enough for me. They have so much, they don't even know when something's gone. So I say we sneak up to the big house one night, and we go into the safe. We take a little bit of money, and depending on how closely they keep track—based on my observations, my guess is not very—they won't even notice. Or they'll each think the other one did it, and is lying about it, because how could anyone else know the combination to the safe? There's no way you or Dad or Henrietta or anybody could know that."

"How do *you* know that?" said Theresa, staring at Cynthia with awe.

Cynthia smiled wickedly.

"I'll show you," she said.

IT WAS EVENING. The sun had set and it was dark and cold. The Meades were in the parlor playing backgammon. Richard knew them well enough by now to know exactly what they were doing at any given point in the day.

Cynthia led them up to the house with an authority that annoyed Richard. The house was his territory. Even if he didn't like it, it was still something only he knew about, and she couldn't even let him have that.

Richard forgot his private resentments when Cynthia slipped under the stairs leading up to the back door and moved aside the pile of wood against the wall, log by log.

"Hurry up and help me!" she snapped. "I don't want to be here all night."

Richard and Theresa quickly joined her and within moments they'd moved the wood pile two feet to the left, revealing a small door set low in the wall. Richard stared.

"How did you find this?" he asked.

"Easy," said Cynthia. "While you were busy pulling weeds and painting shutters, I was exploring. And I, unlike you, notice *all* of what I see."

She opened the door and pulled a pen light out of the pocket of her jeans. She disappeared through the door. Richard couldn't see anything beyond the pale pinprick of light she held. Beyond that was nothing but darkness. He hesitated at the entrance.

"Come on!" Cynthia's voice drifted, impatient and exasperated, from the darkness within. Theresa scuttled in immediately. After another moment's hesitation, Richard complied. It was bad enough his sister had a cooler fort than

259

he did; he didn't want anyone to know she was also fearless, while he was afraid of the dark.

RICHARD AND THERESA trailed Cynthia closely as she led them through the intricate network of secret tunnels in the walls of the big house. They went to the attic, where Cynthia bragged she'd nicked a bunch of stuff and sold it to consignment stores or sometimes just went there to dress up in old clothes. "I even fell asleep up here once," she said. "Nobody even noticed. They never come up here."

They went to the bedrooms, which were opulently decorated and looked more comfortable than any room Richard had ever seen. There was never any reason for him to go in any of the bedrooms when he worked at the house, and it was the first time he'd seen them. He was immediately jealous: jealous of Cynthia, for discovering this first; jealous of the Meades, for their personal fireplaces in each room and the chandeliers dripping crystals and the deep, thick, wine-red rugs. The rugs alone looked more comfortable than Richard's own bed and he wondered, not for the first time, why some people got to have so much while others had so little.

At last, they stopped by the parlor. They could hear the gentle laughter of the Meades, who still loved each other after many years of marriage, and the polite inquiries of Henrietta: would Mrs. Meade like another sherry? Was Mr. Meade ready for his whiskey and his cigar? Cynthia shook her head, frowning, her eyes squinty and mean. Richard knew she hated the sound of Henrietta's pleasant serving voice, because he hated it, too.

Cynthia turned to them and whispered, "This is where they keep the safe. The old man talks to himself, and he always says the code out loud while he turns the dial to the numbers. The idiot."

Richard didn't think it was all that foolish of Mr. Meade to remind himself of the code aloud as he had no reason to believe that a small girl was hiding in the walls of his home, watching him, but there was no point in vocalizing that to Cynthia. She thought everyone was a fool but her. And though he hated to agree with her about anything, he couldn't deny that while his sister was many bad things, a fool wasn't one of them.

Cynthia gestured to them with her pen light, and they followed her down the tunnel and out of the house.

THEY STOLE many things from the house over the years: money from the safe, knickknacks from the attic they knew wouldn't be missed, as they'd been packed away in boxes with enough dust on them to imply they'd been there since the Danforth children had been born. The money they made from the house granted them little luxuries they wouldn't have otherwise: Theresa bought make-up and new clothes so she could fit in with the girls at school. Richard bought a car when he turned sixteen. Thoughts of running away still tugged at his mind, but then he met a girl. He had a car, so he could take her out on dates. He stayed out late and went to work early when he wasn't in school and the rest of the time, he slept, his mind too tired for dreams.

He never knew what Cynthia bought because he never saw the evidence, not until her senior year of high school. Richard was still working up at the house. Cynthia got into college. She was as smart in school as in life and knew it was her only ticket out. She got scholarships and paid for her plane ticket with a hidden cache of money Richard couldn't imagine the proportions of. Money had gone missing from his secret stash over the years, no matter where he moved it: his money from the Meades that they paid him, and the other money that they didn't know about. Cynthia took all her money and she got away.

Theresa's grades were terrible. Richard hoped for a baseball scholarship, or basketball, but he wasn't good enough as his back problems got increasingly worse by his senior year. His girl broke up with him for the quarterback. It seemed like the plot of a bad movie, but instead of making a comeback, getting his due, and having his day, Richard's life seemed to grow paler and paler until he could no longer remember where he once dreamed of escaping.

He thought that perhaps, when the Meades passed on, they might think of him and his family in their will after so many years of service. They didn't. They left all their money to charity and gave the house to their granddaughter, Matilda.

It was then that Richard realized that to the Meades, some nameless, faceless organization had been more deserving than his family, who spent countless hours, days, weeks, months, years making the Meades' lives better and easier than they already were. And that blood was always thicker than water.

The thought of a lifetime of servitude and dissatisfaction enraged him to the core. He watched as Matilda moved in. He watched as she brought in all the children with nothing. Just like the children with nothing who existed unnoticed in her very backyard for all her life. The hypocrisy of it unhinged Richard over time. At first, it was just a nagging thought, and for a while, it remained one. Then the thought grew bigger. It ballooned into a fixation, which became an obsession.

Why them? Why not us?

He watched her. He watched them. He watched her give them a better chance, but where was the better chance for him? Who had helped him? Cynthia would have said you have to help yourself, unless you want to end up helpless. But he *had* helped himself. He helped himself, his father, his sisters, his mother, and the Meades—but who helped Richard?

No one. He was just the help.

CYNTHIA CAME BACK FROM SCHOOL, and she was crazier than ever before. She'd gotten everything she wanted, and it still hadn't been enough. All the girls were effortlessly more beautiful, poised, educated, well-dressed, and well-liked than she was. They knew all the right things to say to all the right people. They looked down on Cynthia, but politely, as if she was merely the salesgirl helping them try on their shoes. It made her completely insane.

She couldn't find a job. She went to the most competitive city in the world where everyone around her started out far, far ahead of her. They had families who helped them get started. She had nothing and no one. She couldn't steal her way out of it. The social stigma of getting caught would be more shame than she could stand. She would be ostracized; exiled.

In the end, Cynthia exiled herself. She came back home and met an insurance salesman. He lived in a large and beautiful house, and Cynthia figured, why not? Better to be in a large house with one person you didn't like than a small one with five. (Cynthia didn't always like herself, either.) But she was wrong. Ray was so devoted to her, so insufferable and needy, it was all she could do not to drown herself in their vast Jacuzzi tub at night just to get away from him.

She appealed to Richard. His original suggestion was to bump off Ray—his life insurance was obscene. It would be the perfect crime. It took him awhile to get Cynthia to admit the truth: her mother-in-law hated her so much and was so distrustful of her that she'd threatened to write Ray out of her will if he didn't get a pre-nup. Ray believed they'd need his mother's money to one day send their many children to college (Cynthia was a very good actress, when she wanted to be), so he'd asked Cynthia to sign. She could have refused, of course, making something up on the grounds that if he really, truly loved her, he'd never prepare for the end. But he wasn't. For him, it was a step to ensure their future—their long, endless future—and to refuse would have looked suspicious.

"What about Matilda?" Cynthia wanted to know. "What's happening at the big house these days?"

Richard told her. He told her all about Matilda, and the kids, and the orphanage. Cynthia snorted with disgust in all the right places, and he thought of how he missed her. It surprised him. But sometimes, she was the only one who understood.

"What a waste," Cynthia said. "What a complete and utter, terrible, ridiculous, awful waste. That idiot of a woman. I get that orphans can net you a lot of money, if you foster enough of them at once, but I mean, why? Why not just sell the house and retire to Cabo?"

"I don't think people retire there," said Richard. "I think it's more like a vacation type of place."

"Who cares, Richard? What does a distinction like that matter? The point is, we should be there now, rather than freezing to death in this godforsaken town for yet another year of our lives. While that woman sits up there frittering away the most massive investment imaginable. Our father spent his life maintaining that investment, if you think about it. She wouldn't even have it to ruin if he hadn't nearly killed himself painting the walls and cleaning the gutters. We're entitled to that house, Richard. Think about it. It should be ours."

And Richard did think about it. He thought about it when he was sweeping the steps and painting the walls and cleaning the gutters. He thought about it while he performed the same mindless work he had for decades now, decades of his life spent devoted to the upkeep of a single house, a house that wasn't even his own and never would be.

But what if it could?

At first, Cynthia made it sound like they would just wait. She would get a job working for Matilda, on the inside, and get close to her. She would get into her good graces and into her will. They'd never once seen or heard about any living member of Matilda's family, and concluded they were all either dead or hated her or she hated them or both. Matilda was getting older. She couldn't live forever.

But she could live for quite a while, Cynthia pointed out a few months into her employment. There was really no telling how long a person could live. Obviously, it would be best if they expedited the process.

Richard was reluctant. He didn't like the idea of killing Matilda. It had been much easier to picture bumping off Ray, whom he neither knew nor particularly liked. He knew Matilda well enough at that point to know what kind of person she was: earnest, honest, and kind. She never had a bad word to say to, or about, anybody. Wouldn't killing a person like that send you straight to hell?

"I've got news for you, Richard," said Cynthia, when he vocalized his concern. "We're already there."

Then Richard thought about his life. He thought about continuing on this way, in perpetuity, until he lived no more. The thought was worse than he could stand. Worse, even, than killing Matilda. He told Cynthia this, and she smiled.

"All right, Richard," she said. "All right. In that case, if you're on board—I have a plan..."

---

*E*mily stared at Richard. She felt many things, at that moment, which were hard to distill—fear, resentment, hostility, and under all this, a powerful undercurrent of pity, which astounded her. He killed Matilda and the children. He planned to kill them. How could she feel pity for a murderer? But something in Richard's story was painfully relatable: the quiet desperation of living hand to mouth, dreaming of a better life. But why like this?

"Why like this?" Emily asked. "Why does it have to be like this?"

Richard was still staring into the fire, as if still caught up in the throes of the past he'd just re-lived, and she hated to remind him that she was there: his final problem. But she had to know. "If you were just a good person who couldn't get over being poor, then why resort to murder? Do you expect me to feel sorry for you? We have our problems, too. But we'd never hurt anyone."

Richard snorted with contempt. "You had each other, is what you had. What kind of problems can you possibly have? A few unpaid credit cards and a student loan or two? I never went to college. I never even imagined it. Cynthia went, and it did her no good. I watched over people with more of everything than I had for over half my life, but who watched over me? Nobody. Sooner or later, you've got to watch over yourself." He turned from the fireplace to look at Emily and Jesse. "I really did like you, you know. It's a shame it had to be this way. But I've waited far too long for this."

Emily closed her eyes and wished for a solution: any solution. She was surprised to feel Richard undoing the duct tape bindings from her ankles. Had he changed his mind?

"I'm a fair man," he said as he sawed at the tape with a pocket knife. "That's the difference between me and Cynthia: she's the snake in the grass you never even see coming. She'll throw dirt in your eye and hit below the belt. But I believe in giving people a fighting chance. So I'm going to take you outside and give you exactly thirty seconds. Then I'm going to come find you."

Emily stared at him. He was giving them a chance to get away?

Richard looked at her and laughed. It was as if he'd read her mind. "Oh, you won't get away, of course. I'm not *that* fair. Been hunting for years now. Lately, there hasn't been that much to shoot."

With these chilling words, he released first Emily's feet, then Jesse's. He left their hands tied and Jesse's gag secure. Then he brandished the gun at them and gestured for them to get up from the couch.

"Now walk," he said.

Emily walked ahead of Jesse and Jesse walked ahead of Richard. He marched them to the front door. Richard kicked it open with the toe of his black cowboy boot. He nudged them onto the porch.

"Stop," he said. They froze in place.

Richard set his handgun on the small round table next to the Adirondack chair. He picked up a hunting rifle leaning against the wall next to the door. From behind her, Emily heard the sounds of a gun being loaded. Fear coursed through her, followed by adrenaline.

"Remember what I told you?" Richard said.

At first, she wasn't sure whether he was speaking to her or Jesse, or what specifically he was referring to. He'd told her many things over the course of the last hour, most of which she'd like to forget.

"Keep your finger off the trigger until you're ready to fire," he said. Then he laughed. It was the high, maniacal cackle of a madman. He nudged Emily in the back with the rifle. "All right, girl, you got thirty seconds. Better make 'em count. They'll most likely be your last."

Emily looked at Jesse. Jesse looked over at her. They stumbled off the porch side by side. It was hard to run after being bound for so long, and her feet felt numb. After about ten seconds, when they were just out of Richard's eye line, Jesse pulled her down behind a hollow tree.

He'd worked most of his duct tape gag off by rubbing his face against the couch arm while Richard was talking. Richard, lost in memories of his childhood, hadn't noticed. Jesse loosely refastened the tape over his mouth before Richard unbound their feet and led them outside. He reached his bound wrists up and ripped the tape off. He scrabbled around on the ground for a sharp rock and sawed quickly at the tape around Emily's wrists. He whispered very quickly while he looked directly into Emily's eyes.

"We can't outrun him. I haven't eaten anything or had anything to drink since they took me, and I'll slow you down. We won't get far. I've seen him shoot before. He's a perfect shot."

"Ten seconds!" shouted Richard gleefully from the porch.

The tape around Emily's wrists gave. She took the rock and went to work on his.

"We have to overpower him," Jesse said.

"But how?" whispered Emily. "He gave me a gun, but I'm

sure it's not loaded." She gave a final hack at the tape and Jesse pulled his wrists apart.

"Let me see." Emily lifted her shirttail, and Jesse lifted the gun out.

"Five...four...three...two...one..." Richard counted down from the porch.

"It's not," Jesse said grimly, checking the chamber. "But that doesn't mean we can't use it."

"Olly, olly, oxen free," called Richard. They froze and listened as he stepped off the porch.

"He probably thought we'd run as far as we could," whispered Jesse. "Be quiet and keep still. Wait for him to pass."

Emily clutched Jesse and closed her eyes, trying to regulate her breathing so that it was inaudible even to her own ears. Richard's footsteps crunched closer through the underbrush, and Emily felt Jesse's intake of breath as he held it.

Richard paused near the tree. Emily and Jesse froze. Then the footsteps continued.

"I know you didn't get far," shouted Richard. "Might as well give yourselves up now. I'll make it quick."

His footsteps passed them and receded. Jesse turned to Emily again. "I'm going to distract him," he said. "When he aims at me, you've got to sneak up behind him and hit him with this rock. It's our only chance."

Emily shook her head. "It would be better if I distracted him."

"I can't let you do that, Em. If he shoots you, I don't think I could live with myself."

"I know, but listen: he's much taller than me. Unless he's lying flat on the ground to aim at you, I'm not going to be able to hit him over the head. And if I don't hit him hard enough the first time, he'll shoot both of us. You have to do it."

Jesse bit his lip. He knew that she was right, but he didn't want to admit it. Emily knew this without him saying anything. They'd known each other for a long time now and knew each well enough that they no longer needed to speak. Emily thought of Richard's story. She thought of the original Meades, laughing gently in the parlor while they played backgammon. She thought of Richard's mother, who loved his father no matter what his station. She squeezed Jesse's hand. Without giving him a chance to argue, she got up and ran into the woods.

Emily ran in a straight line from their hiding place, so Richard would pursue her directly in sight of Jesse. He might be a masterful hunter and an excellent shot, but there were two of them and only one of Richard. It seemed possible that their gambit to distract him could work. At least, that's what Emily told herself as she purposely ran into Richard's crosshairs.

He raised his gun to fire at her. "I see you've decided to take my advice," he called.

Emily turned and ran back towards Jesse's hiding spot so that when Richard followed, Jesse could get behind him. She heard his footsteps behind her. She was winded and frightened, and it required only the slightest effort on Richard's part in order to keep up with her. She had only run a few yards when the footsteps stopped. Emily glanced over her shoulder. He was taking aim.

In a particularly lean time, she and Jesse had moved to a neighborhood where the cost of living was low and the level of safety was questionable at best. One night, gunshots went off in the apartment below them. They hid in the bathtub. Jesse told Emily that if anyone ever fired a gun at her, to run in a zigzag and make it harder for anyone to aim at her. It's very difficult, he said in the bathtub, to hit a moving target.

Emily ran back and forth and hoped that Jesse had time to sneak up behind Richard. The gun went off. Emily screamed as the dirt next to her exploded. There was a shout in the near distance. Jesse? Or Richard?

Emily heard the sounds of a scuffle and turned. She could just barely make out two figures grappling, just out of range of the floodlight that illuminated the yard. *Jesse.* Without thinking, Emily ran toward the pair.

The gun was lying on the ground a few feet away. Jesse had disarmed him, but hadn't succeeded in knocking him out. Richard, taking advantage of Jesse's weakened state, had pinned him on the ground and was now strangling him. In her brief glimpse of the expression on Richard's face, Emily thought with revulsion that he looked like he was enjoying himself.

That doesn't mean we can't use it. Emily reached into the waist of her jeans for the seemingly useless gun Richard gave her in the truck, right before she went inside the cabin. Just as Richard was about to take his next swing, Emily was on him. She pistol whipped him across the face, driving the barrel into the side of his skull. Richard grunted and looked up, startled, as a thin trickle of blood slid down the side of his face. Beneath him, Jesse kneed him in the groin and Richard toppled over sideways.

Jesse raised the nearby rock he'd used to hit Richard and disarm him. He brought it down hard against the back of Richard's skull. Richard was still.

Emily stood over him, shaking, more from adrenaline than fear. "Is he dead?" she asked.

"I don't know," said Jesse grimly, struggling to his feet. "But I'm not taking any chances." Jesse picked up the hunting rifle and aimed it at Richard. "Get the duct tape from inside and we'll tie him up. I'll stay here in case he comes to."

As Emily ran to the cabin, she had the strange thought that this was why Richard and his sisters had chosen to work together. It was much easier than trying to be in two places at once.

Emily returned with the duct tape and securely bound Richard's hands and feet. She taped his mouth so he couldn't issue a warning to Cynthia or Theresa if they returned before Jesse and Emily could flee. She sat back on her heels and surveyed him.

"What should we do?" Emily said. "If we leave him out here, he'll freeze."

"I can think of worse things," said Jesse.

"We're not killers," she said. "I want him to go to jail for a long, long time."

"That's a good point," he said with a sigh of resignation. "Grab his feet. I'll get his arms. We'll drag him back to the cabin." Jesse slung the strap of the rifle over his chest and grabbed Richard's bound hands, pulling them over his head. They dragged him as far as the front porch steps when Emily saw the old wooden door set in the ground and stopped.

"Is that a cellar?" she said.

Jesse dropped Richard with a careless thud and went over to the door. He slid back the black metal latch. A steep flight of cement steps led down into the darkness below.

"Let's throw him down here," he said. "He'll be out of the cold, anyway."

They dragged Richard's limp form over to the cellar and rolled him through the open door. His body slid down the steps and out of sight, the heels of his boots the only thing visible in the porch's floodlight. Jesse slammed the door shut and was about to slide the latch in place when Emily remembered.

"Wait, Jesse!" Emily exclaimed. "The keys!"

"That's right, I forgot." Jesse pulled the door open and Emily scurried down the stairs. She made a horrible face as she scrabbled through the pockets of Richard's coat. It revolted her to touch him. Her hand closed around cold metal. Richard's body gave a lurch and thrashed toward her. He swung his bound hands wildly. Emily screamed and scrambled up the stairs. Jesse slammed the door again and latched it firmly shut.

Emily reached out for Jesse's hand and together they ran for the truck. Emily looked over at Jesse. He looked terrible.

"I'll drive," she said, opening the passenger side door for him. "There's some water in the glove compartment, I think. Here it is." Emily uncapped the bottle and handed it to Jesse after he struggled into the truck and collapsed against the seat.

"Thanks," he said gratefully, taking a long swallow.

Emily climbed in the driver's side and started the truck. She executed a quick tight turn in the small yard and drove down the narrow, steep trail back to the main road.

"We have to tell the police," she said.

"Sheriff Oglethorpe? We can call him from Florida," said Jesse. "When we're safely two time zones and two thousand miles from here."

Emily took a hard right at the fork in the road.

"Are you going back to the *house?*" Jesse said incredulously. "We still don't know where Cynthia and Theresa are. They could be waiting for us, Em."

"We can't let them get away with this, Jesse." Emily shook her head, grim determination etched on her profile. She thought of the letter in the basement and the hundreds of photographs of children whose lives had been changed by Matilda and the house.

"They seem pretty close to getting away with it, Em," said Jesse. "We're in over our heads here. I got kidnapped by a dead woman and held hostage by her sister. Richard, the dear old handyman next door, just tried to murder us. I'd suggest calling the police, but knowing Oglethorpe, it will take him three days to do anything about it. We need to get out of here. Once we're safe, we can leave it to the authorities. Maybe they'll actually do something about it this time."

"And what if they don't?" asked Emily. "These people will never leave us alone. If we try to run, they'll find us. You heard Richard. He has no intention of letting us live. He's going to kill us. They're going to take the house and they have no right—no right whatsoever—to what Matilda built there. We can't just let them win."

"But what can we do?" asked Jesse. "We don't even have a gun."

"That's true," said Emily. "But we do have the element of surprise. As far as Cynthia and Theresa know, Richard is with us at the cabin. He's not going to let us escape, at least not in their minds. They're heading back to the house now to steal whatever they can get their hands on. They have no idea where we are or what we're doing. If we use the passageway, we can sneak up on them. We can catch them in the act and stop them. There will be no denying what they were up to. If we just run and hide and disappear, all we're doing is buying them time—not the other way around."

One of the things that Emily loved best about Jesse was that he never tried to undermine her ideas or belittle her. He listened to her, and however opposite his opinion might be, he took what she had to say into consideration and valued it —sometimes, Emily thought, even more than he valued his own perspective.

Jesse's priorities tended to lie with whatever kept them safe. But he was also strong, brave, and bold. Like Emily, he was a fighter. They were the most important traits they shared, and these traits had kept them together from the day they met through this, their darkest day yet.

"Okay," he said simply, but Emily could sense that the fighting spirit had awakened in him and knew that he wouldn't go down without a fight. "Let's make sure they never mess with us again."

Emily reached for his hand and he took it. Then she laid on the gas. The truck sped down the mountain toward whatever awaited them below.

. . .

JESSE ROLLED down the window of the pick-up truck. The truck was extremely old, and neither the windows nor the locks were automatic. The air was cold, but he felt like he needed a little bit of wind in his face to keep him conscious. His entire body ached and he felt like he needed to sleep for about a thousand years.

Emily glanced over at him. He could tell she was worried, but there was no time to slow down and rest.

"Are you okay?" she asked.

"I'm okay," he said. "I mean, I've seen better days. But I'm alive and kicking." He gave what he hoped was a convincing smile, but it came out more like a sickly grin. Emily looked alarmed.

"I'll be fine," he said. "I'm just dehydrated." He drank the water from the glove compartment, as if to prove his point.

"I was so afraid," said Emily, and her voice broke. "I thought I might never see you again."

Jesse looked over, moved at the sight of the tears that slid down her cheeks. She wiped them hastily away. He knew she felt guilty that he was the one who was hurt.

"What happened to you? After you dropped me off to meet with Darla and Roger?"

"I met with Watkins," he said. "That's when everything went wrong..."

*J*esse had left Watkins's office in a hurry. Something about that guy gave him the creeps. He couldn't quite put his finger on it. Emily had always described him as pretty trustworthy, but Jesse thought it was the complete opposite. Almost like he tried to seem trustworthy for the exact reason that he wasn't.

Jesse took out his phone to call Emily. She answered on the first ring.

"Are you okay?" he asked.

"I'm okay, sorry I didn't text you," she said. "I got caught up eavesdropping on Roger and Darla."

"What did the dynamic duo have to say this time?" He glanced over his shoulder, as if expecting them to appear at any moment, break his kneecaps, and roll him into the gutter.

"They didn't do it," said Emily. "They threw the rock through our window and painted the wall, but they didn't do anything to Matilda, Cynthia, or the kids. They didn't know I was listening, they had no reason to lie."

"The lawyer finally gave me the will," said Jesse. "I have it with me now."

"What does it say?"

"Haven't looked yet. On my way back to the truck."

"Can you meet me at the coffee shop on the corner from where you dropped me off?" asked Emily. "I don't want to hang around Three Star. I snuck out the window."

"Way to go, Nancy Drew." He smiled. "Yeah, I'll meet you there."

"Okay, see you soon."

"See you soon."

Jesse ended the call as he got to the truck. He unlocked the door and got in. He opened the folder Watkins had given him and sifted through the pages in his lap. Buried within the legalese, he saw where Matilda had named Emily the inheritor of the property. It was the next line that made Jesse drop the folder, sending papers sliding across his lap and onto the floor of the truck. In the event that Emily declined or that Watkins was unable to locate her, the property would revert to Richard Danforth.

Jesse stared at the document in shock. This changed everything. If Richard was the next in line for the house and had known it all along, then he was the most likely suspect behind all of this. In flashes, Jesse remembered how the intruder the night of the blizzard had sabotaged his truck by taking the distributor cap, and how Richard had conveniently shown up with one the next day. He remembered Richard helping him paint the living room after the latest round of vandalism, pouring poison in his ear about the property managers. And they were rats, it was true, but it turned out there had been something even worse in the walls all along.

Jesse shook his head and reached for his phone. He had to get to Emily, immediately. They were supposed to meet at that coffee shop, but he couldn't take a chance that she might go home first and run into Richard.

Jesse was about to call Emily when the driver's side door

was yanked violently open. Someone in a ski mask pulled him to the pavement. The last thing Jesse saw was the crowbar sailing toward his face. The last thing he heard was the whistling sound it made as it cut through the air.

JESSE WOKE up with an ache in his head and what felt like a welt the size of Montana covering half his face. He was certain he had a black eye and wouldn't be surprised to discover his nose was broken, or possibly his entire face in general. He moved his head tentatively and flinched. Even this minor motion sent waves of pain washing through his head. He bit his lip and tried moving his eyes instead. This, too, was painful, although slightly less bad.

He was on his back in the backseat of a car. Through the window, he could see the sky rushing by at an accelerated pace. He tried to move his arms and legs, but found that he was securely bound at both the wrists and ankles. He thought about sitting up, but didn't think his head could take it. Plus, he assumed that whoever was at the wheel would probably turn around and shoot him.

After what seemed like hours but was probably only twenty to thirty minutes, the car slowed. It turned sharply and began what felt like a steep climb up a large hill. Jesse winced as he was thrown against the seat. The car leveled out and came to a stop.

Jesse was filled with dread as the driver got out, closing the door. What would happen now? He imagined being dragged from the car and shot. He'd once heard that during a kidnapping attempt, it was imperative to prevent the kidnapper from taking you to a second location. Well, here he was. The second location. They could do whatever they wanted now and no one would ever know.

The door to the backseat opened. Jesse looked up, helpless, as the assailant who hit him in the face with the crowbar pulled him roughly from the car. Jesse assumed it was a man by how easily he dragged him from the car towards the old log cabin a few yards away. *Richard.* The figure was still shrouded in the ski mask, the same as it had been when Jesse saw him at the house during the storm, but Jesse thought he could make out Richard's build beneath the black clothing, boots, and parka. It was hard to say. In any event, Jesse didn't express any recognition, just in case there was any chance Richard—or whoever it was—might let him go. The less he knew, the better.

Jesse bit back a yell as the masked figure, having dragged him up the porch steps, through the front door, and into the cabin, tossed him roughly on the couch like a rag doll. Everything hurt again.

The figure stomped back out of the room. Jesse could hear muffled voices arguing on the front porch and strained to make out who they belonged to and what they said. He could just barely hear the sound of what he thought might be Richard and a second, female voice.

"...get them out here, because..."

"We're so close...can't afford any mistakes..."

Jesse slumped against the chair, defeated. He was no closer to understanding what was going on than he'd been in the car. Who were they? What were they doing? What were they planning to do? All he wanted to do was call Emily to warn her, but he couldn't reach his phone and even if he could have, he was sure they had taken it.

Jesse heard footsteps approach the couch. He looked up with dread. Was this it? Was this the end?

It was a second, smaller, slighter figure in a ski mask. This one sat on the hearth across from the couch and studied him briefly before reaching up to pull off the mask. Jesse immediately closed his eyes.

He heard the sound of a harsh laugh. A woman's laugh, but cold and cruel. "That's not necessary, really. Although if you'd like me to blindfold you, I'd be more than happy to do so. But we're really not planning to kill you. Assuming, of course, you cooperate."

Warily, Jesse cracked open one eye. He was finding it harder and harder to open the other one. He opened his good eye the rest of the way as best he could to stare at her, utterly confused.

"Who are you?" he asked. He'd never seen this person in his life.

"That's a good question," she said. "An existential one. Who are any of us, really?" The woman reached into the pocket of her black jacket and removed a pack of cigarettes. She pretended to offer Jesse one, then glanced down at his bound hands, as if remembering. She laughed again. She reminded Jesse of a schoolyard bully who punches you in the face, laughs, then punches you again. She pulled a cigarette out and lit it.

"I'm surprised you don't recognize me," she said, blowing a long stream of smoke into the air, like a dragon. "Wifey's been all over town, trying to track me down."

Jesse narrowed his good eye. "Cynthia Harkness?"

"I don't go by that name anymore," said Cynthia. "Except on paper, of course. I'll probably change it back to Cynthia Danforth, not that I liked my father any more than my husband. I'm thinking of trying something new: what do you think about Coco Channing?"

"I think that's the dumbest name I've ever heard," mumbled Jesse.

"I admire your candor, Jesse. I always did like that about you. I've admired you for a while now, from afar. There's something kind of charming about having you up close." She leered at him.

Jesse eyed her warily. "Are you going to do something weird?"

"Don't flatter yourself. I'm a little more professional than that." Cynthia ashed on the hearth. "Aren't you wondering what you're doing here?"

Jesse remained silent. He couldn't bring himself to give this woman what she wanted. Cynthia waited patiently and when it became apparent that he wasn't going to answer, she continued. "All right, I'll tell you then. We're going to have ourselves a nice little party here—don't worry, nothing weird —until wifey shows up. Then we're all going to sit down and hammer out the details of how you're going to give us the house. I'm going to buy your silence with a bag of money and then you're going to leave town, get lost, and never come back."

"Aren't you supposed to be dead?"

"The key words are 'supposed to be.' 'Supposed to' and 'actually' are two very different things."

"Why are you doing this?"

Cynthia stared at him as if he was naïve, stupid, or both. "What do you mean, why? Why does anyone do anything? Why did you pack up your miserable little life and move to the middle of nowhere, only to have your life threatened on a daily basis by me? For the money, of course." She ground out her cigarette on the hearth and tossed it into the fireplace.

"Please don't hurt Emily," Jesse said. Ordinarily, his pride would forbid him from pleading with such a person, but the idea of this woman getting anywhere near Emily was more than he could stand.

"That's very chivalrous of you, Jesse, but I've never actually seen your wife," said Cynthia, before amending, "Well, I've *seen* her, but I haven't met her. And I don't plan to. The less our paths intersect, the better, as far as I'm concerned. I have other people to deal with that. I don't like to get my hands dirty."

"What about when you killed Matilda?" asked Jesse. "What about then? All those kids, you don't call that getting your hands dirty?"

"Little old me?" Cynthia pretended to look shocked. "I would never kill anybody. Not out of ethics, of course. If they're in the way, and that's the surest way to get them out of it." She shrugged. "Well, in that case, good riddance. But that's precisely why I don't plan to kill you. You're in my way, but killing you is actually not the surest way to get rid of you. If anything, you'd create more problems for me dead than alive. Anyway, actually killing somebody, or felony murder, involves doing time I have no intention of ever doing. Having someone *else* do it means I can set up a plea deal if everything really goes to the dogs. You know?" Cynthia cocked her head at him as if this was a normal thing to ask.

Jesse felt sick. He wanted her to go away so he could lie down, but he was afraid if he went to sleep, he'd never wake up. And even listening to the horrible things she said seemed preferable to not knowing. Maybe if he accumulated enough information, he'd learn enough to get out of the situation. Or he'd learn something that might save Emily later. Ideally both of them, but even in the worst-case scenario, he could at least save Emily.

"Who are you working with?" asked Jesse. "Was it Richard? What about the lawyer? Was it him, too?"

Cynthia eyed him pityingly. "I think you know the answer to that already, don't you, Jesse?" She lit another cigarette and looked into the empty fireplace. "It's a funny thing about family, isn't it? Can't live with them, can't live without them, am I right? I love my brother and sister, but they're like two brainless pawns I have to move around in order to get everything done. Can't I at least have a rook? A bishop? A knight? Do I really have to make every single vital move on the board for us to succeed? But that's family for you. You don't choose your family. You can, however, choose to get away from them, which is hopefully where all this is leading to."

Cynthia got up and went over to the couch, extracting a roll of duct tape from the large pocket of her black parka.

"Not that I don't enjoy talking to you, Jesse, but if you don't mind, I just need to make a quick phone call." She taped Jesse's mouth shut. Then she reached into the pocket of his jacket and pulled out his phone. She shook her head at him.

"You didn't even look, did you?" she said mockingly. He glared at her. She chuckled. She scrolled casually through his phone, as if she had all the time in the world. She tapped on the screen.

Jesse could hear ringing, and he knew that Cynthia had put the phone on speaker just to torment him. She made Richard seem passive as a kitten. His heart contracted when Emily answered the phone.

"Jesse?" she said. "Are you okay?"

Jesse tried to make a noise, but all that occurred were a series of helpless, muffled groans. Cynthia snickered at him.

"I'm afraid Jesse can't come to the phone," she said. "He's feeling a little...indisposed."

"Who is this?" Jesse could hear the fear in Emily's voice, now frantic.

Cynthia explained and told her the terms of the arrangement. When she demanded to speak with Jesse and Cynthia lied, telling her he was unconscious, he tried to kick over the coffee table so that she could hear him.

For the first time, Cynthia's cold mask of phony jocundity dropped. She marched over to the couch and slapped Jesse right across his bruised and tender face. He sank into the cushions in agony.

"I'm afraid you'll just have to take my word for it," she said into the phone before she hung up. "Nice try, Romeo. Pull something like that again and I'll shove this poker through your eyeball." Cynthia picked up the iron poker next to the fireplace and tapped it menacingly on the hearth.

Jesse mumbled something through his duct tape gag. Cynthia studied him, as if debating whether or not it was worth it. Finally, she peeled back a corner of the tape over his mouth.

"What was that?" she said.

"I thought you didn't like to get your hands dirty," Jesse said.

Cynthia smiled. Even her smile was little more than a sadistic little smirk.

"Just because I don't like to," she said as she tapped the poker against the hearth, "doesn't mean I won't."

JESSE DIDN'T KNOW how long it was before Emily came. It felt like days, though he assumed it was only hours. He nodded off for a while, and when he came to, there was a different Cynthia sitting on the hearth. She looked similar to the Cynthia of before and for a moment, Jesse wondered how hard they'd hit him on the head. Was it the same person?

The woman glanced over at him and he saw it was Theresa Plumber, Cynthia's neighbor. Or the woman he thought was Cynthia's neighbor. They were clearly related. Sisters, even.

"Oh, hello," she said. "You're awake. Can I get you a sandwich?"

Jesse's head swam. He felt a wave of nausea wash over him at the very thought of a sandwich. He shook his head, but just barely.

"You probably need water," she said, nodding. "I'll get you that."

Jesse marveled at the difference between this person and Cynthia. It was as though someone added a generous helping of empathy, put Cynthia back in the oven, then set the timer for twice as long. Maybe he could use it to his advantage. Jesse made a noise, hoping she would take the gag off.

The woman giggled. "Oh yeah, I see what you mean. Can't really drink anything with that over your mouth, can you?"

He thought she would take it off, but she had apparently merely made the logical connection required not to get him water, and she went back to staring into the fireplace. Jesse stared at her incredulously.

"It won't be much longer now," she said comfortingly, almost as much to herself as to him. "She'll show up and I'll get the deed and give her the money and then you guys can go. This will all seem like a bad dream."

Jesse saw then that Theresa wasn't kind, just delusional. She probably believed whatever Cynthia and Richard told her and followed them blindly.

Theresa's phone chirped and she pulled it out to look at it. "Oh, it looks like your favorite person is here!" She got up and reached into her pocket for what Jesse felt certain was a gun. He hated the feeling of knowing Emily was in danger and he couldn't do anything to stop it.

"I'm just going to tuck you out of sight for a few minutes, for safekeeping," Theresa said. She got up and came over to the couch, grabbing Jesse by the collar. She was shockingly strong. Where Cynthia was frail and waif-like, Theresa was built like a linebacker. She dragged Jesse out of the room only slightly less easily than Richard had dragged him into it. He watched the floor of the hallway scrape by under his heels before she dropped him into a bedroom and shut the door.

Jesse looked for something he could cut his bonds with, but the room was pitch black and he couldn't see a foot in front of his face. He wasn't sure how much time went by before he heard voices in the living room. *Emily.*

He had to warn her. Jesse thrashed his way across the floor, startled when a beam of light fell across his face.

"Oh, look," said Theresa. "You were already on your way out to join us."

She grabbed him again, proceeding to drag him back the way they'd come earlier. At this point, Jesse didn't know which one he feared and disliked worse: Cynthia or Theresa.

Cynthia was pure evil, but he felt certain he could take her in a fight. Theresa, he wasn't so sure about.

Relief washed over him in waves when he saw Emily, unharmed, in the living room. He thought that everything would be okay if they could only make it through this together.

As Jesse finished his story, he rolled the window up. The stinging cold air was too much for the pain on his face. It was beginning to snow. Emily reached over for his hand and squeezed it tightly in hers. He squeezed back.

"We'll make it out of this together," she said. "I'm sure of it."

Emily slowed as she reached their street, in case Cynthia and Theresa had gotten there first. Theresa had left the cabin before their showdown with Richard, but Emily had no way of knowing if she was meeting Cynthia at the house, or if the two were off plotting somewhere, or meeting Watkins before they came by to loot everything Matilda had owned. Emily felt a fresh wave of anger at the thought of them not only taking Matilda's life, but everything in the house. Inwardly, she vowed that she wouldn't let them get away with it. Not for a second time.

There was no sign of a vehicle in front of the house and no lights on inside the house, either. Emily turned off the headlights on the truck and crept cautiously around the side of the house to the back, where there was no sign of Cynthia or Theresa, either.

She pulled into the shed out back. "Even if they do see the truck here, they'll just think it's Richard," she said.

"Good point," said Jesse. "But how are we going to take them out? You know they're both armed. And we're not. I don't think Matilda owned a gun. If she did, I've never come across it. And we have no ammo in the one we got off Richard."

"They're going to have to split up at some point," said Emily. "They won't think anything of it because they'll think it's just them in the house. As far as they know, we're still duct taped to a couch in the mountains. They're armed, but I don't think they'll have their guns out. They won't have any reason to. We'll just have to sneak up on them. Do you still have that baseball bat you used to chase Richard the night he broke in during the storm?"

"It's in the basement," said Jesse.

"Okay, here's what I think we should do: we go in the house through the tunnels and get Widget. We bring her out here to the truck. We get the baseball bat and whatever else we can find to use as a weapon: maybe the poker from the fireplace. We wait for them to get here. We follow them through the walls and when they split up, we can take them out, one by one. It worked on Richard, and he was a lot bigger than us and he had a gun. But between the two of us, we were able to outsmart him."

Jesse nodded, and Emily could tell by the set of his jaw that he was determined to overpower the people who had overpowered him. "I think we should sneak in low-key, in case they're already in there with the lights out. We'll grab Widget and get her out here in the truck where she'll be safe. Then, we go back in and wait for them."

He opened the trapdoor in the corner of the shed that led to the hidden passage through the house. He went down the ladder first, so he'd be beneath Emily if she fell. She lowered herself after him and pulled the door closed over their heads, surrounding them in darkness.

*E*mily pulled out her phone and opened her flashlight app. She shined it into the tunnel to illuminate their way. They ascended the gently sloping rise that led past the kitchen and stopped at the small door that opened to the inside of the pantry. She pushed it open and crawled through, nudging open the pantry door as quietly as possible. The house was dark and silent. Emily reached into her pocket and pulled out her keys. On it was Widget's dog whistle. She put it to her lips and blew.

Relief washed over her as she heard the familiar clicking of Widget's black toenails on the linoleum floor. She trotted across the kitchen and into the pantry, her tags jingling. Emily picked her up and buried her face in Widget's thick fur. She turned and handed her to Jesse. Then she pulled the door shut as quietly and carefully as possible.

"I'll take her to the truck and meet you back in here," said Jesse. "Where do you think they'll come in?"

"Probably the back door," said Emily. "They'll want to hide the car from the street, so they'll probably park behind the house. I'll get the poker from the fireplace and find the bat.

Do you remember where it's at in the basement?"

Jesse shook his head. "It's all kind of a blur, to be honest. It's probably pretty close to the opening, because that's where I was when Richard got away."

"I'll find it," she said. "You'll need a light for when we split up." She quickly crawled back through the door and into the pantry. She ran across the kitchen to the drawer next to the sink, where they kept a spare flashlight, and brought it back to the passage, where she handed it to Jesse. She pulled the doors to the pantry closed and then shut the doors to the passage.

"I'll be in the passage by the living room when you get back," she said.

Jesse squeezed her hand. Then he turned on the flashlight with his free hand. They made their way back down the passage. Emily turned right toward the basement and Jesse turned left toward the shed.

She opened the passage door that led into the basement. It was pitch black and Emily held the light of her phone high to see. She tried to visualize the basement. The last time she'd been down here, the ghosts had protected her from Richard. Jesse had chased him from the basement into the secret passage just as the police arrived. What had he done with the bat?

A thin beam of light illuminated the corner closest to the secret passage. Emily stared at it. As she watched, it seemed to glow brighter and brighter.

"Matilda?" she whispered.

Soon the corner was as bright as if the overhead light was on. Emily could clearly see the outline of a bat. She went over and grabbed it.

"Thank you," she said softly as the light dimmed and faded out.

. . .

JESSE HELD Widget tightly as he ran down the passage toward the toolshed. Widget wagged her tail excitedly. She seemed to think they were playing a game. When he got to the end of the tunnel, he climbed the ladder built into the wall with Widget tucked carefully under one arm.

Once he emerged into the shed, he opened the door to the truck and placed Widget gently in the cab. She cocked her head and looked at him.

"Stay here," he cautioned her. It was then that he heard it: the sound of a car.

Jesse cracked the door of the shed and peered through the narrow opening. The first thing he saw was snow. In the brief time since they'd hidden the truck and gone in the house to get Widget, it covered the ground. Fat flakes fell from the sky with no sign of stopping.

The second thing he saw was the black Town Car. The sight of it immediately brought back the memory of being hit in the head and thrown in the backseat. Jesse narrowed his eyes as he watched the car glide into the backyard and park flush with the steps that led to the back door.

Cynthia got out and popped the trunk. She opened both the doors to the backseat, then pulled on her ski mask. Theresa got out of the passenger side, already wearing hers. The sisters trudged up the back steps and into the house.

Jesse shut the door and went over to the trap door. He opened it and lowered himself down into the tunnel, pulling the door closed over his head. He swiftly scaled the ladder down and dropped to the hard, packed dirt floor. He ran swiftly down the tunnel toward the house to find Emily.

EMILY HEADED up the passage back toward the living room. The hidden door that opened to the room was concealed behind the couch. Emily slipped through it and darted across the room to the hearth, clutching the bat from the basement.

She tested the weight of the fire poker, giving it an experimental swing.

It was then that she heard the car engine out back. Emily froze at the sound of car doors opening and closing. Then she ran back into the passage carrying the poker and closed the door firmly behind her.

Emily was focused so intently on the sound of Cynthia and Theresa entering the house that she didn't hear Jesse come up behind her until he was practically on top of her, his breath in her ear. Emily bit back a scream as she backed into something warm and solid before realizing it was Jesse. He put a finger to her lips. She handed him the bat.

The back door opened. It was followed by the sound of urgent voices. The voices were muffled in the kitchen, but grew louder as they walked down the hallway and toward the living room.

"What do you want in here?" came Theresa's curious voice from the hall.

"I want that hideous painting over the fireplace so I can throw it on a bonfire and dance around it while it burns," said Cynthia. Her voice grew louder as they entered the living room. "Other than that, just the Ming vase on the end table and the Waterford crystal from the mantel."

Emily and Jesse huddled together in the passage. They were barely breathing, not daring to make the slightest sound.

"What if they go back on the whole deal? They could be talking to the cops right now."

"They're not talking to the cops," said Cynthia impatiently. "I'm telling you, I know these people, and they're predictable. All good people are. If they decide not to take the money, she'll take him to the hospital, putting his well-being above everything else, including her own. Then she'll come back for the dog. And if she does that, it's time for Plan B."

"How are we going to explain *that*?"

"We're not," said Cynthia. "Richard did it, obviously."

"Frame Richard? Cynthia, he's our brother!"

"And when he goes to jail for murdering six people, his latest acquisition will go to us," said Cynthia. "We'll get Watkins to take care of it. We'll just give him a bigger cut. If we're not buying off Tweedle Dumb and Tweedle Dumber or splitting the money with Richard, we'll have plenty extra. Like old times. In the fort. Remember?"

"Oh yeah," Theresa said fondly.

Emily was amazed she was this easy to manipulate. She almost felt sorry for her.

"Get the stuff from the parlor while I go upstairs and hit the old lady's room. Do you have the list I gave you?"

There was a pause while Theresa consulted something. "It's on my phone."

"Good. Don't take anything not on the list, and don't miss anything that is. This money has to last awhile until we own the house free and clear, and even then, we still have to sell it. That could take a while. So, don't forget anything and don't mess this up."

"I'm not gonna mess anything up! Why do you always act like I mess things up?"

"I do not act like you'll mess things up. I tell you repeatedly not to, so that way you don't. Get going."

Their voices receded back down the hallway as the pair carried off their living room acquisitions and split up.

Jesse turned to Emily. "I think it would be best if I went after Theresa. She's a lot bigger than you." He paused. "Come to think of it, she's a lot bigger than me. But I don't like the idea of you going after Cynthia alone."

"I'll be okay," said Emily. "Her hands will be full. I'll make sure her back is to me."

"I know, but she's wily," said Jesse. "You know? It's like fighting a weasel."

"I know," said Emily. "But so am I. And I have an idea."

THEY OPENED the passage door that led into the basement.

"Do you remember where the fuse box is?" Emily whispered to Jesse.

"It's on the far wall, next to the stairs. I'll get it."

Emily heard the faint shuffling and bumping sounds of Jesse sneaking across the basement. She heard a faint click from the corner across the room by the stairs, followed by someone cursing loudly somewhere above their heads as the house was plunged into darkness. She felt Jesse rejoin her side.

"It's funny how easily the power goes out during a storm," he said.

*J*esse opened the passage door that led to the parlor. He could hear Theresa blundering around in the inky black darkness. The light from her phone was the only thing he could see, illuminating her scared, pale face in the dark. She looked both angry and upset.

"Hurry up and get back here, the power's out...because I can't see anything! How am I supposed to find it? Fine!"

There was an especially loud bang followed by a yell. It sounded like Theresa had inadvertently kicked one of the heavy wooden pieces of furniture.

"Ahhhh, my foot! What is this thing? How am I supposed to get this out to the car?"

Jesse paused and listened. Had Cynthia ordered Theresa to move the gramophone? It seemed like a Herculean task, even for someone of Theresa's size.

He slipped out of the passage, clenching the bat tightly. Across the room, Theresa grunted and groaned as she struggled to move the gramophone. She gave up, momentarily winded. She hunched over, gasping, her hands on her knees. Jesse approached her and silently raised the bat.

He was unprepared when Theresa whirled around, grabbing the end of the bat and yanking it towards her. Jesse swung out blindly with his right fist, and Theresa batted it away as if it was nothing more than an angry fly. The bat slipped from his grasp and she threw it across the room. There was a harsh chuckle in the darkness, and Jesse realized she had duped him.

"I grew up in the mountains, boy," she hissed. "It takes more than that for me to lose my wind." She grabbed a handful of his hair and twisted it as she raised her large and meaty knee, driving it into his gut. Jesse gasped and doubled over, trying not to throw up.

"Everybody thinks they can mess with Theresa," she said. "Poor old, dumb old Theresa. Well, she's not as dumb as she looks, is she?" Theresa brought her elbow down onto the tender part of Jesse's face, and he immediately dropped to the rug.

"You think I can't beat a man?" she asked. "I can beat a man. I can do whatever I want. Nobody tells me what I can and can't do." She dragged Jesse to the coat closet and shoved him in among the coats, wedging what sounded like a chair under the door. "I can take anybody who tries to take me on. I'll make you sorry you were ever born. I can—" Theresa's tirade of what she could do came to an abrupt halt and gave way to a prolonged scream.

Jesse rattled the door from the inside and succeeded only in knocking the chair loose enough to open the door a couple of inches, just enough to see the gramophone sliding across the floor of its own accord. It sped full tilt into Theresa, driving her into the opposite wall and pinning her there. She screamed and kicked at the wall, and the heavy frame above her head, which contained a soothing pastoral scene of bucolic countryside, tumbled from its hanging and slammed into her skull. Theresa collapsed on the floor in a heap of tangled hair and overalls.

In the closet, white spots danced in front of Jesse's eyes. His head throbbed. He slammed his shoulder into the closet door in an attempt to knock the chair loose. A wave of dizziness overcame him and he slumped to the floor.

EMILY CLIMBED the steep and narrow passage that led to Matilda's bedroom. She stopped just outside the passage door. She clutched the poker tightly and waited.

Emily heard the door creak as Cynthia entered the room. There was a pause as she tried the lamp on the bureau, then the switch on the wall. When neither of these turned on, there was a slight click of a flashlight turning on and Cynthia resumed prowling around the room.

She didn't even react to the power outage. She immediately adapted and moved on. This, more than anything, scared Emily. It reminded her of an apex predator on a nature show: the shark cutting dead-eyed through the water; the crocodile slipping up to a boat and rolling its unsuspecting prey until it becomes too disoriented to escape.

Cynthia's phone rang and her footsteps paused as she answered. "I'm aware that the power is out, Theresa. Whatever would I do without your remarkable powers of observation? Get the stuff from the parlor like I told you to or I'll burn you like you'll never forget...I don't care. And make sure you get the gramophone." She stopped talking and the footsteps resumed.

The passage entrance into Matilda's room was inside the small square created by her vanity. When Emily heard Cynthia open the bureau drawers on the other side of Matilda's bed, she quietly pushed the door inward and crawled silently onto the rug. She reached back in behind her and pulled the poker from the floor of the tunnel. She crouched behind Matilda's bed as Cynthia went through all the drawers.

"Well, well, what have we here? Most people keep their jewelry in the freezer, but not you, Matilda..."

Emily felt a flare of anger in her heart on Matilda's behalf. It wasn't enough to murder her and rob her; she had to belittle her on top of it.

Cynthia finished rifling through the drawers and opened the armoire. Once Emily heard the creak of the doors opening, she knew Cynthia's back was to her. She stood up slowly, her hands shaking from all the adrenaline coursing through her body. Just as Emily swung the poker to bring it down onto Cynthia's skull, she turned. It was as if she'd known Emily was there all along. The blow glanced off her shoulder. Cynthia grabbed the poker and used it to pull Emily toward her.

"Couldn't stay away, could you?" she hissed. "I'm so glad we have a chance to say good-bye. I'd never forgive myself if I left without giving you a proper send-off." She yanked the poker from Emily's hands and raised it to hit her across the face.

Emily reacted on instinct. She slammed her head into Cynthia's, and the other woman staggered and fell back on the bed. Jesse always told her she was hard-headed. He meant stubborn, but Emily guessed it could also be interpreted literally.

Emily grabbed the poker back and swung at Cynthia again. She rolled out of the way. It was dark and Emily could see little beside her shadowy outline. She knew it was of paramount importance to take her out before she could reach for her gun, which Emily felt certain was in one of the pockets of her coat. Frustrated and frightened, she threw herself on top of Cynthia, grabbing her by the hair.

Cynthia emitted a surprised grunt. It was as if she hadn't expected Emily to fight very hard and was unprepared to deal with her on this level. She reached up and tried to get her hands around Emily's throat, but Emily bit her on the hand. Cynthia screamed shrilly as Emily pulled her off the bed onto the floor. She heard a hollow thunk as Cynthia's head slammed into the nightstand. She collapsed like a rag doll on top of Emily, and she was pinned on the carpet beneath the dead weight of her opponent.

Unconvinced it wasn't a trick of some kind, Emily wiggled frantically out from under her enemy. Cynthia lay prone on the rug, silent and unmoving. Emily nudged her with a toe, then rifled through the pockets of her coat, pulling out the gun she found in Cynthia's coat pocket and putting it in her own.

She shined the light of her phone around the room. She wouldn't feel safe until Cynthia was securely tied and bound. She looked for something to tie her up with.

One of the dresser drawers hung open, revealing an array of brightly colored scarves, and Emily sifted through them quickly, grabbing what felt like the strongest one. She turned back to Cynthia, shining the phone's light on the floor where Cynthia had fallen.

She was gone.

EMILY RAN DOWN THE STAIRS, blinded by rage and fueled by adrenaline. She couldn't let her get away now, not after all this. Not after she'd come this close to stopping her.

Emily reached for the gun, remembering what Richard had told her in the truck before she went into the cabin: *keep your finger off the trigger until you're ready to fire.* She clutched the gun in one hand and the fire poker in the other.

She ran down the stairs and into the kitchen, kicking the back door open. The car was gone. *No.* She immediately ran to the front of the house, out the front door, and down the steps. If she could catch her in the act of driving away, she could shoot out the tires, she could—

Emily stopped in the yard, puzzled. There was no sign of

either Cynthia or the car—no dull roar of an engine as its driver escaped, no taillights fading out of sight. Then Emily heard the sound of an engine turning over. She turned.

Cynthia had hidden the car behind the forsythia bush in the yard, its bare tangles of dry dead brown limbs concealing her from view until the moment Emily ran from house. The headlights blazed on and the engine revved. Emily understood then that Cynthia planned to run her down.

She turned and ran toward the backyard. There was a large tree on the side of the house, forming a narrow passage between the wall and tree. Emily thought if she could only get there in time, she could get around it and Cynthia wouldn't be able to pass.

The sound of the engine grew louder behind her and Emily thought, *I'll never make it in time.* She slipped and slid across the snow. The fat flakes swirled madly around her, blinding her. She could feel the heat from the car just behind her.

Emily squinted ahead and saw an impossibly strange sight: illuminated by the high beams of Cynthia's car were Matilda and the children, clear as day. They stood together in front of the tree, as if posing for the portrait in the living room. Unlike the portrait in the living room, their faces were identical masks of pure wrath.

Emily glanced over her shoulder as Cynthia lost control of the car. She was close enough to see her expression of white-faced terror and helpless rage as the car's tires skidded through the snow.

The car smashed into the tree with an earsplitting crash of metal against wood. Emily threw herself against the side of the house, covering her face and head with her arms. She remained that way, huddled in a small ball, until the sound of twisting metal and shattering glass fell silent and the air was heavy and still.

Emily looked up. Great gray plumes of smoke billowed

out from under the hood of the car. The airbags had deployed and it was impossible to make out anything inside. Emily got to her feet cautiously. Was it over? Was Cynthia dead?

In answer to Emily's silent question, the driver's side door opened. Emily stared in shock as the bloody, battered figure dragged herself from the car. Her face was horribly disfigured and barely recognizable but for the bright, burning eyes in her skull, which blazed with hatred. It was like a fuel that kept her from death and made her invincible.

Cynthia clutched a tire iron in her hand. It was the same one she'd used to knock Jesse unconscious. She bore down on Emily with that crazed, unstoppable look in her eyes.

Emily had dropped the poker when she ran for the tree. She plunged her hands into her coat pocket, reaching for the gun, and found nothing. She looked wildly around and saw it lying a few feet away. She stumbled backward through the snow towards the gun, thinking if she could only reach it—

Cynthia brought the tire iron down in a long swinging arc, the metal whistling through the air. Emily screamed and rolled out of the way just in time. The iron hit the ground, spraying snow in the air.

Emily was on her back, looking up helplessly as a turtle as Cynthia towered over her. Her face was covered in blood and she wore a depraved smile of triumphant lunacy. She raised the tire iron, preparing to bring it down directly on Emily's face.

Emily threw her arms up to protect herself, covering her face. But the blow never came.

Instead, there was a scream: prolonged and anguished, it reverberated through the cold night air. Emily opened her eyes, which she'd squeezed shut in anticipation of the blow, and cautiously uncovered her face.

Cynthia glided away from her, heels dragging across the snow, as if pulled by an invisible wire. Her arms dangled loosely as a kitten being held by the scruff of the neck and her eyes were wide with terror. Her mouth hung open in an endless scream.

The driver's side door hung open from when she dragged herself out of the wreckage. She flew back into it in reverse and the door slammed shut behind her. Emily could hear the click of the automatic locks and Cynthia's muffled screams through the rolled-up windows as she tried to free herself from the burning wreckage. The doors would not open. The windows would not go down.

Emily, sensing she needed to get as far away as possible, struggled to her feet and ran for the backyard. Behind her, the car erupted into a fireball, and an enormous plume of smoke billowed into the air over top of the inferno.

Emily ran for the door beneath the back stairs and let herself into the passage, closing the door shut behind her. She squeezed her eyes shut and covered her ears with her hands, but even in the darkness and silence, she was convinced she could still hear Cynthia's screams.

*E*mily ran through the passage toward the parlor, holding the light from her phone aloft so she wouldn't trip and fall. She had to make sure Jesse was okay. Had he taken out Theresa, or was she still lurking somewhere in the house? Had she done something to Jesse?

Emily burst through the door that led from the passage to the parlor. The first thing she heard were muffled thuds from the closet. There was a chair wedged beneath the doorknob and Emily went over and yanked it loose, throwing open the closet door.

Jesse stumbled out of the closet and put his arms around her in the darkness of the parlor. She hugged him, but her mind was still racing ahead to what could go wrong, and she pulled away immediately.

"Where's Theresa?" she asked.

"Indisposed," he said. Emily shined her light into the corner of the room, revealing the crumpled heap of Theresa, slumped over unconscious on the floor. "Where's Cynthia?" he asked.

Emily thought of the inferno in the front yard and shivered. She shook her head. "I don't think we need to worry about Cynthia anymore," Emily said. "We had better call the cops." Even as she said it, she could already hear the sound of approaching sirens. The billowing smoke in the front yard must have attracted attention from the neighbors, on edge after smelling smoke in a dry climate.

"Probably a good idea," agreed Jesse. "I guess I should go turn the lights back on."

"Probably a good idea," agreed Emily, smiling.

She went into the living room as Jesse disappeared down the hallway to go to the basement. She had never been more tired in her life. At that moment, she craved nothing so much as the warmth and light of a fire. She quickly built one in the hearth, a large and roaring blaze. After she lit the logs, she immediately gasped and stumbled back from the fireplace.

Illuminated by the flames were Matilda and the children. They were gathered together in front of the fireplace, beneath the painting that portrayed them. They looked much the same as she had seen them outside, but now their expressions were peaceful and benevolent.

As much as this reassured Emily, the sight of them was shocking. She had only ever experienced contact through a secondary medium, and only ever seen them as shadows or lights. To see them this vividly was both startling and, Emily realized, emotionally overwhelming. She had not seen her aunt in many years, and regarding her now, she felt the tears well up in her eyes.

Matilda didn't say anything, just smiled at her warmly. Andrea stood next to Matilda with the two younger children by her side. They smiled at Emily, too.

The lamp on the end table flared on. Jesse had thrown the switches in the breaker box downstairs. A moment later, he appeared at the doorway to the living room. As soon as he saw the ghosts in front of the fireplace, he stopped dead.

"It's okay," said Emily. "They just want to say good-bye."

Jesse slowly entered the room and came to stand beside

her. Emily knew it took a considerable amount of willpower for him not to run screaming into the night. Jesse had never liked anything that couldn't be explained with a logical explanation, and she imagined it was taking everything he had to accept the scene before them.

Matilda smiled sympathetically, as if she knew how mind-boggling this was for him.

She nudged the youngest children forward. They waved at Emily and Jesse. Matilda reached out for their hands, and they went to stand by her side. Andrea smiled at Emily. She reached up to her neck and touched the necklace there lightly. Emily saw that it looked very much like the one she'd found upstairs and returned to Andrea's parents in the park.

In the distance, sirens wailed, the sound gradually amplifying as they grew closer and closer to the house. Matilda blew Emily a kiss. Andrea and the children waved. With these final gestures, the four of them faded from sight until the only thing left was the light of the fire behind where they had once stood.

THE FIREFIGHTERS USED the Jaws of Life to get Cynthia out of the car after they put out the flames. She was unconscious when they took her away in the ambulance, burned beyond recognition. Sheriff Oglethorpe assured them she'd be heavily guarded at the hospital so that when she did regain consciousness, there would be little chance of her escaping. Although, he added, it seemed highly unlikely, in her condition.

Theresa came to just as the police arrived, groaning "Where am I?" from the floor of the parlor. One of Oglethorpe's deputies, Officer Tapper, cuffed her once the EMTs examined her. He put her in the back of a squad car and gave the roof a sharp slap. The car pulled away from the house with Theresa in the back of it, staring out the back window, her eyes dead and her mouth slack. She looked shell shocked, as if she didn't fully comprehend what was happening. Emily wouldn't have been surprised to find that she didn't, without Cynthia there to tell her what to think and how to feel.

Jesse brought Widget inside from the truck and Emily held her while they sat in front of the fireplace, describing the events of the past twenty-four hours to Sheriff Oglethorpe. Emily gave him the address to the cabin where Richard was locked in the cellar. He sent several officers up into the mountains to retrieve him.

"So, Cynthia Harkness has been alive all this time?" Oglethorpe said to Emily and Jesse. "Do you know what made her swerve right into that tree?"

"No idea," said Emily, shaking her head. She thought of Matilda and the children. She was glad they'd finally gotten their revenge.

"She was crazy," added Jesse. "I think she'd lost her mind at that point. She also may have been drunk, or on something."

The sheriff nodded. "I've seen people do some pretty crazy things when they're under the influence. Wouldn't surprise me. Sounds like she was crazy enough to begin with, trying to murder her way into owning a house." He shook his head. "I mean, most people would just take out a loan, y'know what I mean?"

Emily remembered Richard's story in the cabin. "I think it was about more than that to them. They thought of Matilda as a Have, while they were the Have Nots. It seemed like they wanted to even the score."

"Money will make people do crazy things," said the sheriff with a sigh. "I've seen some strange things in my time. But rest assured, with your testimony, they'll be behind bars for a long, long time. I'd be surprised if they ever saw the light of day again."

"Will you find out what they did with the bodies?" asked

Emily. "Matilda and the children, I mean. I would really like to give them a proper funeral."

"We'll find them," said the sheriff. "It's the least she and those kids deserve. Right now, I want to have the EMTs look you over and take you down to the hospital." He glanced over at Jesse, whose face had swollen to Quasimodo-like proportions. "You look like you need some medical attention. We'll get the rest of your story afterwards." The sheriff went to find a paramedic to take care of Jesse. Emily reached for his hand and he took it.

"Do you think it's over?" she asked, resting her head on his shoulder.

He squeezed her hand. "The ghosts are at peace. Cynthia has been thoroughly incapacitated. Richard is going from that cellar straight to a cell. And Theresa left here in the back of a police car. So yeah, I think we're pretty much safe. Don't you?"

Emily gazed into the fireplace and thought of Matilda.

"Yes," she said. "I do."

a year had passed since Emily and Jesse moved into the rambling old house on the hill. It had once been a haven of criminal activity when the original Meades lived there. It became a beacon of hope for children with nothing when Matilda took over the home. And for a while, it became the site of a tragedy. Though for many months it had been a place of mystery, dark secrets, and fear, it was finally the place Matilda had always dreamed of it being: a safe haven for the less fortunate, for the kids who otherwise might have nothing.

Emily opened the Matilda Meade Home for Wayward Children two years after the death of her great aunt, and she knew that if Matilda had been there—and that in a way, she still was—it would have been the proudest day of her life. The proudest day of Emily's life had been seeing her name on the New York Times bestseller list, after her book about the events of the previous year became a bestseller. She'd taken her earnings and the advance on her next book and used it to get out of debt and realize Matilda's dream. Jesse had built an addition onto the house, and there were now no fewer than ten foster kids there at any given time. Emily and

Jesse bought his parents a house nearby and Jesse's mother, who had always dreamed of him having a large family, came over every day to help them with the kids.

Cynthia, Richard, and Theresa were all doing hard time in federal prison for murder, kidnapping, and assault, among their myriad of other crimes. Watkins was disbarred and landed in a white collar minimum security prison in exchange for the plea deal he struck for providing the details of their conspiracy.

As for Roger and Darla, they'd been driven out of business when Emily posted the video she took of them online, the one she took on her phone of the pair sneaking out of the house after vandalizing the living room. The video quickly went viral, and there was now a class action lawsuit against them, formed on behalf of the numerous outraged home-owners who'd been subject to the same harassment and intimidation tactics that Roger and Darla had inflicted on Emily and Jesse.

Without the money from the property managers pouring into his campaign, Sheriff Oglethorpe lost the election. He lost to one of his own deputies, Jake Tapper, an idealistic young officer whose increasing frustration at Oglethorpe's lackadaisical style of law enforcement and whiff of corruption had led him to take a stand against his superior in the name of making a change.

Now, Emily sat in the library. She regarded the portrait of Matilda and the children she'd moved to hang above her desk for inspiration. She thought of how much had changed in so short a time. While Emily and Jesse had once been two people struggling on their own, they were now a large and flourishing household, filled with laughter, noise, and love. It happened so quickly and unexpectedly, and she thought of the remarkable series of events that had led them to where they were today.

It had inspired the book she'd written in a frenzy: never

had the words and ideas come so quickly and fluidly to her before, and it was as if the writer's block that had plagued her for so long had never existed. And it hadn't returned to inhibit her since.

Today, Emily was at work on her next book. It was about the lives of the children who lived at Meade House: the various hardships they experienced, and their future hopes and dreams. She had already written a story about death. Now, she wanted to write one about life—life, and all its endless possibilities.

Emily rolled a fresh, clean sheet of white paper into the typewriter. Now that the ghosts were at rest, the only words she ever wrote on it were her own. Emily closed her eyes, and the first lines came to her as easily as breathing: *It was an old house, a house filled with history, whose walls had been witness to many a mystery, hope, and struggle. The house had seen many stories pass through its doors and was now home to the numerous stories of the children who lived there. And while many of those stories were of the tragedies that comprised their pasts, the house was now a vessel that contained the promise of their hopeful futures.*

She opened her eyes and began to write.

Printed in Great Britain
by Amazon

61156358R00180